BORROWING
DEATH

Books by Cathy Pegau

MURDER ON THE LAST FRONTIER

BORROWING DEATH

Published by Kensington Publishing Corporation

BORROWING DEATH

CATHY PEGAU

k

KENSINGTON BOOKS
www.kensingtonbooks.com

KENSINGTON BOOKS are published by

Kensington Publishing Corp.
119 West 40th Street
New York, NY 10018

All Kensington titles, imprints, and distributed lines are available at special quantity discounts for bulk purchases for sales promotion, premiums, fund-raising, educational, or institutional use.

Special book excerpts or customized printings can also be created to fit specific needs. For details, write or phone the office of the Kensington Sales Manager: Kensington Publishing Corp., 119 West 40th Street, New York, NY 10018. Attn. Sales Department. Phone: 1-800-221-2647.

Kensington and the K logo Reg. U.S. Pat. & TM Off.

eISBN-13: 978-1-4967-0057-5
eISBN-10: 1-4967-0057-0
First Kensington Electronic Edition: July 2016

ISBN-13: 978-1-4967-0056-8
ISBN-10: 1-4967-0056-2
First Kensington Trade Paperback Printing: July 2016

10 9 8 7 6 5 4 3 2 1

Printed in the United States of America

Acknowledgments

Once again, thanks to the folks at the Cordova Museum and the Cordova Library for all of their help with research. Any mistakes are completely my own.

Thank you, Natalie and John, for all you've done to make these books happen.

Special thanks to Paula and the copy editor. Your expertise and patience are greatly appreciated.

Chapter 1

How can we, as Americans, claim to support individual freedoms while advocating for such a restrictive amendment? Not to say overindulging isn't an issue, but even with current prohibition laws in some States and here in the Alaska Territory we have seen a rise in the illegal production and sale of alcohol and associated criminal behavior. There has also been an increase in wood alcohol deaths as the common man attempts to slake his thirst with his own poisonous concoctions. Is this the price we're willing to pay in what can only be a futile attempt at national sobriety?

Charlotte Brody typed the final lines of her editorial for the next day's edition of the *Cordova Daily Times*. She grinned as she swiped an errant strand of hair out of her eyes. "That'll give the ladies of the local Women's Temperance League something to grouse about."

She just hoped Andrew Toliver, the *Times*'s owner and publisher, liked it. Since Charlotte started working for him, Toliver had relinquished the roles of chief reporter and typesetter to her and was able to concentrate on his neglected executive duties, as well as edit and run the printing press itself. He was neutral on most major topics, at least as far as what he put in the paper, and it delighted him to have the town talking about what they found within its pages. This would get some tongues wagging, for better or worse.

With the twist of one of the Linotype's several levers, Charlotte sent the sequence of steel mats to the molding mechanism. The machine clattered and whirred, the small motor by her left knee buzzing. In a minute or so, the new lead slug would be molded, dropped into place, and cool enough to handle.

How would Cordovans react to her take on National Prohibition? A fairly even split, she reckoned. No matter what side they supported, she hoped it sold papers. Then again, as the only news source in a town full of folks who enjoyed a good debate, she was more than certain it would.

But that's not why she wrote the article. Increasing sales, while financially beneficial, wasn't her goal as a journalist. Seeking justice, informing the public, and getting them to talk about issues was what she loved about her calling.

Despite President Wilson's attempts to veto it—though not for the reasons she espoused—the Eighteenth Amendment would take effect in less than two months. Perhaps if enough people considered how ridiculous it was, and called for its repeal, this waste of time and energy would be a mere footnote in future history books.

Charlotte slid the stool away from the massive Linotype's keyboard and bent down to flick off the electric motor that ran the gears and chains of the machine. The buzz in her ears subsided. After three months as Mr. Toliver's assistant, she hardly noticed the tang of hot lead from the crucible any more, but silencing the motor was always a relief. She felt her head clear, like cobwebs swept from rafters.

Now, the Nineteenth Amendment, *that* was a change that truly mattered and would have positive lasting effects. Nearly twenty states had ratified the voting amendment so far, and it looked like more were poised to join in. All the marching, protesting, and arrests of good women and men had made for a long, often painful journey, but it was worth it. Charlotte would never forget the stories of sacrifice and bravery that had paved the way, and couldn't wait to celebrate national suffrage someday soon.

Would she still be in Alaska when that happened? Hard to say. Charlotte's original plan had been to stay over the winter, then she pushed her unofficial scheduled departure back to later in spring. Perhaps she'd spend the summer in the Great Land before returning to New York. She was looking forward to seeing the territory in more pleasant weather. Why not experience all the seasons while she had the chance?

The late November wind rattled a loose panel of the metal roof of the *Times* office, reminding her pleasant weather was a long way away. It was probably snowing again.

Anxious to finish and get home before the streets were too messy, Charlotte picked up the cooled lead slugs and aligned them in the frame on the proofing table. Seeing no obvious defects in the dull gray reliefs, she rolled ink onto the raised letters, then laid a fresh piece of newspaper over the frame. She used a second, clean roller to create a proof and lifted it carefully. With the eye of an editor, she searched for errors that would require retyping a corrected slug.

Satisfied, Charlotte put the rollers and ink away. Mr. Toliver would be in soon to run the large printing press across the room. First, they'd go over the next day's issue, making changes as necessary, then she'd go home while he stayed overnight to mind the machinery. He preferred working at night, he'd said when he hired her, listening to the rhythm of the press as he perused articles or created special advertisement pages.

The shared tasks suited Charlotte. She was able to write local stories, gather the social notices, tidbits, and comings and goings endemic to a small town paper during the day, and still work on her serialized account of women in Alaska for *The Modern Woman Review* in the evenings. What made for news in a remote Alaska town wasn't usually as exciting as back in New York, but you learned who threw the most popular dinner parties.

She closed the door of the press room behind her and entered the main office. It was much cooler away from the Linotype, despite the coal stove in the corner. Quieter too, with only the ticktock of the cuckoo clock to challenge the periodic howl of the wind. She checked the time as she sat at Toliver's messy desk. After eight already? He should be here soon.

Charlotte slid a piece of scratch paper under the circle of light made by the desk lamp and jotted a note about the thunking she'd heard earlier within the Linotype. Toliver had instilled in her the need to keep the intricate machine in tip-top shape, as it was their bread and butter.

Setting the note where he'd see it, or at least eventually find it, Charlotte was drawn to an article that had come in over the Associated Press Teletype on coal miners threatening to strike down in the States. Though she'd seen the articles hours ago, she often only scanned pieces as she organized them for printing.

Goodness, what sort of things are happening to those poor people? She started to read, frowning at their plight. A triple knock on the front door jerked Charlotte's eyes open. She'd meant only to rest them for a moment. Late nights and early mornings were starting to catch up with her.

All she could see through the frosted glass was a vague, dark figure. The streetlight must have gone out again. Who would be out on a night such as this? Toliver wouldn't have knocked, as he had his own key.

"Michael or James," she answered herself as she rose, her voice rough in her own ears. Her brother or the deputy marshal occasionally checked in on her at the office. Chances were good it was one of them.

Back in New York, she would have ignored a nighttime visitor. Or taken one of Michael's old baseball bats with her. Here, she was fairly confident the person outside wasn't going to hurt her. Besides, she'd left the bat at her parents' house.

She opened the door. A gust of cold, wet wind blew in, making her shiver.

Deputy Marshal James Eddington stood at the threshold, melting slush dripping off the brim of his hat. "You shouldn't be opening the door without asking who it is."

"Are you saying you're unable to keep the streets of Cordova safe enough for a woman to be at her own place of employment without worry?" Charlotte smiled as she said it, letting him know she was just teasing. James was a very good deputy, committed to his job, and most everyone in town knew he and Marshal Blaine weren't to be trifled with when it came to breaking the laws of the territory.

James's black eyebrows met in a scowl, but there was a glimmer of amusement in his eyes. "Common sense should come into play, even here. There are some unsavory elements about."

She'd certainly learned that in her three months in town.

"I'll be more careful from now on," she promised. "Come in and warm up. I'm almost done."

James slipped in when Charlotte stepped aside. She closed the door after him. He swept his hat from his head, shook off the excess water carefully to avoid wetting her, and hung it on a peg screwed into the wall alongside her own hat and coat.

"More snow since early evening. Cold and slick out there," he said as he unbuttoned his coat. "Wanted to make sure you get home okay."

Though warmed by his concern, Charlotte rubbed her chilled, bare arms, her sleeves held up by an old pair of garters so they wouldn't get dirtied by the Linotype. "That's very kind of you. Sit for a minute while I finish a few things. Mr. Toliver should be here soon. Would you like some tea? I think the water's still hot."

"Toliver doesn't have anything stronger stashed in his desk?" James asked with a sly smile.

He did, but friend or not, Charlotte wasn't about to admit it to a deputy who enforced Alaska's dry laws. "Just tea."

"Then tea'd be great, thanks." He sat on the straight-back chair on the other side of the desk while she went to the stove to check the kettle. Still hot enough to make a decent cup.

Charlotte prepared their tea and brought the cups to the desk. She sat in Toliver's padded chair, suddenly at a loss for what to say to James. They'd been friendly enough since she'd arrived in Cordova in August, and he was easy to talk to. They'd even gone to dinner, and another time a show at the Empress Theater with her brother and her friend Brigit. And they'd shared a kiss. That was as far as she'd allowed herself to take their relationship in a physical sense. Charlotte was pleased that they engaged in enjoyable conversations on all manner of topics most of the time they were together.

So why was she unable to come up with small talk now, as they sat in a dimly lit office while the wind blew outside?

"Anything exciting in tomorrow's paper?" He watched her over the rim of the cup as he sipped.

Relieved to break the silence and have something to focus upon, Charlotte passed him the originals of the articles she'd transcribed. "Mostly the usual, though there are a few that should get some attention."

How would Deputy Eddington and Marshal Blaine take her editorial? They already knew her personal stance on Prohibition, and Blaine had more or less agreed with her that enforcement was difficult. Putting it in print for all of Cordova to see was another matter.

He glanced through the drafts, stopping at a page and frowning. "This damn arsonist is driving us crazy."

"At least there hasn't been any serious damage or injury."

Charlotte had written three pieces about fires set over the last month. Abandoned sheds and piles of brush seemed to be the arsonist's main source of entertainment.

"Not so far," James said, "but this is the third year he's done it. Sets a few fires, then stops. I'd rather not have this be an annual event."

"How unusual. Are you sure it's the same person?" There was no evidence pointing to anyone or any particular pattern other than the timing.

"Not really, but in a way, I hope so." He shook his head slowly. "We don't need a copycat—"

A muffled boom from somewhere not too distant cut him off, followed by three more smaller ones in quick succession. The explosions weren't loud, more like when she'd stood on the street in New York City for a parade and heard the bands' bass drums while they were still a couple of blocks away.

James set his teacup down quickly, sloshing liquid onto the pages on the desk, and bolted from his seat. Charlotte followed him. Throwing open the door, he stood on the walk looking up and down Main Street. His eyes widened as he faced west, toward the canneries.

"It looks like Fiske's. Call the firehouse," he said, already running in that direction.

Charlotte took a quick look. Though she didn't see flames, there was an unnatural glow coming from two streets away. She about-faced, dashed back to the desk, and snatched up the candlestick phone. Placing the earpiece against her ear, she flicked the bracket several times.

After a few long moments, a drowsy voice answered. "Operator."

"There's been an explosion and a fire," Charlotte said. "At Fiske's Hardware."

"I'll call it in," the operator replied, perkier now. "Anyone hurt?"

"I don't know. Deputy Eddington went down there. Hurry."

Charlotte hung up before the operator. She grabbed her notepad and a pencil from the desk and practically broke her neck hopping from one foot to the other as she pulled off her shoes. Thank goodness single buckles and slip-ons had replaced high-laced styles, but they weren't good in snow. She hurried to the door, shoved her feet into her heavy boots, on top of her wool socks stuffed inside, and yanked her hat and coat off their pegs.

Struggling to get her coat on while she slipped and slid in the slush, Charlotte made her way to the end of the street. By the time she turned toward Fiske's, fire licked at the side window of the building. Luckily, there was some distance between the hardware store and its nearest neighbor. The idea of a block-long inferno scared the hell out of her.

"James!"

He was nowhere in sight. The door was open and black smoke poured out, dimming the streetlight on the far corner. The acrid stench of burning chemicals made Charlotte's eyes water. Her heart raced and her palms were clammy, despite the cold. She stepped back, rubbing the thin scar beneath her left eye. Not long ago, she'd been caught in a burning room, and the memory was too fresh to allow her to get any closer.

"James!" She called again, praying he hadn't gone inside.

The smoke was getting thicker, the flames growing larger and louder. The upper floor seemed untouched, for the moment, but that wouldn't last long.

Charlotte heard the bell clanging from the firehouse near the harbor. If any of the volunteers had spent the night there, they would be on the scene soon. But would it be soon enough?

She reached into her pocket for the notebook and pencil. Taking notes and focusing on the facts for the article she'd write kept her worry for James at bay, for the moment.

Several people joined her on the corner, some with coats pulled on over nightclothes.

"Anyone call the fire department?"

"I heard the bells going."

"What the hell happened? Anyone inside?"

Charlotte glanced up at the building as the flames snapped and flashed through the windows. God, she hoped the building had been empty. A shudder ran through her. She shoved her notebook into her pocket, buttoned her coat, and crossed her arms against the cold. Thank goodness she'd worn an old pair of long johns under her skirt.

By the time the sound of yelling and the clang of the fire engine bell came up the road, the fire had grown and smoke billowed out of the upper floor window. The two-horse-drawn pump cart with six men hanging on was followed by the three-horse tank cart. The firemen leaped off their carts before they came to a complete stop, boots squishing in the icy mud. Two men connected the tank hose to the pump. Others connected the fire hose to the other end of the pump and unrolled the rubberized canvas toward Fiske's.

Three men donned hard leather masks that covered their heads, the eyepieces giving them an insect-like appearance. Hopefully the air canisters attached to the back of the mask would sustain them long enough to extinguish the flames. When their equipment was secure, they hurried to the hose.

"Ready!" came the muffled cry of the man at the front as he waved an arm. He pointed the nozzle toward the open door. Four men operated the pump mechanism, two to a side. After a few pumps, water shot out of the nozzle. The man in the front slowly walked forward, the others behind keeping step.

James came around from the back of the building, and Charlotte breathed a sigh of relief. He strode directly to Chief Parker, who wore a black, hardened leather helmet with a metal crest on the front, and began talking and gesturing. Charlotte couldn't hear what they were saying over the rush of water, the roar of flames, and the chatter of the men near her.

"Charlotte, are you all right?"

She turned toward her brother. Like some of the other men,

Michael wore his mackinaw over a stripped pajama shirt and hastily donned trousers.

"I'm fine. Did you get a call? Is someone hurt?" Charlotte hadn't seen anyone come out of Fiske's with an injury. Maybe he'd been contacted as a precaution.

"No, I heard the commotion. But I have my bag, just in case." He held up his leather satchel, then turned his gaze to the building. "I pray I won't need it."

James nodded at something the chief said, then walked over to them. Melted snow plastered his hair to his head, but he didn't seem to be feeling the effects of the wet or cold. "Doc," he said, greeting Michael. "Shouldn't have been anyone inside, but if you'll stick around to make sure the firemen are okay, I'd be obliged."

"Of course," Michael replied. "Has anyone gotten word to Fiske?"

"One of Parker's sons was sent to the house. He's not back yet."

The men manning the hose hadn't gone far beyond the front door. One inside shouted something. The men stepped back several steps as a loud crash sounded within the building. Black smoke billowed out of the windows and over their heads.

The onlookers startled and stepped back. Though they were far enough away to be safe from the flames, the chemical smell burned Charlotte's nose and eyes. Several men wiped sleeves across their faces.

"There's the chief's son," James said, nodding toward a lanky youth jogging down the road as fast as the slick surface allowed. He joined Parker and his son. The young man was shaking his head as he spoke. James returned to Charlotte and Michael, his brow deeply furrowed. "Fiske wasn't at home. No one but the housekeeper was there."

"Caroline's out of town," Charlotte said. She recalled placing the travel announcement and Caroline Fiske's promise of a holiday party upon her return on the social page of the paper. "She gets back any day now."

"That's what the housekeeper told the kid. Helluva home-coming," James said.

All of them looked back at the building. Dread solidified in the pit of Charlotte's stomach.

"Maybe he's at one of the clubs or something," Michael suggested.

"I'll check around." James raked his fingers through his wet hair. "I need to catch that damn arsonist. This has gone too far."

It seemed like hours before the firemen trudged out of the building, smudged with soot and dripping water. The outer walls of the hardware store had scorched, but remained intact from what Charlotte could see. Thank goodness they lived in such a wet environment. The interior, however, was likely a total loss.

The chief met with one man as he and his companions helped each other remove their masks, taking care with the air canisters. Charlotte couldn't hear their conversation, but the man gestured back to the building, curving his hand as if giving direction. Parker's frown deepened. Even from where she stood, Charlotte heard his emphatic, "Son of a bitch."

He looked out toward the crowd, his gaze falling on James. "Deputy," he called, waving James over. "You too, Doc."

The three of them exchanged glances, and the dread in Charlotte's gut turned to a bilious cramping. There was only one reason to request Michael, the town's coroner as well as one of its doctors.

"Damnation," James muttered, heading to the chief.

Michael and Charlotte followed. Both men stopped and turned to her.

"No," James said, holding up a hand. "This is no place for you."

Irritation bristled at the back of her neck. "I beg to differ, deputy. As a journalist I have an obligation to report suspected crimes."

Michael rolled his eyes. "Here we go again."

She scowled at him.

"And as Deputy Marshal," James said, "my investigation into suspected crimes trumps your journalistic obligation. I'll relay any pertinent information to you, Miss Brody, but right now I'm ordering you to remain out here. If you don't, I'll handcuff you to the light post. Understood?"

He'd do it too. Charlotte resisted her natural inclination to argue with anyone who told her she couldn't do this or that and gave him a curt nod. James nodded back. They'd known each other only a few short months and had quickly come to respect each other's duties. When James felt it was time to disclose information for public consumption and safety, he'd do it. Pushing him too far, too fast, would likely land her in one of his jail cells. Or cuffed to a post.

Charlotte would comply, but she didn't have to like it.

James and Michael made their way to the door of the hardware store with the chief. Two firemen loaned them their masks. The fire may have been out, but smoldering embers and toxic fumes from whatever chemicals Fiske had in his inventory could prove dangerous, if not outright fatal. The three men disappeared into the blackened store. Charlotte caught a few glimpses of smoky light from Parker's flashlight.

Worry gnawed around the edges of her irritation. What was inside the charred store? No amount of craning her neck allowed her to see past the front door.

"What's happening, Miss Brody?"

Charlotte gave Henry, one of her paper boys and a server at the café, a nod of greeting. What was he doing out so late? "The chief asked Deputy Eddington and Michael to look at something inside."

Under the wan electric streetlight, Henry's ruddy cheeks

paled. "What would they need the doctor for? Someone inside get hurt?"

She wouldn't be the one to start rumors or set off wild speculation. James would never forgive her that transgression. "I couldn't say."

Henry stared at the front door and broken window leaking smoke, his expression the same as the few remaining gawkers who stayed to see what James and Michael might find. "It's not Mr. Fiske, is it? I mean, who else would be in his store at this hour?"

"We don't know what's what, Henry, so let's not jump to conclusions." She sounded a lot like James, but the words offered a small amount of hope that Lyle Fiske was all right.

"Even so," Henry said, "the store's a goner." He glanced at Charlotte. "Do they think the arsonist did it?"

Charlotte and others had entertained the same thought. "I'm sure the fire department and the marshal's office will investigate every possibility. But the three other fires were smaller, in places where no one was around. This seems like a significant increase in destructive intent to me."

Henry nodded, his attention back on the building and the firemen putting their equipment away.

Finally, Michael emerged from the hardware store. A fireman helped him with the mask. Michael took a deep breath of fresh air, but his face was drawn.

Charlotte started toward him. "Excuse me, Henry."

Her feet slid in the slushy road. It was particularly mucky where the water tank had been dripping, adding to the mess of the wet snow. As she reached Michael, James exited the building with the fire chief, the two of them talking in hushed tones, but their expressions were similar to Michael's. James held something heavy wrapped in cloth and under his jacket to protect it from the snow.

"It's bad, isn't it?" Charlotte kept her voice low and her back turned so the onlookers wouldn't pick up on their conversation. No need to get rumors started. "Lyle Fiske?"

Michael nodded. "It looks like it. They'll bring the body over to the basement of the hospital. The new morgue is up and running. Just wish we didn't need it so damn soon."

"You'll confirm who it is and manner of death for an article, won't you?" Charlotte had no desire to attend this autopsy. One was enough for her lifetime.

Images of Darcy Dugan's autopsy three months ago flashed through her mind like a jittery nickelodeon. Charlotte quickly pushed them aside. Insisting on attending that examination might have been a mistake, despite the fact that the results explained why the young prostitute had been murdered. She'd rely upon Michael's explanation alone this time.

"I don't want anything out about this yet," James said as he joined them. He looked cold and wet, his hair dripping. "There are circumstances that need clearing up."

"Like what?" she asked. "How the fire started? Do you think it was the arsonist?"

"Those questions, and who'd want Lyle Fiske dead."

"You're sure it was intentional?" What a terrible idea.

"The fire may not have been," James said, bringing the cloth-wrapped items out from under his coat, "but the knife and hammer near his body suggest his death was deliberate."

Charlotte shifted on the uncomfortable chair in Michael's outer office. Staying late at the *Times*'s office the night before, she'd typed up a short piece for the morning edition, just a few lines of facts and observations of the fire department's activities. Mr. Toliver had arrived by the time the fire department was finishing up. He manned the Linotype, encouraging Charlotte to go home and get some rest.

Sleep had been nearly impossible. Speculation about how the fire had started, why, and the identity of the unfortunate victim were left out of the article, but not her thoughts. The discovery of a possible murder weapon contributed to theories about what had happened.

Poor Mr. Fiske. Charlotte hoped he was dead before the fire started. Awful as that sounded, she couldn't imagine the terror of being conscious while the building burned around him.

The outer door opened and Michael came into the office, quickly closing out the cold and wind. Charlotte caught a whiff of burnt flesh under the "hospital" smell of carbolic acid and cleanser. Probably just her imagination, but she rose and cracked open the window for some fresh air despite the winter chill.

"How'd it go, Michael?"

He hung up his hat and mackinaw, then sat in the chair behind his desk. In his usual manner of preparing to deliver bad news, Michael straightened his tie and smoothed back his hair before meeting her gaze.

"I do believe it's Lyle Fiske," he said. "Build and clothing— what's left of it—are consistent with Fiske. His features had been damaged by flames, but not completely burned away. Still, since no one's been able to find Fiske in town, I believe it's him."

"Did the fire kill him?" She knew that often people were overcome by smoke before burned by the flames of a fire. With so many chemicals in the hardware store, it wouldn't have surprised her if toxic fumes had rendered him unconscious first. But unless he'd been asleep in his office, how had he not been capable of escaping? The presence of the knife and hammer became more than a little suspicious.

Michael scrubbed his palms over his face, the whiskers on his cheeks just long enough to become disheveled. She'd gotten used to the mustache he sported, but a beard was something else. Though understandable, given the climate. "I think he was dead before the fire."

Thank goodness for small favors, Charlotte thought. "Why do you say that?"

"His clothes and skin were burned, and he smelled of chemicals as if he'd been doused with paint thinner or something. That obliterated any obvious wounds on his front. I think the debris that fell on him after the explosion smothered the flames, essentially preserving the rest of the body. The clothing and skin on his back was relatively unscathed. But when I opened him up—"

Her stomach flipped, but she quickly suppressed memories of Darcy's body. How Michael managed to distance himself from such gruesome elements astounded her. It must have been difficult to be detached, especially in a small town where he was often familiar with the victims. On the one hand, she knew he was sympathetic to his patients' conditions. On the other, he managed to dictate graphic details of injury and illness with nary a hitch in his voice.

"—blood in his chest cavity," Michael said.

"Blood? How?"

"A slit in his heart's apex. There was an obvious cut on the inside of his thoracic cavity and into the heart muscle." Michael pointed at his own chest, just under his sternum. "The killer thrust upward. Not an easy task, but the knife we found was large enough to do the trick. Still, whoever killed Fiske was pretty strong, and either lucky or skilled."

A shudder ran through Charlotte. The idea of a "skilled" killer in Cordova brought to mind the terrors of a Jack the Ripper–type. *Let's not blow this out of proportion.*

"Why would someone kill him?"

"That's Eddington's job, not mine. All I can say is he was likely dead, or close to it, prior to the fire." Michael shrugged and slowly shook his head, looking weary. "Fiske was a decent sort, as far as I knew him. He and his wife were well-liked."

"Not by everyone, perhaps." Charlotte had met the couple only a few times. Caroline was ten or so years older than she, Lyle another ten years older than his wife. They were friendly enough, and Caroline seemed to enjoy being among Cordova's

growing number of society matrons—wives of the more prom-
inent and successful businessmen.

"Poor Caroline."

After checking back issues of the *Times* earlier, Charlotte had
found the social page where Mrs. Fiske's travel plans had been
mentioned. On a more practical note, the fact she was out of town
meant she wasn't a suspect. Michael had said killing Fiske took
some strength as well. That covered a number of men and women
who lived in a place that required muscle and skill to survive.

"Eddington will be questioning the housekeeper and whoever else works for them to ask about any problems and her return plans. In the meantime, we'll have Fiske taken over to the
funeral parlor. I don't envy them this preparation." Michael
rose, stretched his back, and crossed to stand with her at the
window. "I know that look in your eye, Charlotte. Keep your
nose out of this and let Eddington do his job."

She held up her right hand in the Boy Scout salute. "I promise not to impede his investigation."

Michael squeezed her fingers. "That isn't the same thing as
staying out of it."

Charlotte eased her hand out of his and rose up on her toes
to peck him on the cheek. "I wouldn't want you to call me a
liar. Let me know when you want me to type up your report
for Juneau."

As his sometime secretary, Charlotte helped keep his patient
files and official reports organized. Sending copies to the territorial capital was one of the tasks she helped with.

"About that," he said, cheeks pinkening under his new
beard. "I'm getting someone to help me with paperwork and
some interpretation issues."

Charlotte couldn't help the surprise widening her eyes. "You
are? Since when?"

They saw each other every day, or just about, and he'd never
mentioned getting help.

"Well, it's not official yet, but with more of the Natives coming into town for work and whatnot, I thought it would be a good idea to have someone with me who knew them better."

That made sense, but it didn't explain why he'd never mentioned it to her.

"And I've been busy with the newspaper and unavailable," she said.

Michael's mouth quirked into a crooked grin. "That too. But mostly because Mary can really help me communicate with her people. And she needs the job."

"Mary?" Charlotte wasn't nearly as familiar with the local Eyak population as he was, and there were a number of Marys around.

"Mary Weaver. You might have heard her called Old Creek Mary. She's worked at the grocer off and on."

"Oh, yes." Charlotte recalled a young Native woman stacking shelves or behind the counter at McGruder's. A lovely girl. Well, not a girl. She was probably the same age as Charlotte. "She has a couple of kids, doesn't she?"

"That's right. A boy and a girl, five and around three. The grandmother watches them when Mary's working." Michael returned to his seat at the desk. "Her husband died last spring."

"How terrible."

"It was. When she mentioned she was looking for something more challenging than stacking shelves, I sort of offered her a job." He winced. "You don't mind, do you?"

"Of course not. In fact, I'm looking forward to talking to her." Charlotte crossed the room and retrieved her coat and hat from the peg on the back of the door.

Just as she lifted the mackinaw, the door opened and she quickly stepped out of the way to avoid getting hit.

James came in and shut the door behind him. Removing his hat, he said, "Shoulda known you'd be here before me."

Charlotte grinned. "Early bird gets the worm." The deputy shot a questioning look at Michael. "Don't worry, James, I promise not to write or say anything until you give me the go-ahead. I won't compromise your investigation. But you'll inform me of any developments, right?"

James and Michael exchanged glances. After the terrible situation with Darcy Dugan, they knew Charlotte couldn't help but get herself involved. But they could also trust her to keep her word and not spoil the case.

"You've told her how Fiske died?" James asked Michael. There was a hint of irritation in his voice.

"She's my current secretary of record," Michael said. "I trust her with keeping pertinent evidence and case information to herself."

He'd just told her that a different person would be performing that task, yet here he was, covering for her, practically lying to James. Though it was possible Michael wouldn't want to frighten his soon-to-be assistant Mary with the horrible details of an autopsy.

Charlotte suppressed a grin of appreciation. Not only for him standing up for her, but for the renewed closeness they'd achieved since she arrived in Alaska. Terrible things had transpired for each of them, inspiring them to regain the relationship they'd shared as children. In a way, Charlotte was glad for the challenges and heartache they'd both endured. Without them, they may never have reconnected.

James shook his head, resigned for the moment. "Fine. Was there a stab wound, or was it the blow of the hammer?"

"Stab." Michael recapped his autopsy findings. "Any idea why someone would kill him?"

"Robbery. The till was open and empty."

Charlotte could see that scenario play out in her head. The thief broke into Fiske's store after hours, thinking it empty. Lyle happened to be there, working late while Caroline was out of town. Surprised, the thief killed Lyle, then set the fire to cover up the crime.

"Whoever did this is looking at a life sentence, if not worse," James said.

Robbery was bad enough, but compounding it with murder—intentional or not—was almost a surefire way for the culprit to get hanged or sent to the electric chair.

"Have you been able to contact Caroline?" Charlotte wasn't close to the woman, but couldn't imagine returning from holiday to such horrific news.

James rubbed the back of his neck. His eyes seemed sunken in with weariness. "Just talked to the housekeeper. She comes in on tomorrow's steamer. I'll get a message to the naval office outside town. They'll wire the ship to have everyone kept on board when they get in. Better she wonder about the delay than come down the gangplank to a dock full of gawkers."

Charlotte nodded, appreciating his sensitivity about the matter. "You may want to have a friend of hers or at least the housekeeper with you."

"Good idea." He eyed her warily. "And no, not you."

Indignation heated her face and neck. "I'm a journalist, not a ghoul, deputy. The woman deserves her privacy at a time like this."

"I'm glad we agree on that." James set his hat on his head and touched the brim in his standard salute. "Get me a copy of the autopsy report as soon as you can, Doc."

"I'll do that, but I think a nap is in order first." Michael covered a yawn, as if the very idea of sleep made him more weary.

Charlotte buttoned her coat and donned her hat. "I think that's a fine idea. Walk me home, deputy?"

James's eyes widened, but without pause he opened the door. "Of course, Miss Brody. See you later, Doc."

As she walked with James, Charlotte pulled on a pair of mittens she kept in her coat pocket. The colorful wool cheered her, and reminded her of her friend Kit, who'd sent them as an early Christmas present. The sun had supposedly risen an hour before, but thick, dark clouds that were low enough to obscure the tops of the surrounding mountains made it feel much later.

Few people were out on the snowy street, though there was inviting light from within businesses.

So far, the cold and wet of Cordova, Alaska, in late November hadn't been any worse than what she'd experienced back East; it just felt colder and wetter because of the shorter days. Sunrise around nine or ten and near dark by four in the afternoon took some getting used to. Some people never got used to it. Add that to being cooped up when bad weather hit, further darkening the skies, and folks tended to get a little antsy. Maybe the bears had the right idea, to hibernate until warmth and light returned.

Those who could stick it out loved it in the Great Land. She enjoyed interviewing those people and sharing their stories with *Modern Woman* readers. It was a matter of keeping busy, she'd been told more than once. That explained the frequent changeover of shows at the Empress Theater and the weekly community dance or two. Keeping entertained and social was a good prescription for fending off cabin fever.

"I didn't mean to imply you'd harass Mrs. Fiske as soon as she got off the boat," James said as he took her arm and guided her around a large, slushy puddle. "If you weren't a journalist, I'd have asked you to come with me. I just don't want her to feel overwhelmed."

"Apology accepted," she said. "Did you get much information from the Fiskes' housekeeper or employees? Was Fiske having trouble with anyone?"

James shook his head. "I spoke to Mrs. Munson, but she's only been working there a month and didn't see Mr. Fiske all that often. Fiske had two men working with him at the store. I'll interview them later this morning."

"Michael said Fiske seemed like a decent sort." Charlotte watched him for a reaction. James tended to have a spot-on opinion of most people in town. They both knew a person's public life could conceal unpleasant private activity.

He flicked a glance her way and shrugged. "Nothing reported to us."

"But you have your suspicions." What could James think Fiske was up to?

"I'm suspicious of just about everyone, Charlotte. It's my job."

She grinned. "Mine too."

In about ten minutes, they'd navigated the slippery incline of a side street—most everyone lived uphill of Main Street—and stopped in front of the little green house where Charlotte was staying. The owners, Harold and Viola Gibbins, were in the States for the winter. Having Charlotte live there gave them peace of mind that their home would be cared for while they were away. And since the first place Charlotte had lived in had burned down in August, she now had a roof over her head.

The house, with its footings set to compensate for the angle of the road, was large enough to provide plenty of room, but small enough to feel cozy. The wood stove heated the place quickly, which Charlotte had appreciated each and every morning since late September.

James held her elbow as they ascended the stairs. The staircase wobbled a bit, and Charlotte made a mental note to have it looked at. Standing in front of the black door, James said, "All settled, are you?"

"I didn't have much to move in, thankfully, but yes." Her parents were shipping more of her things, but storms had delayed arrivals from Seattle.

She glanced up at the quaint little home and the neighbors' similar houses. She'd only briefly met the folks on either side, but felt comfortable here, like she belonged. "I'll need to find another place before Mr. and Mrs. Gibbins return in March. It'll have to be bigger than a room at a boarding house, though. I rather like having the space to move about."

She tended to pace and putter about while mulling her writing, a challenge in a single room.

"So you're staying past spring."

Charlotte eyed him curiously. Was he asking or concluding? "That's my current plan."

James nodded. "Good. That's good."

"I'm glad you approve." She poured as much sarcasm into the words as she could while grinning.

He started at her tone. "I'm not approving anything." She laughed, and his face pinkened beneath his dark beard. "What I mean is, you don't need my approval or anyone else's. I'm glad you're staying. If you are."

The urge to tease him diminished, but only a little. "Even if I'm bothersome?"

"I'm hoping you'll grow out of that," he said with a mock scowl.

Charlotte laughed again. "Don't count on it." She unlocked the door and glanced over her shoulder. "Thank you for walking me home."

James put his hand on the door frame, leaning slightly toward her. "Why did you ask me to, Charlotte?"

She turned and stared at him, her body suddenly tense, aware of his proximity. Why *had* she asked? Honesty seemed the best course with James Eddington. "Because I enjoy your company."

Even if he did seem to tie her tongue at times.

The smile he gave her brought out the dimple in his cheek. "The feeling's mutual, Miss Brody." He tugged the brim of his hat. "Good morning."

"Good morning, deputy," she said, more breathlessly than intended.

He made his way down the stairs and strode back toward Main Street. As she watched him turn the corner, Charlotte wondered for the umpteenth time if she'd ever be able to let herself truly relax around him.

Chapter 2

By the time she rested, washed up, and managed a rough draft of a slightly more detailed article on the Fiske fire, it was early afternoon and Charlotte was ready for lunch. Nothing in the icebox or pantry caught her fancy. A visit to the café for a bowl of soup sounded perfect on a blustery day. Afterward, she'd go into the *Times* office and start on tomorrow's paper.

With her satchel packed and her coat buttoned to her throat, Charlotte headed out. A deep breath of clear, cold air brought the fishy bite of low tide to her nose. Blue sky peeked over the mountains to the east. Perhaps a reprieve from the cold, wet, gray was on its way, but she wouldn't hold her breath waiting for it.

The train whistle sounded at about mile two of the rail line, warning of its arrival. The CR&NW carried copper ore from the Kennecott mine over one hundred miles to the north, rumbled through town on its way to pick up cargo at the canneries, then continued out to the ocean docks to fill freighters. Passengers utilized the small station closer to town, taking the train from Cordova into the interior of the territory to Chitina and Kennecott.

Charlotte hurried as fast as she could without slipping. If the train was on time, and it usually was, it was after two and she had a busy workday ahead before press time.

She waved to business neighbors shoveling slush off their walks as she picked her way down to Main Street. Arriving at the café, Charlotte pulled open the door and was immediately met with the welcoming aroma of coffee and bacon. The lunch crowd was gone, with only a few folks finishing up their meals or lingering over the paper. She was always tickled to see readers intent on the *Times*. Were they reading her piece?

Charlotte claimed her usual seat at the counter, placed her satchel at her feet, and unbuttoned her coat. She was too chilled to remove it, but sitting in the toasty café would remedy that soon enough.

"Afternoon, Miss Brody." Henry hurried behind the counter, coffeepot in hand, and took a cup and saucer from the stack against the wall. He poured out a cup for Charlotte. "What can I get for you today?"

"What's the soup of the day?" She wrapped her hands around the heated cup.

"Beef barley. Might be a bowl left. We were busy." He set the pot back on the small stove. Reaching along the counter, Henry placed a sugar bowl and a small pitcher of cream near Charlotte's place.

"That sounds wonderful. A bowl of soup and a chicken sandwich, please." Her stomach gurgled in anticipation.

Henry poked his head into the kitchen, called out her order, then took a rag out to clear a table where a couple of patrons had just left.

Charlotte added a little sugar and some cream to her coffee. She sipped it as she surreptitiously observed the other diners. Three older men sat at a corner table, laughing and chatting. Two women Charlotte recognized, but whose names she couldn't recall, drank coffee and spoke quietly together.

Henry served her soup and sandwich, made sure she had everything she needed, then dashed off again to clear tables. Between his job here at the café and his early-morning duties as paper boy—as well as the occasional assistance with proofreading and printing—he was a busy young man. When did he have time to sleep? Henry rarely spoke of his personal life, and Charlotte wondered if he was on his own or helping his family make ends meet.

When he returned to his post behind the counter, Henry asked, "How's your lunch, Miss Brody?"

"Delicious, thank you. Tell the cook this chicken salad is top-notch. I haven't had anything like it before."

Henry leaned over the counter a little and winked. "Apples," he whispered, "and something called curry."

Charlotte had no idea how a short-order cook in Alaska had come up with the idea of putting apples and curry in chicken salad, but it ruined her forever for the standard variety.

"Any official word on who died in the fire or what caused it?" Henry asked, absently wiping the counter.

It didn't surprise Charlotte that he knew someone had perished; more than likely most of the town already knew. Putting the location and the absence of Lyle Fiske together, one could easily conclude Fiske was either the culprit or the victim.

"Nothing I can say for now." She daubed her napkin against her lips. Keeping her voice down, she asked, "Why? Have you heard anything?"

Henry was in a good position to glean bits of town gossip and chatter. Patrons of diners and cafés often forgot their servers had ears. "Invisible staff" was also a good source for private society tidbits, but Charlotte had found those employees tended to be more loyal.

Henry glanced down at the rag in his hand, as if a particular dusting of crumbs needed his rapt attention. "Folks reading the paper earlier figured it was Mr. Fiske."

"What about anyone who might have set the fire or been upset with Mr. Fiske?" she asked. "Does anyone think the arsonist is responsible?" His head came up. It was difficult for

Charlotte to read his expression. Surprise at the suggestion it was the arsonist? Had someone mentioned the connection, or did he know something? "Henry?"

"Nobody's said anything more than that, Miss Brody. The Fiskes are good folks. Always nice and left good tips when they came in. Took care of their own. I heard that when their house-keeper, Mrs. Derenov, passed, they gave the family a week's wages as a . . . a what do you call it?"

"Grievance pay," Charlotte said. "That's very generous of them." And a rare occurrence in any employment situation. "What about Fiske's employees at the store?"

Henry shrugged. "No complaints near as I can tell. I gotta get Mr. Skinner more coffee."

He snatched up the pot and hurried toward the table of men.

Charlotte sipped her coffee. *Was* the robbery a random act? Would a thief be so surprised that his reaction was to kill a man? Why not just knock him out? Unless Fiske put up some sort of a fight.

She finished off what was in her cup and paid the bill. Henry barely met her eyes as he took her money. Definitely not his usual smiling, chatty self. Maybe he was tired, having been up late last night, then early this morning to deliver newspapers. The last twelve hours had been taxing on her, and she hadn't gone to work in the wee hours.

"I can get Jacob to cover your deliveries tomorrow," she offered.

He shook his head, still not meeting her eyes. "No, that's fine, Miss Brody. I'll be there, same as always. Have a nice day."

He shoved the till drawer closed and disappeared into the kitchen.

Charlotte left a tip beside the till, then left the café. The rain-snow mix continued to fall, adding another layer of slush to the walkways. Clive Wilkes, in the Studebaker that he used as a taxi, rolled by, throwing a wave of icy muck just in front of her.

"Thanks a heap," she muttered as she shook bits off her skirt.

She resumed walking to the office, mentally prioritizing what needed to be done. Her step faltered when she looked down the walkway. Standing at the door of the *Times* building was a trio of women, arms crossed as they watched her approach. Their fur-collared wool coats and fashionable hats were almost identical, as were their pinched demeanors.

Well, that hadn't taken long at all. Had the Women's Temperance League called an emergency meeting after the paper came out that morning? Were they watching for her arrival at the office?

When she was within polite conversation distance, Charlotte smiled at them. "Good afternoon, ladies. To what do I owe the honor of a visit from the League?"

She knew why they were there, but teasing the women was better than outright calling them fools.

Mrs. Walter Hillman—Charlotte wasn't sure of her given name, as Mrs. Hillman only introduced herself as such—a stout lady in her mid-forties, pressed her lips together. "You know perfectly well why we're here, Miss Brody."

Flanking her, Mrs. Cron and Mrs. Burgess wore equally displeased expressions.

Charlotte fished the key out of her coat pocket and fit it to the lock, wriggling and jiggling it while she spoke. The damn thing stuck in icy weather. "I'm not about to presume anything, Mrs. Hillman. Why don't you come in and have a cup of tea?"

The lock clicked and she opened the door, gesturing for them to go inside.

None of them moved.

"This isn't a social call," Mrs. Hillman said. Apparently she was spokeswoman, given her ranking position in the League. "We want a retraction printed."

Charlotte went inside. She wasn't going to stand on the street for this conversation. Besides, it was too cold. If the ladies wanted to talk, they'd have to follow her in. After a few moments of standing in front of the open door while Charlotte removed her hat and coat, they entered the office, shutting the door behind them.

"And what is it you're retracting?" Charlotte asked.

By the pursing of Mrs. Burgess's lips, Charlotte's little "misunderstanding" wasn't appreciated.

"*We* aren't retracting anything," Mrs. Cron said, her nasal voice full of irritation. "*You* need to take back that article from this morning's paper."

Charlotte didn't let her own irritation at the audacity that they demand she do anything of the sort show on her face. "Which one is that?"

Mrs. Hillman took over again. "You know which one, Miss Brody. The article you wrote regarding the Volstead Act making things worse. It's irresponsible for the *Times* to produce such gibberish that will only serve to undermine the fabric of this community."

"You mean the irresponsible reporting of facts about crime rates going up in dry areas or the gibberish about people poisoning themselves?" The fun of teasing the ladies was quickly waning. "The statistics are clear, Mrs. Hillman. These things are happening right now, and Prohibition isn't even fully enacted yet. Ignorance like yours will only force people to take dangerous risks."

"I don't appreciate your attitude," Mrs. Hillman said. "As a woman who champions what's good and right—yes, I know you were active in the suffragette movement back East and you support equality—how can you condone the terrible conditions the consumption of alcohol creates? The financial burden on families? The violence from drunken brawls involving men desperate for a drink?"

Men weren't alone in their desperation, but now was not the time to quibble.

"I condone nothing of the sort, Mrs. Hillman, and said as much in my article." Heat crawled up Charlotte's neck as she spoke. "It's possible to advocate for social justice and equity while allowing for adults to make personal choices. Complete prohibition won't fix those ills you've mentioned. People will come to realize how restrictive it is, and I doubt the law will be tolerated for very long."

Mrs. Cron's pointy chin lifted. "The best way to stop a scourge is to eliminate the source."

Mrs. Hillman and Mrs. Burgess nodded.

Charlotte clenched her hands at her sides, overcoming the desire to rage at the woman's ignorance. "And the best way to get someone to break an overly invasive law is to make them feel like they can't be trusted with their own choices, be it alcohol, deciding who will represent them in Washington, or the use of birth control."

The women's eyes grew large and round at the mention of such a delicate matter.

"Well, I never," Mrs. Burgess said, aghast.

Charlotte focused on her. "Perhaps you should. It's very liberating."

There was a perverse pleasure in seeing each of them pale, but the small voice in the back of her head warned Charlotte she just made three of the most affluent women in Cordova exceedingly uncomfortable. Probably not her smartest move in the last several months.

"Mr. Toliver will hear of this," Mrs. Hillman said, her voice low and threatening.

Without allowing Charlotte to respond, she about-faced and swept past Mrs. Cron and Mrs. Burgess. They waited half a beat, long enough to give Charlotte a pair of disdainful glares, then followed their leader out the door.

Charlotte slowly relaxed her clenched fists. She'd encountered more than a few of their ilk, well-intended women who were so shortsighted they couldn't see the real world past their turned-up noses. She took a deep breath and let it out slowly, attempting to relax. Mr. Toliver would be talking to her, she was sure, but he'd approved her piece and she expected his support.

Still, it was a concern. What if Mrs. Hillman had enough influence over Cordovans to call for a boycott of the paper?
What if businesses pulled their advertisements, even for a short
time? A drop in revenue could be the thing that got to Toliver.

Would she have a job by the end of the week?

Damnation.

Charlotte turned toward the back of the office, but the sight
of Toliver's desk and its blanket of papers just made her want to
sweep them all onto the floor. Nothing against him; she just
needed to *do* something. She grabbed her coat and hat. A brisk
walk might clear her head.

Charlotte found herself standing in front of Brigit O'Brien's
house. Its white clapboards and green shutters made it look like
most other homes in Cordova, even down to the window boxes
that would have flowers come spring. The house could have fit
in any neighborhood in any American city. This one happened
to be owned by one of the more successful madams in town.
Many Cordovans ignored the inside activities, while others par-
ticipated eagerly.

It was also the best place for Charlotte to find a sympathetic ear
in which to grumble about the visit by Mrs. Hillman and friends.

She knocked on the door and was startled when it was opened
almost immediately. Young Charlie O'Brien, Brigit's son,
blocked the entrance with his slight body. He was dressed to go
out with a cap, heavy coat, scarf, wool pants, and boots. One
hand rested on the jamb, the other held the edge of the door.

"Good afternoon, Charlie. Is Brigit available?"

"Afternoon, Miss Charlotte," he said, and turned to look toward the parlor. Worry creased his smooth brow. "She's here,
but . . ."

The absence of the boy's normally stoic expression concerned her. "Is everything all right?"

He shrugged and shook his head, unsure and unhappy about
whatever was going on.

"Let her in, Charlie," Brigit called from the parlor. "Go to Davey's and play for a bit."

Charlie gave Charlotte a helpless look, then ran past her, leaving the door open. She watched him trudge through the snow to the road, then disappear around the bend, heading up toward town. She knocked the snow off her boots and went in. The entry to Brigit's house was tastefully decorated, if a little worn around the edges.

Leaving her mucky footwear near the door, Charlotte entered the parlor through the wide arch on the left. Brigit rose from one of the three couches to meet her near the doorway. She wore an orange and blue kimono-like robe with silver thread accents. Tendrils of hair framed her face, having escaped from the loose bun at the nape of her neck. Her dark eyes, usually so full of fire and mischief, were dull and red-rimmed.

"What happened?" Charlotte asked, hurrying toward her friend and gathering Brigit's hands in her own. Not Charlie, obviously, thankfully.

Brigit drew her back to the couch and they sat. On the low table in front of them, a crystal tumbler of amber liquid was beside several cream-colored pages and a matching envelope. Both the pages and the envelope had elegant script covering them.

Brigit picked up the letter. "From a friend in Cincinnati," she said, her voice rough. "One of the girls I started out with down there—" The words caught in her throat, and her hand gripped Charlotte's hard. "She died."

Charlotte squeezed back. "Oh, Brigit, I'm so sorry."

"Camille, Tess, and I were at the same house for a few years. Camille was always laughing and carrying on. Every day was a party." Brigit smiled sadly at the memory. "Everyone who came in wanted to see Camille. Smart as a whip, pretty, quick-witted."

"She sounds lovely."

Brigit nodded, dashing tears away. "We had it all planned. Work the houses rather than the street. So much safer. Save enough to buy our own place or set up a business. A flower shop. Camille loved flowers. But then Tess got this idea into her head to go to Alaska. There was gold still coming out of the hills and things were booming. Tess wanted part of that, and it sounded good to me. Camille decided to stay in Ohio, said she'd follow later."

Brigit, her sister, Tess, and Tess's husband, Frank Kavanagh, the former mayor of Cordova, had come to Cordova several years before. Their path from the States to the Last Frontier was a story unto itself, and not one many knew the truth of.

Brigit lowered her head, breathing deeply, unable to continue.

Charlotte drew her into a hug. Brigit shook as she cried on Charlotte's shoulder.

"Is there anything I can do?" Charlotte knew there wasn't, but she had to ask.

Brigit lifted her head, sniffling and dabbing her eyes and nose with a handkerchief from within her sleeve. "Find the bastard who killed her?"

Charlotte's breath caught. "She was murdered?"

The life Brigit and her friends lived had its risks. Whether they chose it or were forced into it through circumstances, prostitution was inherently dangerous. But that didn't make a sporting woman's murder any less heinous, as Charlotte had seen firsthand three months earlier.

"Might as well have been." Brigit's eyes hardened, anger equal to the grief now. "Camille died after going to some back-alley butcher."

A chill ran up Charlotte's spine. "Back-alley—she died after having . . ."

The word wasn't used in polite company, or any company Charlotte had been in of late. She said it to herself on plenty of occasions, but to speak it out loud? She just couldn't.

"A so-called 'delicate operation,' yes," Brigit said. "Victoria, the friend who wrote me, said Camille had gone to a good doctor. Paid top dollar. But it didn't matter. He practically shoved her out of the room right after because he got wind he was about to be raided."

Charlotte's stomach clenched like a fist. How lucky had she been that the doctor who had performed her own "delicate operation" hadn't been a drunkard or incompetent or caught up in a police raid? A woman with money had a better chance at surviving her decision, but the risk was real no matter what you paid. How many women took that chance and lost every day? Every week? Every year? Hundreds? Thousands? Tens of thousands?

"Charlotte, are you all right? You're pale as a ghost." Brigit rubbed Charlotte's cold hands between hers. "I shouldn't have said anything about it. I assumed that as a journalist and all you'd be somewhat used to atrocities like this."

"No, it's not that." Meeting Brigit's gaze, Charlotte managed a wan smile. "It's not that. I have dealt with some distasteful things, of course, but this . . ."

This was too close, too personal.

Brigit stared at her for several seconds. "You've lost someone to a botched abortion."

Charlotte shook her head and stared down at their entwined hands. She could trust Brigit with the truth, but the words stuck in her throat. How did you explain feeling guilty for *not* feeling guilt and shame?

In her head, in her heart, she absolutely believed in a woman's right to make her own decisions about having children or not. Charlotte knew she wasn't ready. Not then, and not now.

So why did her stomach ache and her head pound when she thought about what she'd done? The option of living with Richard as his wife had been no option at all. Having the child alone? Out of the question, even if Richard hadn't threatened to besmirch her family. Father would have been livid, Mother would have been appalled. Charlotte would have been responsible for ruining their carefully orchestrated lives.

Instead of a suffering a loveless, resentful marriage, or having a child she didn't want, she'd opted to have an illegal abortion.

Breaking that particular law had still put her own reputation and her family's reputation at risk, but the procedure was shorter than a pregnancy and easier to hide. At least on the outside.

"Let me get you something to drink." Brigit gently extricated her fingers, patted Charlotte's hand, and rose. She crossed to the credenza where she kept the house's liquor supply locked up, in defiance of Alaska's dry laws.

A voice came from the stairs behind Charlotte. "I-is everything all r-right?"

Charlotte looked up, knowing it was Della from her soft tone and stutter even before seeing the girl. Della stood halfway up the stairs, wearing a red dressing gown. Her face was clean of makeup, her black hair loose about her shoulders, and her blue eyes full of worry.

"It's fine, Della," Brigit poured a tumbler of whiskey and came back to Charlotte, bottle in hand. "Go finish getting ready, please, and tell Lizzie to wear the dark blue dress. Mr. Copper sent a message he'd be visiting and prefers that color on her."

There was no "Mr. Copper" in Cordova, of course, but pseudonyms told the girls which preferred customers to expect. Brigit was usually tight-lipped about who came to her house, be he councilman or cannery man.

Della glanced between the two of them, then went back upstairs.

"Here," Brigit said to Charlotte, giving her the glass and setting the bottle on the table. "You look like you could use this."

Charlotte held the tumbler with both hands. How long had it been since she'd had a drink? Not since she and Richard had started seeing each other. Not since the days following her procedure, when a dram or two or three helped her sleep without nightmares.

God, the nightmares. Endless crying coming from all around her. Images of herself pounding on doors along a dark and rainy city street while the feeling that something black and wicked was making its way toward her. Something that would eat her whole.

Her reasons for having the abortion were selfish. Her shame was selfish. She publicly called for equality and rights, yet she couldn't bring herself to admit her own decision. Society would never look at her the same if they knew what she'd done.

Charlotte knew she was a hypocrite. That was what haunted her.

"Want to tell me about it?" Brigit asked gently, her dark eyes searching Charlotte's face.

"It's just that—" Charlotte's voice broke, and she took a drink. The whiskey burned down her throat, then up into her sinuses. It hit her stomach. Heat spread through her gut. Her eyes watered, and she coughed as she peered into the glass. Half gone. How had that happened?

"We can go into my office," Brigit offered. "No one will bother us in there."

Della's interruption was both a blessing and a misfortune. She would have told Brigit everything, but now . . . Now, she just couldn't bring herself to say it. Charlotte had practically perfected the façade she showed the outside world. She wasn't ready to reveal her truth to Brigit. Telling Michael had been difficult enough.

She swallowed another mouthful of her whiskey and blew out a cooling breath. "No. Another time, perhaps. Today, we'll celebrate Camille."

Concern clear on her face, Brigit nodded, then held out her tumbler. "Death ends a life, but not a friendship."

She touched the side of her glass to Charlotte's and both drank. The alcohol went down much more smoothly this time.

Brigit smiled sadly. She finished her drink and poured them each another two fingers.

"To friends past and present," Charlotte said.

"To friends."

They drank again to the delicate ringing of glass.

Chapter 3

Miserable was the only word to describe the weather two evenings after Lyle Fiske's death. Shivering, Charlotte tugged her collar up as the steamship *North Star* arrived in port, its whistle sounding in the icy air. The snow and rain mix chilled to the bone. Even the extra pair of wool socks she wore wasn't quite enough.

The *North Star* sidled up to the lighted dock and blew a final burst of exhaust, its engines roaring, then settling into a low rumble that Charlotte felt in the soles of her boots. The ship had the capacity to carry a couple of hundred passengers, but according to the published list only half that were aboard. The most important one, in her reckoning, was the woman whose life was about to change dramatically.

"What are you doing here?" James growled low in her ear so the other dozen or so people waiting on the dock wouldn't hear.

Charlotte didn't bother turning around. Instead, she watched the dock men secure thick lines to the massive posts. "I really should do a piece on them," she said offhandedly. "These men work in some wretched conditions."

"You know that's not what I'm asking. I told you I didn't want you here."

Now Charlotte faced him, anger hot in her chest. He looked as mad as she felt. "This is a free territory, deputy. You have no right to tell me any such thing, and you can't order me away from a public place when I've done nothing wrong. Did you honestly think I'd go against your wishes and pelt poor Caroline with questions? What sort of person do you think I am?"

His scowl softened into contrition. "I'm sorry. You're right. I should have trusted you'd keep your word." He rubbed a gloved hand over his beard and watched the gangplank being lowered to the dock. "I have to go. Everyone is being kept on board until I get Mrs. Fiske. I want a clear path to the car so we can get her home right away." James met her gaze again. "I am sorry, Charlotte."

"That's twice in several days that you've insulted my integrity," she said.

"Reckon I owe you something for that. Dinner tomorrow?"

She blinked at him. After all that, he was asking her to dinner? She should have said no. Instead she heard herself say, "All right."

There was nothing wrong with friends having dinner, especially when one was asking as a way of apology for boorish behavior. It would be rude to turn him down. Wouldn't it?

He touched the brim of his hat, and without another word jogged up the gangplank.

Charlotte shook off the funny little feeling she had in her gut and pulled her notebook out of her coat pocket. Protecting the pages from the snow as best she could, she took notes on the crowd and atmosphere while everyone waited for James to conduct the ugly business of informing Caroline Fiske of her loss and escort her to the waiting car.

The steamship company's Cordova agent stood near the rear door of a Model T, anxiety etched on his thin face beneath the dock's floodlights. His collar was turned up and his bowler dripped. What was his name? She'd have to remember to get it for the article. People usually liked seeing their names in print, even under less than positive circumstances.

It was a cold twenty minutes, according to her pendant watch, until James and Caroline appeared at the top of the gangplank. The glare of the dock lights washed out the normal glow of Caroline's fair skin. A sable hat and matching long coat enveloped her, as if they were too large for her frame. She wasn't a tiny woman, but she seemed fragile now. The news James had to deliver would certainly have made anyone shrink in on themselves.

James took Caroline's arm as they descended. The dozen or so people waiting at the dock fell into respectful silence. The only sounds were the low rumble of the resting steamer's engine and the lap of waves against the piling. Even the dock workers paused in their duties, sensing something was amiss. James looked straight ahead at the car waiting for them, one arm now around Caroline's shoulder, the other supporting her elbow.

As they passed, Charlotte noticed tear streaks through Caroline's makeup and the smudged mascara. No one said a word. The steamship company agent opened the rear door of the car. Inside, an older woman peered out at the approaching pair, her face lined with anxiety. Charlotte assumed she was the housekeeper or a friend James had mentioned calling upon to help tend Caroline.

Caroline slid onto the backseat. Charlotte saw the older woman's lips move, but couldn't hear what she was saying. All she caught was Caroline's expression crumbling into tearful sorrow.

Without a glance or word to anyone, James closed the door and climbed into the front passenger seat. The agent hurried around to the driver's seat. The black car had been left running, and smoothly eased forward toward the road.

The crowd started talking at once. Most sympathized with

the new widow, and wondered who could have done such a thing to Mr. Fiske. No one mentioned the robbery, but several speculated that the arsonist had gone too far.

The ship's passengers began disembarking, making their way to waiting friends and family with questions about the delay.

Charlotte pocketed her notebook and pencil and withdrew a flashlight from her coat. The snow had abated for the moment, at least, so the walk back to the office wouldn't be intolerable. She could have hired one of the two waiting taxis, but wanted some quiet time to get her thoughts in order. Her article would touch on Caroline's emotional state, without disrespecting the woman.

A car roared up behind her, its headlights throwing shadows. Charlotte moved as far to the side of the road as she could, but the taxi splashed slush onto her boots anyway.

"Thanks another heap, Clyde," she muttered. He seemed to have a knack for finding her.

A second vehicle approached from the same direction, but rather than pass her it slowed.

"Charlotte, is that you?"

Charlotte turned as the car stopped. She shielded her eyes from the glare of the headlights. Brigit's rosy-cheeked face peered out from the rear window. "It's me. What are you doing out here?"

"Not getting wet." Brigit opened the door. "Get in here before you catch your death."

Realizing she'd lost the feeling in her toes, Charlotte climbed in. The backseat of the Ford was worn in places, but clean. Brigit sat in the middle of the bench seat. A younger woman in a knee-length dark green coat sat near the other door. She was no more than twenty, with short curly blond hair beneath her cloche.

The driver, a man Charlotte knew as Brigit's handyman and muscle when things at the house became a bit too boisterous, nodded to her. "Miss Brody. Where can we take you?"

"To the *Times* office please, Mr. Larsen."

Their conversations never went beyond a few words. He focused on the road again and moved forward when she was settled.

"Charlotte, this is Edie," Brigit said. "She's come up from Juneau. Edie, this is my friend Charlotte. She's with the paper."

Brigit rarely referred to her girls by last name, and she afforded Charlotte an appreciated familiarity by introducing her by her given name. "Nice to meet you, Edie."

"Likewise." She gave Charlotte's sogginess unabashed perusal. "Ain't such a good night to be walkin'."

Charlotte and Brigit exchanged amused glances. If Edie was one of Brigit's new girls—and Charlotte remembered her saying she was looking for fresh faces—her forthright manner would serve her well in Cordova.

Now that Brigit had her blonde, maybe she'd stop teasing Charlotte about coming to work for her. Though Charlotte would miss their little personal joke.

"No, it's not," Charlotte said. "I appreciate you stopping."

"I thought I saw you on the dock," Brigit said, "but everyone is covered head to toe. Were you there to talk to Caroline Fiske?"

"Not talk to her." Charlotte didn't want to rehash the argument with James here. "Just making observations. Did you know Mr. Fiske?"

Brigit's mouth quirked into a crooked smile. "Do you mean professionally? He stopped by now and again."

"How about Caroline?"

"No, she never came to the house," Brigit said with a wink. She put on a show of jocularity and cheer, but Charlotte could still see the pain of the loss of her friend in the shadows beneath her eyes. "I saw her in a shop or on the street now and again, but we weren't familiar."

"Just a nice, upstanding couple who've met with tragedy." It was a story Charlotte had heard all too often.

"I never said they were upstanding."

Charlotte stared at her friend, a woman who knew more than a few secrets about Cordova's citizens. "What do you mean?"

Brigit shook her head. "Not here."

The car stopped on Main Street in front of the *Times* office. Mr. Larsen got out and came around to the rear door.

"Come by for lunch tomorrow," Brigit said, and delivered a quick peck to Charlotte's cheek.

"I will. Thanks for the ride." Charlotte smiled at Edie. "Good night."

The young woman responded with a halfhearted smile, her eyes on her employer. Was she curious about the Fiskes or Brigit? Probably both.

Charlotte stepped out of the car, thanked Mr. Larsen, and went to the office door. She waved as the vehicle pulled away.

Brigit would have trusted Mr. Larsen with whatever she knew, but Edie was of untested reliability. Discretion had kept Brigit in business; she wouldn't risk that by talking in front of the new girl. But did Brigit know something pertinent to the murder of Lyle Fiske?

Mr. Toliver strolled into the office a couple of hours after Charlotte had returned from the steamship dock. His fur hat and coat on his bulky figure made him look like a bear that had woken too soon from hibernation.

Flicking snow off his coat, he grinned at Charlotte. "How's she running, Miss Brody?"

His typical greeting encompassed both the Linotype and herself.

Charlotte rose from the chair behind the desk where she'd been working. "Going well. I just finished the bit on Caroline Fiske's return this evening."

He shook his head sadly as he hung up his things and changed out of his boots. "That poor woman."

Toliver straightened his tie and smoothed down his hair. He

made sure his vest, jacket, and trousers were neat before striding over to her. Out from under the bulk of his furs, he was
graceful and light on his feet for a large man. At every dance
Charlotte had attended where he was present, ladies practically
stood in line for a chance to be whisked across the floor by the
newsman. There were eligible bachelors aplenty in Cordova,
but few could fox-trot as finely as Andrew Toliver.

"She was quite shaken, as expected," Charlotte said, stepping
aside and allowing Toliver to take his seat. "But I kept the piece
short and to the point. No sense in getting overly emotional or
gruesome."

"Good, good." He picked up papers, perusing them as he sat.
"Speaking of emotional . . ."

He quirked a graying eyebrow at her.

Great. What had Mrs. Hillman said to him?

"I take it you spoke to the president of the Temperance
League?"

"More like she spoke *at* me," he said, rolling his eyes. Charlotte smiled, but knew he had brought up Mrs. Hillman for one
reason. "She had definite ideas about how things should be."

Her smile tightened, and she felt flushed with irritation as
she recalled the conversation with the women. "And no qualms
about telling others their opinions are wrong."

Toliver nodded. "True, but feuding with her or the Women's
Temperance League is not in our best interest."

She folded her arms across her chest. "She wanted me to re-
tract my opinion piece. I said no."

"I'm pretty sure you said more than that. I believe you called
her ignorant?"

Charlotte felt the heat of that truth, but Toliver was wearing
a wry grin while he said it. "And shortsighted, but only to myself after they were gone."

Toliver stared at her, wide-eyed, then chuckled as he shook
his head. Maybe he wasn't terribly angry with her. "I can only
imagine the look on her face."

"I thought Mrs. Cron and Mrs. Burgess were going to die of the vapors right over there." She gestured toward the doorway. "I guess I was a tad unprofessional."

Toliver looked serious now. "She wants me to fire you, you know."

That didn't surprise her in the least. "I'd expected her to call for a public flogging or lock me in the stocks in the town square."

"I'm sure it crossed her mind. If we had a town square, and stocks, she's the sort of woman who'd call for their use on a regular basis." He leaned back in the chair, thumbs hooked inside the pockets of his vest. "I reminded her this was a fair and balanced newspaper, and we'd be happy to run something she and the ladies penned."

"And?"

He reached into his inside jacket pocket and withdrew several pieces of paper folded lengthwise. He held them out to her. "We'll include this in tomorrow's edition."

Charlotte took them and read. There was nothing within the essay she hadn't heard countless times before from Temperance Leagues from New York to California. The evils of alcohol, the deterioration of American society, particularly the looseness of morals and mores. That last bit, Charlotte was sure, was aimed at her own reference to using birth control. And of course there was the less-than-subtle potshots at anyone who thought differently.

The position Mrs. Hillman and the others took made her blood boil, but the First Amendment was near and dear to Charlotte. She'd make sure the article was typed just as it was written.

"I'll get to work on it right now." She started toward the printing room.

Toliver called her back. "I appreciate you standing by your convictions, Miss Brody, but can I offer you a word of advice?"

Charlotte frowned at her boss. "If it's 'make nice' with Mrs. Hillman and her friends, you may as well fire me now."

"Oh, good Lord, woman, no one expects miracles." He smiled and she grinned back, relieved. "Just be careful. This is a small town and social politics are a local pastime. There's a certain 'us versus them' attitude you need to be aware of."

"I won't kowtow to the likes of that woman." Charlotte had learned long ago that letting bullies get away with threats only made things worse.

"I'm not asking you to do that at all. As a journalist, neutrality on issues is key. You're supposed to report the news, not necessarily make it." Toliver wasn't quite lecturing her, and Charlotte tried not to take it as such.

"As a human being and a citizen of this country," she said, "I have the right to my opinion."

He nodded. "Of course you do, which is why your article ran as an opinion piece. The League also has that right. But Mrs. Hillman can be a force to be reckoned with."

"She's not the only one."

"I know that too," Toliver said with a gentle smile. "That's why I asked you to come aboard in the first place. Try not to let her get to you, eh? Weigh the risks and consequences of challenging her, or anyone."

Charlotte understood his dilemma. Andrew Toliver did his best to let all voices be heard, but the *Times* was his life. If Hillman and her friends pushed hard enough, they might influence businesses to pull advertisements, or start a skirmish within the pages of the paper. While that might increase readership, there was also a potential for boycotting.

She didn't think the entire town backed either her or Hillman, but Toliver shouldn't risk his livelihood on her stubbornness. No blaming him there. She'd withstood threats and vandalism when she wrote for the papers back East and knew all too well how personal opinion or activity could influence the newspaper business. Readership waxed and waned with controversial articles, but Toliver and the *Times* didn't have the resources to keep afloat if too many stopped reading.

"I'll be civil to Mrs. Hillman and her friends."

"That's all I ask." He squared himself behind the desk and shuffled through more papers. "All right, get on that article, please, Miss Brody, and get yourself home at a decent hour."

Charlotte started toward the print room again, then stopped and turned back. "Thank you, Mr. Toliver."

He waved absently. "Just keep doing what you're doing."

"Oh, I plan to, sir."

Chapter 4

Charlotte stayed home the next morning to work on her series for *Modern Woman*. She'd interviewed the proprietresses of Frankle & Taylor Ladies' Finery, who had come to Alaska nearly twenty years before during the Nome gold rush. Theirs was an exciting tale of two young women succeeding in a rough and wild mining town that tested the toughest of all who were drawn there. Penelope Frankle had been an assayer, buying gold, and Rowena Taylor made herself a nice little nest egg mining on the crowded beach of the remote town. Now in their forties, the two friends had settled down together in the more amicable Cordova.

Charlotte's readers would love it. But only if she got it to New York and into the hands of her *Modern Woman* editor and best friend, Kit Cameron. Kit was understanding when it came to the inherent hiccups of the postal service between Alaska and the States, but Charlotte tried to avoid escalating hiccups into all-out distress for her and Mr. Malone, the publisher.

Just after noon, she finished the draft, promising herself to go over it later and get it out on the next ship, and headed to Brigit's. Careful to keep her footing on the icy road, she descended the hill to Main Street, then down toward Michael's office. There was a shortcut to Brigit's just about behind Michael's, but chances were good that no one had cleared it of snow. Rather than risk a bad fall, she went the long way, around the corner and down the street.

Charlotte knocked on the door. It wasn't so early in the day that Brigit and the girls would still be asleep. Charlie was likely in school, since it was Tuesday, otherwise he was the unofficial answerer of the door before business hours.

The filigreed brass peep box didn't slide open, as usual, before the door latch clicked. Brigit smiled as she held the door for Charlotte. "I saw you from the upstairs window. Come in."

She followed Brigit into the entry. Someone was in the parlor running a sweeper and singing. Della's sweet voice, and not a stutter to be heard. Brigit took Charlotte's hat and coat and had her change her boots for a pair of soft slippers.

"How are you doing?" Charlotte asked as she accompanied Brigit into her office.

The madam shrugged, a sad smile on her face. "Getting on as best I can." She tilted her head. "How are *you* doing? You were more than a little affected yourself the other day."

Charlotte swallowed hard; the reminder of their conversation caught her off guard. "I'm fine. Really."

She was lying, and Brigit probably knew it.

"Let me know if I can do anything for you, all right?" Brigit's sincere offer was accompanied by a warm squeeze of Charlotte's arm. Charlotte's throat tightened and she could only nod.

"Have a seat," Brigit said, indicating one of the two chairs at a small table near her desk. There were matching plates, cups for tea, and bowls at each place. Beside the table, a rolling cart held an ornate soup tureen. "I'll get the sandwiches. Is there anything else you'd like?"

Recovering from the unexpected emotion, Charlotte smiled at her friend. "No, thanks. This is wonderful."

Brigit grinned and left the room. It was funny how she and Brigit had become friends, yet they hardly knew anything about each other. Charlotte had discovered a little about Brigit's past during the whole ugly business of the Darcy Dugan murder, but Brigit rarely volunteered information. The news about her friend Camille had been an exception. Then again, Charlotte wasn't exactly forthcoming with her own flawed history.

"Here we go." Brigit returned in a few minutes and closed the door behind her. She set the plate of sandwiches between them, ladled soup from the tureen, then sat down. "Split pea soup. My mother's recipe."

"You cook?" Charlotte couldn't help the surprise in her voice. The women usually took turns preparing meals and taking care of the house, though Brigit had hired someone to help out with some chores.

Brigit laughed and winked. "I have many skills outside of the bedroom."

Charlotte knew she was a savvy businesswoman as well. Brigit's house was one of the few remaining in Cordova, known to have a reputation for quality entertainment, be it in services or gaming.

They each enjoyed a few bites of their food—the soup was marvelous—and made small talk before getting to the true point of the visit.

"You alluded to something last night," Charlotte said, "about the Fiskes not being all they appeared to be. What did you mean by that?"

Brigit wasn't one to gossip; her livelihood depended on discretion. She wouldn't say anything if she didn't think it was important to the investigation of the fire or the death of Lyle Fiske.

The madam dabbed at her lips with her linen napkin. "Everyone has their secrets, don't they, Charlotte?"

Charlotte stared at her friend. Brigit certainly had hers. Was she referring to Charlotte's reluctance to tell her own secrets the other day? Everyone kept things to themselves, but what secrets were worth killing a man over?

"The Fiskes had an open marriage," Brigit continued, "though neither broadcast the fact. Appearances and all that. He quietly saw girls here or at other houses from time to time. She's said to have a lover who's more . . . satisfying than her husband."

Having an affair wasn't anything new, but people usually tried to be more discreet. Maybe the Fiskes figured living in a small town meant everyone would know sooner or later anyway.

"Who?"

Brigit shrugged. "I don't know and really don't care. I'm sure Lyle knew, but he wasn't complaining. He was just talking. That's what he usually did here. Talk."

That didn't surprise Charlotte. A lot of men visited brothels just for a little companionship. "Were you the one to have conversations with him?"

"Sometimes," Brigit said. She sipped her tea. "More often than not it was one of the other girls. He was partial to Marie for a while."

Marie had left not long after Charlotte had arrived in Cordova. She wondered how Marie was doing back in the States.

"If they weren't happy with each other, why stay married?" Charlotte asked.

"Why divorce? He gets a wife who has social acumen to help his business and standing in the community. She benefits from the financial and social stability. As long as they're both in agreement of expectations, no one gets hurt, right?"

But someone did get hurt. The question was, did their arrangement have anything to do with the fire and Lyle's death?

"Maybe Lyle got tired of being the cuckold," Charlotte suggested. "Maybe he called Caroline's lover in to tell him to leave her be, and the lover refused."

"They fought and things got out of hand," Brigit said, finishing the scenario.

"Or Caroline wanted out of the marriage and Lyle refused," Charlotte said. "Maybe she sent her lover to make him change his mind." Though that was less likely, it wasn't completely out of the realm of possibility.

"And *then* things got out of hand." Brigit nodded, a thoughtful expression on her face. "Men can become possessive, even when they've given up claim, be it woman or object."

Love and jealousy did strange things to people, to their ability to act and think logically.

"What about other people who may have had problems with Fiske?" Charlotte asked. Businessmen sometimes made enemies, whether they ran large corporations or small town stores.

"Nothing unusual," Brigit said. "Folks grumbled here and there. He and Otto Kenner had a yelling match in the middle of a Businessmen's Association meeting, I heard."

"Otto Kenner?" The name sounded familiar, but Charlotte couldn't quite place him.

"Big, burly guy." Brigit held her hands over her shoulders to illustrated Otto Kenner's physique. "He's a builder and carpenter. His brother Adam has an office just across from yours, above the barber shop."

Charlotte still couldn't picture either man. They probably didn't cross paths often.

"Anyway, Fiske was the only game in town, really, as far as the hardware store went. It's expensive to bring goods up here. I think he was decent about not gouging customers. Much."

Something was missing at the end of that sentence. "But?"

"There are things you shouldn't know, that I can't tell you." When Charlotte started to protest, Brigit covered her hand with her own, stopping her. "Not because I don't trust you. I do. But your relationship with a certain deputy puts you—and me—in a precarious position. If you know something and don't tell James, and he asks about it, you could get into trouble. None of us wants that." She smiled at Charlotte. "Especially James, I'd wager."

If she was speaking to anyone else, Charlotte would have

pushed for more, but Brigit was her friend. "Can you give me a hint? Something I can try to work out for myself? That way if I happen to learn anything you won't get into trouble."

Brigit pressed her lips together, her brow furrowed as she contemplated Charlotte's request. "Let's just say the Fiskes were better off than they seemed."

"Was he doing some creative accounting?"

Lying about business income and expenditure wasn't new, though Fiske didn't have investors to steal from. None that were known, at any rate.

Brigit shook her head. "I can't say more. Truly, Charlotte."

Charlotte squeezed her hand in understanding. "Thank you for that much. It gives me something else to go on."

"Are you going to talk to James about the Fiskes' marriage?"

She wasn't sure how to read the look on Brigit's face. "I think I should, don't you? It could be vital to finding out who killed Fiske. I promise not to tell him where I got the idea. You can be my anonymous source."

Brigit laughed. "I'm sure James Eddington will have a good idea where you got your information, but as long as I don't say anything specific, we should both be all right."

"Exactly." Charlotte spooned up some more soup. "This really is delicious."

"I'll give you the recipe, if you'd like."

"Oh, no," Charlotte said. "I'd much rather visit you to get some."

She grinned at Brigit's pinkening cheeks, and the two of them finished their lunch.

On her way back to the office, Charlotte saw James standing in front of the federal building, talking to a woman. She wore a fashionable cloche hat despite the cold and wet. Her back was to Charlotte, making it impossible to identify her. Bundled up as everyone was in this weather, it was difficult to recognize who was who most of the time. The woman patted James on the arm and leaned forward to peck him on the cheek before she hurried up the street.

A pang went through Charlotte, stopping her momentarily. Who was that?

Charlotte shook off whatever it was she felt. Not jealousy, exactly. Surprise? She had no claim on him, nor he on her. They were friends, free to see whomever they chose, to have another person kiss them, if that's what they wanted.

She started toward him again and called out before he went inside. "James, do you have a minute?"

He turned his head as he unlocked the main door. The marshal's office occupied the ground floor. Up a wide staircase was the post office, which was closed for the afternoon. "About that," he said. "I have a meeting with the fire chief."

He held the door for her, then unlocked the interior office door as well. The room smelled of leather, gun oil, and tobacco. Both James and Marshal Blaine enjoyed a pipe or cigar now and again.

"I won't hold you up. How did it go with Caroline last night?"

James went to his desk and rifled through a drawer. "Much as you'd expect."

"Did she have any idea who'd try to rob them or hurt Lyle?" It was a long shot of a question, of course. Chances were good the robbery was a random act and the murder of Lyle Fiske a terrible result of circumstances.

He closed the drawer with a bit more force than necessary. "No, she didn't. According to Mrs. Fiske, he had no enemies, and no one in his employ had reason to hurt him or the business."

Charlotte narrowed her gaze. "You don't sound convinced."

"It's the rare businessman who becomes successful without ruffling at least a few feathers. Or being ruffled himself."

"I was just saying as much." She always felt heartened when she and James seemed to follow similar thought processes. "I heard he and Otto Kenner weren't exactly friendly."

"Yeah, I heard that too, but that isn't motive for murder."

"But what if it turned into something more?"

James lifted one eyebrow. As much as they seemed drawn to similar conclusions, she also knew that look of skepticism. "Do you know anything specific, or are you just flinging things out there?"

She shrugged. "Mostly flinging. Never hurts to speculate."

"No, but I need more than a list of who didn't like the man." He came around the desk and gestured for her to precede him to the door. "Right now, it looks like a robbery that got out of hand. The thief, caught by surprise, grabs the closest thing he could use as a weapon. This time it happened to be a big hunting knife from the display case. People make mistakes when a situation gets excitable. They don't think straight and it goes from bad to worse."

It certainly had at that.

He held up the folder. "Your brother's report. That's what I'm meeting Parker about, to confirm the explosion of the solvents covered Fiske with debris that snuffed out the flames on his body. Had Fiske's body burned further, Michael might not have found the fatal wound. This case is now officially a homicide investigation rather than an unfortunate accidental fire."

"Do you think the arsonist is responsible?" Charlotte was starting to have her doubts. This event was well beyond the arsonist's typical behavior.

"I'm not ruling anything out just yet," James said. "It's possible our firebug broke in to steal some solvent and got caught by Fiske."

They were back in the shared entry. James tucked the file under his arm and secured the inner door.

"What about Mrs. Fiske?" she asked.

James's head came up, his eyebrows arched. "As a suspect? How? And why? She was on a ship, two days from port."

"But her lover probably wasn't."

His eyes narrowed. "Lover?"

Was he unaware of the Fiskes' open relationship, or feeling out what Charlotte knew?

"I understand Caroline was seeing someone. Whom Lyle knew. Is it possible Lyle confronted him, or vice versa?"

Lovers' quarrels and triangles that led to murder seemed to be the thing of dime-store novels, but they happened. How many men and women were killed "in the heat of passion" by their spouses or lovers or rivals?

"Of course it's possible. A man can only take being a cuckold for so long." James practically spat the words out, angry. Something had touched a nerve. "But unless someone has a name to go with this supposition, there's not much I can do."

"Caroline wouldn't be keen on giving up that information."

"Not likely." James gestured toward the outer door, giving her an expectant look when she didn't move. "What?"

Charlotte considered a possible scenario. "Lyle calls the lover to the store to tell him to stop seeing his wife. Things get heated, out of control, and the other man grabs the knife in rage." She pantomimed snatching the hunting knife out of the display behind the counter. "And in his anger—"

She thrust the imaginary knife upward, hitting James just under the sternum with her fist.

He wrapped his large hand gently around her wrist. "Or the lover goes to Fiske to demand he divorce Caroline. Lyle refuses. Fight. Stab."

He thumped her fist against the same spot on his chest.

"Or," Charlotte said, easing her hand from his grip and lowering it, "there was another reason the killer wanted Lyle dead."

"Other than an interrupted robbery."

"Yes. Keeping a business going is difficult, especially in a small, remote town. What if Fiske's business dealings weren't so legitimate?"

"I'd be more surprised if they were completely legitimate." He cocked an eyebrow at her. "What have you heard?"

"Nothing specific." That was true enough. Brigit had been willing to hint, not divulge. Charlotte was jumping to an awfully big conclusion without any detail. "But it's worth considering, yes?"

"Yes," he said. "I'll see what I can dig up. Probably need to talk to Caroline again."

Charlotte headed toward the outer door.

"We're still having dinner tonight, aren't we?" James asked.

She stopped, her heart fluttering. She'd forgotten about his invitation.

It's just dinner.

"Of course," she said. "Meet you at The Wild Rose at six."

Charlotte left the federal building, fully intent on getting back to the *Times* office to work, but her eye was drawn toward the harbor road. Specifically to Fiske's. She couldn't quite see the building from Main Street, but she could swear she smelled the burnt wood and acrid chemical bite of the air. Bypassing the office, she made her way to the devastated store.

The scorched siding around the open door and broken windows reminded her of a night three months ago. She shivered, recalling the fire meant to scare her, if not kill her. Charlotte had ignored the note she'd received about involving herself in Darcy Dugan's murder, but the fire made it clear she'd been getting too close to the truth. Hopefully nothing like that would happen again. Touching a fingertip to the small scar under her left eye, Charlotte shook off the memory and went through the gaping door.

Even days later, a residual stench hung in the air, though the worst of the offensive aroma from the fire seemed to have dissipated. Watery light penetrated the gaps in the building, leaving deep shadows between the head-high shelves that hadn't completely succumbed to flames or the firefighters' drenching. Tools, boxes, and small appliances littered the floor. Glass crunched under her boots. The deeper she went, the more dank and oppressive the air became.

"I should have brought my flashlight," she muttered aloud. She'd needed to change the batteries and forgot to put it back in her coat pocket. Though she wasn't quite sure what she was looking for. A clue as to who killed Lyle, but what did she expect to find in these ruins?

The charred service counter across the rear of the room separated the store from what she figured was Fiske's office. The blackened door was open and a light flickered within the back room.

"Damnation!" A woman's voice, coming from the office.

Charlotte hurried behind the scorched counter, past the equally blackened gilded till. She peeked around the doorjamb.

In a room dimly illuminated by wintery light coming through the empty narrow windows, Caroline Fiske, in widow's black, knelt in front of a squat safe, her profile to Charlotte. A balled-up coat cushioned her knees. The rear of the office had escaped the worst of the fire damage. The safe sat beside Fiske's sodden but mostly intact wood desk.

Caroline's head was bowed, her eyes closed, and a pinched expression on her face. She took a deep breath and opened her eyes. Staring hard at the combination lock, she turned the dial with care while holding a flashlight in the other hand. Right. Left. Right. She tried the handle. It didn't budge.

Caroline slapped her palm against the safe and let out a frustrated growl.

"Mrs. Fiske?" Charlotte had no reason to hide from the widow, and her curiosity bade her to question the woman.

Caroline startled and swung the light toward her. "Who's that?" Charlotte ducked her head slightly to keep the light from her eyes. Caroline lowered the beam. "Oh, Miss Brody. What are you doing here?"

"My apologies. I was going to do a follow-up article about the fire, and the possible connection to the arsonist, when I saw your light. I'm so sorry about your husband."

Caroline rose, dusting off her skirt. "Thank you."

Dark smudges of sleeplessness marred the pale skin beneath her brown eyes. Despite her foray into the sooty remains of the store, Caroline's face was otherwise clean and clear, and her black hair remained in its neat bun.

"Is there something I might help you with?" Charlotte glanced between Caroline and the safe.

The woman closed her eyes, collecting herself. Her shoulders stiffened, and her back straightened. With an almost regal bearing, she focused on Charlotte again. "I was looking for insurance papers."

Charlotte felt a kick of adrenaline. Insurance? Money was as strong a motivator as love. Perhaps stronger for some people.

"I'm sure that sounds perfectly horrible," Caroline said, pain deepening lines along her mouth and between her eyes. "I've been wandering around the house most of the day feeling out of sorts and useless, and figured at the very least I could look into taking care of the store."

It hadn't bothered her that she was in the place where her husband had been robbed and murdered? Had she no feelings for the man?

"That's understandable," Charlotte said despite the thoughts she had. "But you don't know the combination?"

"I do, or thought I did." Caroline glanced at the safe. "The numbers seem to have left my head. I was sure it was—Oh!"

She quickly knelt down again and spun the dial. Right. Left. Right. This time, when she pushed down on the handle, it clicked.

Charlotte made her way over some debris to stand behind the woman. Had the safe been emptied like the till?

Caroline pulled the heavy door open. She shined her light inside. Papers, folders, several stacks of federal reserve notes, a canvas coin sack. All lay neatly on the shelves, undisturbed.

So much for robbery.

Caroline reached in, shoving aside the papers and cash. A small whimper escaped her. "It's gone. Where did he put it?"

Chapter 5

Caroline jumped to her feet, nearly knocking Charlotte over. She ran to the desk and yanked open drawers. "Where is it? Where'd you put it, Lyle?"

Anxiety raised her voice half an octave. A drawer crashed to the floor. She gave the mess a cursory search, then pulled out another when she didn't find whatever she was looking for. The flashlight's beam bobbed in time with her frantic movement.

"What are you looking for, Caroline?" Charlotte came around the desk, wary of flying papers, pen nibs, and ink pots.

"A black metal box with a gold border around the lid." Caroline straightened from a crouch, turning this way and that as she swept the room with the light. "It's gone. He kept it in the safe, and now it's gone."

Charlotte scanned the room as well, though she had no sense she'd actually find the missing box. "Would Lyle have brought it home? Did you look there?"

Caroline shook her head. "No. No, he kept everything here. This is the most secure place." She turned to a set of shelves behind the desk and began pulling out waterlogged catalogues and papers, scattering them across the floor with wet thuds. "Where could it be?"

"Could someone have taken it?" If the box contained papers important enough for Caroline to be in a panic over it, perhaps the thief had wanted it as well.

Caroline stopped emptying the shelf and her head snapped up. Her dark eyes were wide, the whites visible in the low light. Did she have an idea who might have the box?

"Hey! Who's in there?" a gruff voice called from the other room. Heavy footsteps pounded closer. "If any of you kids— Oh." A flashlight beam cut across Charlotte. She raised a hand to block the light from her eyes. "Miss Brody. What are you doing here?"

Fire chief Donald Parker stood in the doorway. Filled it, more accurately. He was a tall, barrel-shaped man. His hardened-leather chief's hat almost touched the top of the frame.

Before Charlotte could say anything, Caroline stood up, putting herself in his light.

"I couldn't help myself, Donald." She gave Charlotte an unreadable look. "I came to find some papers, but Lyle must have moved them."

The complete opposite of what she'd told Charlotte, that Lyle would never have moved them. That's what Caroline's glance had indicated, a request that Charlotte go along with what she'd told Parker. What sort of game was Caroline Fiske playing?

"Mrs. Fiske. Didn't see you there, ma'am. It's too dangerous for you to be poking around in here." Parker's walrus mustache bristled. "Fire and water damage the structural integrity. The ceiling could collapse and you'd be hurt, or worse." He shined the light on Charlotte again. "And what about you, Miss Brody?"

"Doing a little investigative journalism, is all."

Chief Parker harrumphed and frowned, telling her exactly

how he felt about that. "Nothing to investigate as far as you're concerned. Eddington and I will let you know what we find. I think you ladies should leave. If you want to search the premises again, Mrs. Fiske, please come see me first. I want someone with you, as a precaution."

Caroline casually picked up her coat and walked over to the safe. She closed and locked it. "Thank you, Chief. I'll send Joe and Randall, or Ben, to check in with you before they get this safe and bring it to the house."

Joe Fisher and Randall Towers were the Fiske Hardware employees. According to James's questioning, both men had gotten on well with Lyle and had alibis for the night. Who was Ben?

As Caroline walked toward the door, with Charlotte following, she visually swept the room again, as if hoping the box would miraculously appear. When it didn't, she sighed, her shoulders sagging.

Parker led the way back to the safety of the street. They all blinked as their eyes adjusted to the relatively bright light.

"Charlotte, what are you doing here?" James asked striding toward them, the displeasure clear on his face. His expression changed to sympathetic confusion when he saw Caroline. "Mrs. Fiske. I recommended you not come here."

He wanted to save her the heartache of seeing where her husband died. Once again, Charlotte was impressed by the sensitivity of the outwardly gruff deputy.

"I know, deputy," Caroline said, "but I was beside myself and unable to just sit there at the house. I decided to look for some important business papers, to keep my mind occupied. Lyle kept them in a box in the safe, but the box isn't there. Perhaps he moved it, or the thief you mentioned took it."

But why take the box and not the money? Charlotte wondered. It made no sense.

"It's been such an ordeal," Caroline continued. Tears welled but didn't fall. "I just can't think straight. I should go home."

"Let me walk with you," Charlotte said. Maybe she could carefully question Caroline.

"No, that's all right." Caroline smiled wanly. "I'd prefer to be alone for now."

Damn.

Caroline bade them good-bye. She picked her way through the snowy street up toward the main road. Rather than continue straight, to her home, Caroline turned onto Main Street, away from her house.

"Now, Charlotte—" James began.

"She's hiding something."

James and the chief exchanged startled glances.

"In the office," Charlotte said, "she was frantic, searching for the black box, saying Lyle kept it in that safe and that safe only. Inside the safe is several hundred dollars in federal reserve notes. Why would a thief take the box and not the money?"

James focused on the dark door, eyes narrowed as he thought it through. "Maybe Fiske had the box out already. The thief takes it and cleans out the till. Somewhere in there, Fiske comes along and gets himself killed."

"Then the thief sets fire to cover his tracks," the chief said. He shook his head. "I'll let you work out the robbery and murder angle, Eddington. I'm going back inside to confirm how this damn fire got started."

"I'll be in as soon as I finish with Miss Brody," James said. The chief grunted, flicked on his flashlight, and headed back into the burned-out store. James locked his gaze on her again. "The question is, which came first? Did the thief go after the money, the box, or Lyle?"

"I don't think it's all about the money," Charlotte said. "There's something about that box and whatever's in it. But how would he open the safe?"

"If the box wasn't already out, maybe he forced Lyle to open it." The deputy's lips pressed together. "Or he had the combination."

"From Lyle or from Caroline," she said. James frowned at her suggestion. "Joe or Randall might have had the combination. Caroline knows it. She could have given the alleged thief the combination."

James shook his head. "Then why is she so panicked about the box? If she knew someone was going to get into the safe, she'd realize who else could have taken it."

"We don't know how much money was in the safe to begin with," Charlotte said. "He may have been told to take the money, to make it look like a robbery, but discovered something better inside the box. If she planned it, Caroline wouldn't want the box 'found' until after she returned. She wouldn't have needed to come here today."

"If her hired thief was tasked with getting it, she could have said it was in their home all the time and no one would dispute it. But you said she was shocked that the box wasn't in the safe, maybe on the verge of panic." James looked skeptical. "That's a lot of trouble to go through to avoid divorce."

Charlotte agreed, but she also knew people did strange things when it came to personal relationships, and ending them. "As much as I like Caroline, if she's cheating on her husband— with or without his acceptance—she might be tired of juggling two lives. Perhaps she wanted Lyle out of the way permanently, so she could have the store, her social status intact, and still keep her relationship with her lover."

James stared at her for several moments. "It would take a helluva cold woman to pull off something like that."

They both knew that a woman was as likely as any man to be brutal and coldhearted, despite outward appearances of gentility.

The idea gave Charlotte an uncomfortable feeling, like there was an itch in the middle of her back she couldn't reach. She didn't *want* to think of Caroline as an engineer of murder, but that didn't preclude the new widow from suspicion.

James removed his hat and raked his fingers through his hair.

He hadn't shaved in several days. The scruff on his face and his mussed hair made him look dog-weary. "If we could figure out who he is, we might get somewhere."

Charlotte felt the thrill of his saying "we" when it came to the case. That he did so without thinking made her question his earlier protests of her involvement, and that made her smile.

"I'll talk to the housekeeper again," James said. "They're usually privy to family secrets."

"Mrs. Munson's only been there a month," Charlotte reminded him.

"A lot can happen in a month."

"What if she doesn't know or won't reveal anything about the Fiskes' private lives?"

"I'll figure something out." He scowled at her even before Charlotte opened her mouth to make a suggestion. "No. You may not talk to her or Caroline or anyone else."

Charlotte's joy at his earlier referral to their working together withered. "I just want to help."

"The last time you helped, you nearly got killed." His expression softened. "I won't have you put yourself in danger again, Charlotte."

"I don't think asking the housekeeper a few questions will lead to anything dangerous," she said. "Besides, last time was an unusually brutal case. I don't think this one is like that."

Charlotte forced the memory of Darcy Dugan's bloody and broken body out of her head.

He crossed his arms. "Playing psychologist, are you?"

"Just my observations of human nature." A shiver ran through her, though from the cold or from considering all she'd seen of human nature, she couldn't tell. "I'm going to head to the office to work and warm up. Will you tell me anything you find at dinner?"

"Not the conversation I was hoping for," he said with an overdramatic sigh.

She grinned. He had a subtle sense of humor that was always

a delight to see come forward. "Oh? What were you hoping to talk about?"

James shrugged. "Opera. Literature. World politics. The usual fodder of Cordova existence."

She laughed and patted his arm. "I'll be sure to brush up."

He caught her hand before she moved it away. Gently tugging her closer, he bent down and kissed her on the cheek. His lips were warm against her chilled skin.

"See you later," he said, then headed into the burnt building.

With a flurry of mixed emotions, Charlotte hurried toward the Fiske home.

The Fiskes lived on a quiet side road three streets up—literally, as the road was at a steep incline—from the hardware store. The house, gray with dark blue trim, looked out over the town, with a view of the harbor and clam canneries.

Charlotte stopped and caught her breath before the black-ribbon-draped door. The walk up hill wouldn't have been too bad on a dry road, but the addition of slush and ice had been more tiring than usual. Careful not to disturb the ribbon, she knocked. When no one responded to her second knock, Charlotte made her way around to the side of the house. As she approached the open gate leading to the side yard, she heard the thump of an axe.

A broad-shouldered man took another swing at a wedge of wood on a round section of a tree set on end. His back to Charlotte, his brown coat and hat were speckled with water spots; his canvas trousers were tucked into knee-high leather boots.

He swung, swift and sure. The blade cleaved the wedge in two with a crack.

As he levered the axe out, Charlotte cleared her throat. "Excuse me."

The man whipped around, axe raised. The cigarette dangling from the corner of his mouth jumped. "Christ, woman, don't sneak up on a man like that."

He appeared to be in his early twenties, his features set in a frown and black brows furrowed over almost black eyes. The complexion of his skin suggested Native blood.

Charlotte hadn't thought she was sneaking, but she wasn't about to argue with a man holding an axe. "I'm sorry. I'm looking for Mrs. Fiske."

She was quite sure Caroline wasn't home. Charlotte preferred not to lie so blatantly, but talking to the Fiskes' people while Caroline was away from the house might allow them to relax enough to divulge something. As long as James didn't find out. Defying him wasn't her favorite thing to do, but sometimes he made the most irrational requests.

The man eyed her, smoke clouding his around his face. "Mrs. Fiske left a while ago. Mrs. Munson's inside."

"I knocked, but I guess Mrs. Munson didn't hear me." Charlotte took a step into the yard. "Are you a friend of the Fiskes?"

Maybe he was helping the family now that Lyle was gone.

The man snorted a laugh. He swung the axe with one hand, embedding the blade near the edge of the round of wood he'd been using as a cutting platform. "Not hardly. I'm what you'd call a handyman."

"Oh, so you don't work at the store, Mr.?"

"Derenov. Ben Derenov. No, I don't. No one does now, do they?" He lifted a half-round of wood from a mound of others and set it on the cutting surface.

"No, I guess they don't." Charlotte watched him for a few moments, the fluid motion of his swing and the thud of the contact between metal and wood almost mesmerizing. Swish. Thunk. Swish. Thunk. "Are you from around here, Mr. Derenov? You seem familiar."

Another lie. Good thing she wasn't required to go to confession on Sundays.

"Grew up here." Swish. Thunk. "But I've been down south for the last few years." He stopped and turned to her. "My mother worked for the Fiskes until she died a few months back."

"I'm sorry for your loss." Two deaths surrounding the Fiskes in the span of months. How sad.

Derenov shrugged. Not a man to dwell on emotions, Charlotte figured. "Thanks. You should try up front again. See if Mrs. Munson can help you."

"I will. Thank you, Mr. Derenov."

The swish and thud of the axe were his only response.

Charlotte returned to the front door and knocked louder than before. Within a few moments, a short, roundish woman of fifty or so wearing a navy blue wool dress answered.

"Yes?"

"Good afternoon. My name's Charlotte Brody. I've come to pay my respects to Mrs. Fiske. If she's taking visitors, that is." Charlotte dug one of her cards out of her coat pocket and handed it to the woman. One of the corners was bent, but otherwise it was presentable, with her name in flowing script.

Mrs. Munson studied the simple card, her lips pressed together. "The missus isn't in just now, but I'll tell her you called."

"Thank you. Oh, could I write something the back of the card, please?"

"Of course. Come in." Mrs. Munson stepped aside and gestured for Charlotte to enter the house. "Let me find you a pen." She checked the drawer of an occasional table near the door. Not finding what she was looking for, she headed into the parlor to the right.

Charlotte didn't offer to use her own pencil, which she kept in her other pocket with her notebook. A few moments alone allowed her to take in the Fiske home. Narrow stairs led to the upper floor. The wall along the stairs was lined with framed photographic portraits of men, women, children, and small groups. To the right, the parlor, where Mrs. Munson searched the drawers of a rolltop desk. The room to the left was closed off with sliding pocket doors. The house was eerily silent and smelled of wood oil and dampness.

"We'll have church services tomorrow at noon," the house-keeper said when she returned to the entry hall. She handed Charlotte a fountain pen. "There will be a visitation here between two and four. No casket, of course. A private burial will be in a few days."

Considering the condition of the body, Charlotte wasn't surprised Caroline chose to not have a viewing at the funeral parlor.

"Thank you." She jotted the *Times* office telephone number on the back of the card and left it and the pen on the table so the ink could dry. "Will the church service be private? I work for Mr. Toliver at the paper and can make sure the announcement is in the morning edition."

Mrs. Munson's lips pressed together again. Because Charlotte was a reporter? "I believe a notice was delivered to your office this morning. It won't be private, considering the Fiskes' standing in the community, but we expect more attendance at the visitation here."

"Of course," Charlotte said. "Thank you very much. Tell Mrs. Fiske I'm sorry to have missed her, and I'll be sure to come by tomorrow."

She left the house and, as she walked down the slick street, Charlotte wondered if Caroline Fiske had hurried off to deliver the notice of her husband's service herself after searching the safe, or if she'd gone elsewhere. Charlotte's money was on elsewhere, since she could have handed Charlotte any notice she wanted printed. But where had Caroline been going? Or perhaps the better question was, who had she been in such a hurry to see?

An envelope had been pushed into the message box slot attached to the door of the *Times* office. When Mr. Toliver was the only person running the paper, he relied on that method to have Cordova residents inform him of happenings about town. Charlotte checked the box daily. Now, a neatly written note signed by Caroline Fiske was in her hand, detailing the services and visitation Mrs. Munson had mentioned.

The cuckoo clock reminded her that she had a job to tend, and Charlotte quickly removed her outerwear and boots.

While she worked on rekindling the fire in the stove, she considered the Fiske murder. Both the thief and Fiske must have been inside at eight o'clock. Even a loud argument or fight would have been enclosed in the building. The businesses closer to Fiske's might have heard something, if it was loud enough, but it was likely no one was about at that hour.

James had just been on the street, though presumably coming from town, nowhere near the hardware store. If he had passed it by and suspected anything, he would have stopped.

Once she got the fire going again, Charlotte went to the desk. Mr. Toliver had left instructions for particular articles he wished to have included in the next edition. The teletype hadn't been too busy, or the line was down, limiting the number of news items that had come in for her to transcribe. Charlotte would have to gather a few more stories to fill out the rest of the pages. A call back East was in order.

She took up the telephone, lifted the earpiece, and flicked the bracket.

"Operator. How may I direct your call?"

Charlotte couldn't help but smile at the formality in the voice. "Hello, Mrs. Jensen. This is Charlotte Brody at the *Times*. Could you connect me to Miss Cameron at *Modern Woman Review* magazine in Albany, New York?"

It would be early evening back home, but Kit was known to be at the office until quite late. Since she'd been taken on by Mr. Toliver, Charlotte called Kit if the *Times*'s pages were looking sparse and for any news items that might not have been sent via teletype. The twice-monthly conversations also gave them a chance to catch up. Charlotte felt only a little twinge of guilt about chatting with her friend on the *Times*'s dime.

"I have that number here, Miss Brody."

Mrs. Jensen kept meticulous records, noting names, numbers and times. Charlotte used to suspect the operator secretly listened in on calls, but after meeting the woman once she knew that was not the case. Mrs. Jensen was the epitome of professionalism and integrity. The night operator, however, was a different story.

"I'll put your call in right away and ring you when it goes through."

"Thank you, Mrs. Jensen."

Charlotte placed the earpiece back in the bracket. She collected the articles Mr. Toliver had set out and began perusing them for errors. Fifteen minutes into copyediting, the telephone jangled, startling her out of her thoughts.

She picked up the earpiece and base. "*Cordova Times.*"

"Your call is ready, Miss Brody," Mrs. Jensen said. "Go ahead, please, Miss Cameron."

A few clicks and a burst of static later, Kit's voice came over the line. "Charlotte! How ya doin', kid?"

Charlotte grinned at her friend's usual boisterous tone. Kit had always been the one to grab on to the latest slang and cadence of language, though she was a consummate professional when it came to editing *Modern Woman.*

"I'm fine. How are you? Happy early birthday."

"Ugh. Don't remind me. Mother and Dad are trying to ignore the fact I'm nearly thirty and not married. They don't know what to make of me some days." She laughed, but Charlotte knew the Camerons were anxious for her to settle down. Kit was always busy with *Modern Woman* or some cause. She went out frequently, but had no one steady.

"I know what you mean." Charlotte's parents had been supportive of her career and activity in the suffrage movement, but she suspected they were waiting for her to find a husband. Considering her relationship record, she was in no hurry.

Her nearly yearlong association with Richard had initially pleased the Brodys, and they'd dropped more than a few hints last year about engagements and weddings. Charlotte's sudden termination of the relationship a year ago this past August had raised a few questions from her parents. Surprisingly, they'd been sensitive to her distress and had not pushed for more details. They knew nothing of the real reason for the breakup and probably never would.

"How's that handsome deputy of yours?" Kit asked.

"He's not *my* deputy. And what makes you think he's handsome?" Though James certainly was a good-looking man, Charlotte had never described him to Kit. "He could be grimy, toothless, and bug-eyed for all you know."

Kit laughed. "Is he?"

Charlotte felt a blush heat her neck and cheeks. "No, but he could be."

Her friend laughed louder, and Charlotte hoped no one else was in the office. "Readers sure see him that way. For a periodical dedicated to the idea of women exerting their independence and strengths apart from men, I get letters every week asking for more information about that 'strapping, stalwart lawman who lives in Alaska.'"

"He is that."

"Charlotte Mae Brody! Are you mooning over a man?"

Damnation. She hadn't meant to say that out loud. She hadn't sighed melodramatically, had she?

"No, of course not." Though she missed Kit terribly, Charlotte was glad to be conversing from three thousand miles away via telephone. At least Kit wouldn't see her burning cheeks. Kit and Charlotte shared almost everything, and Kit knew her deepest secret, but she hadn't even told Kit about James kissing her. "He's very good at his job, is what I meant."

"Good to know," Kit said. "But you didn't call all this way to discuss men. Oh! I have to tell you about this meeting I went to."

Every time they chatted, there was another exciting lecture Kit had attended, or some rally or march. It sent a pang of homesickness through Charlotte, but at the same time she was happy to have the opportunity to get her life together in the quiet remoteness of Alaska. Well, relatively quiet, if you didn't count the dead bodies.

When it was Charlotte's turn to share news and happenings, Kit was positively horrified by the circumstances of Lyle Fiske's death. She couldn't believe two murders could occur in the same small town in such a short period of time. It had surprised Charlotte too, that was certain.

After an hour of gleaning articles and catching up with Kit, Charlotte said her good-byes.

"You should come up here," she told Kit. "I think you'd enjoy it, and Michael would certainly be happy to see you."

Michael had been smitten with Kit off and on during their childhood, and she with him. Their relationship had eventually settled into friendship, and Michael considered Kit another younger sister to fuss over and be frustrated by.

"Maybe," Kit said. "It would be quite the lark, wouldn't it?" There was a long pause on the line, and Charlotte thought they'd been cut off. Then Kit said, in a more serious tone, "How are you really, Charlotte?"

Kit wasn't asking about her physical health. It was her recovery from the past year, her dismal relationship with Richard, and the aftermath that worried her best friend.

Charlotte moistened her chapped lips. "I'm good. Truly. It helps to keep busy."

A soft sigh came over the other end. "It does."

There was something in those two words that sounded off. "Kit, are *you* all right?"

She'd been gone only three months, but anything could have happened. Surely Kit would have told her if there was devastating news.

"Oh, I'm fine. Just tired. Good gravy, look at the time. Gotta meet with Malone. Take care, darling!"

"You too. Talk to you in a couple of weeks." Charlotte set

the earpiece in the bracket and stared at the telephone. It was always bittersweet to talk to Kit or her parents, but it was better that she'd come to Cordova. Better by a long stretch.

Charlotte had traveled north not just to have a journalistic adventure, as she'd told her family and friends, but to get away from memories of her failed relationship with Richard. She needed to put physical distance between herself and constant reminders that she'd been a fool. Months after, she'd start to get back on an even keel, then an announcement that yet another of her schoolmates was getting married or expecting would make her cringe. The inevitable "What about you, Charlotte?" became too much.

Telling them she wasn't ready to settle down was met with stares of incomprehension. Of course she was ready, they'd insist. How could it be otherwise? She'd had her fun playing journalist, marching in parades. It was time to become a productive member of society, and that meant a husband and children in their eyes.

She could explain her reasons ten different ways and still not get them to understand: She wasn't wife and mother material. She'd become tired of trying to tell them not all women wanted that life. Coming to Alaska was intended to help Charlotte put her failings and feelings behind her, but moving thousands of miles away also kept her from beating her head against their walls of outdated expectations.

Taking a deep breath and a moment to clear her head, Charlotte pushed the voices and emotions of the past aside. There was work to be done. Focusing on that would be much more productive than dwelling on things she couldn't change now.

Three hours later, Charlotte got up to make herself some tea. She stood in front of the coal stove, hands spread to absorb heat as her tea steeped, her brain whirling with questions for James. Where had the Fiske store employees been that night? Did Lyle have the reputation for having a temper? Had anyone made complaints against him?

While she considered approaching James, an unexpected, completely unrelated question popped into her head: Who was the woman who had kissed James on the cheek? She didn't look familiar, but then Charlotte had seen her only from the back.

A flutter ran through her stomach. She couldn't possibly ask him that. It was none of her business. But as friends, shouldn't they be able to ask each other such things?

Just a friend? Is that what he is?

Of course he was. She wanted to visit with James over a lovely dinner at The Wild Rose. Yet the way he acted toward her, the way he made her feel sometimes . . .

It scared the devil out of her.

He's not Richard, she reminded herself.

No, but even Richard hadn't become the real Richard until after they'd been together. A man's true self emerged when put under pressure, and what happened between them certainly qualified as pressure.

Would James have reacted the same way?

She wasn't sure, and, in a way, preferred the arm's-length distance she kept him at so she'd never find out. It was safer, not knowing who he really was. Safer that he didn't know who *she* really was.

The rattle of the outer door turned her around, teacup in hand. Michael came in, quickly shut the door behind himself, and gave an exaggerated shiver.

"Getting blustery out there," he said as he removed his hat and stamped his slush-covered boots on the rug near the door. "Was coming to ask if you wanted to get some coffee or something, but I see you've got your tea. Mary's organizing my office, and I thought I should get out of the way for a bit."

"I think I could use something stronger than tea, and maybe a slice of pie." It took Charlotte a moment to remember who Mary was. "How's Mary working out? Did she help you get the autopsy report written?"

She felt a small pang of guilt, having not come back to him to finish her secretarial duties.

"I did it myself, actually," he said. "Mary has already spoken to a number of her friends in the village about coming to see me if their own methods aren't sufficient. They have a lot of natural remedies that are quite effective, but sometimes even they don't work. Mostly the women seem more inclined to see me than the men are."

"That's because men don't like to admit they need a doctor unless they're practically at death's door."

Michael nodded. "True enough."

"Was Lyle Fiske one of your patients?"

"No, he and Caroline saw Dr. Hastings."

That figured. Dr. Hastings was the senior physician in town and generally tended the more well-to-do in Cordova. A third doctor, Bergoff, was just getting settled in. "How about Mrs. Derenov, the Fiskes' housekeeper who passed away?"

Michael's expression fell at the mention of the woman's name. Charlotte didn't think he'd had a close, personal relationship with Mrs. Derenov, but as her doctor he would have felt her loss.

"Yes, she was one of mine. Sweet woman. Worked hard all her life and—" He stopped short, frowning.

"And?" Charlotte prompted.

"Other than the Fiskes, she had no one but her son and daughter. The son had been down in the States for quite some time. Mrs. Derenov did well enough, I guess, but she sent money to him for whatever his troubles were."

"And the daughter?"

"Still in school here. A bit younger than her brother. Though with Mrs. Derenov gone, who knows if she'll stay in school past this year."

"Doesn't Ben want his sister to get an education?"

Michael's eyebrows lifted. "How do you know Ben Derenov?"

Charlotte hesitated. Michael had become a bit overprotective since she'd arrived in Cordova and didn't particularly care for her poking about for stories. "I went over to the Fiskes' earlier to pay my respects. He was there cutting wood."

Inside, she cringed slightly at the half truth.

Michael stared at her for a second, trying to see if there was more to it. Which there was, but he didn't need to know that. "I see. I don't know what Ben Derenov has in mind for the two of them. He's the only immediate family Rebecca has. If he decides to stay and can make money, she might be able to finish her schooling."

"I hope that's the case." It would be a shame for the girl to quit school because of money woes. Taking her education as far as she could go would be the best thing for Rebecca Derenov, for all young girls and women. Charlotte set her cup on the desk and joined him near the door. "Is his working for the Fiskes their way to help out after Mrs. Derenov died?"

He helped her on with her coat. "Possibly. Or they needed a handyman and Ben happened to be around for the job."

"That could explain it too," she said, changing into her boots.

"Why do you always look beyond the simple explanation?"

"Because the simple explanation is rarely interesting. Or the truth. Don't you dig a little further with your patients to make sure the simple explanation is the real reason for their illness?"

"Of course," he said, holding the door open for her. "It's the responsible thing to do."

Charlotte locked the door behind them. "And it's my responsibility to get the real story when I write, not just what it appears to be at first glance."

"I'm sure Eddington appreciates your dedication."

The sarcasm wasn't lost on her. She lightly punched his shoulder and he laughed.

Michael took her arm to help keep her footing as they traversed the slick walkway, wind in their faces.

"The visitation for Lyle Fiske is tomorrow," Charlotte said. "Are you going?"

"I wasn't planning on it. Are you?"

"I'd like to. Will you come with me?"

He gave her a curious look. "Since when do you need me, or anyone, to escort you to such a thing?"

Since she decided it might be necessary to have someone who knew more of the people in town than she did to help her identify attendees. But she wouldn't tell Michael that either. "I don't know Caroline all that well and figured your standing and recognition would help."

"Help get you into the house of a murder victim, you mean." He shook his head, eyes rolling to the heavens. "Fine. I'll go with you. If you'll make dinner for me tonight."

"Thanks, and I will, but I'll have to cook for you another time. I'm going to meet James for dinner tonight. Care to join us?" It was bad manners to ask him without James's consideration, but Michael's presence might make her feel more at ease. Keeping the deputy at arm's length when they were alone together was a challenge.

"Oh, no no no." Michael held up his free hand, waving her request off. "I wouldn't dream of intruding on the two of you."

"It's not intruding, it's just dinner," she said more defensively than she'd intended.

"Right." He tugged his hat down over his ears. "I'm sure Eddington would appreciate me horning in on your date."

"It's not a date."

"Uh-huh."

Charlotte took a quick bath and changed before meeting James at The Wild Rose. The navy blue wool serge dress was something she usually wore for more professional appointments and meetings, not for dinner. But it was too cold and wet for anything else she had with her. Besides, neither James nor Cordova seemed particular about fancy clothing.

The snow had tapered off, but the slush remained in the streets. Charlotte hurried along as fast as she could while keeping her feet under her. Lights from homes and the few streetlamps helped her avoid the worst puddles, and soon she turned the corner just before The Wild Rose.

The aromas of roasted meat and coffee, with an underlying bite of the cigar smoke from a table of men, hit her as she opened the door. The low murmur of conversation from the men and an older couple accompanied by the tink and clink of silverware filled the small dining room. With fewer than a dozen white cloth-covered tables under individual pendant lights, The Wild Rose wasn't a large restaurant, even by Alaska standards, but it was one of the more attractive Charlotte had dined in.

"Miss Brody." Will, the owner, came out of the kitchen to her left. "Nice to see you again."

"You too. I'm waiting for James Eddington." It was unlikely he'd made a reservation, but James may have mentioned to Will that they were coming.

Will's face brightened. "Excellent. Let me help you with your coat and you can wait here by the fireplace."

He took her mackinaw, then gestured to a pair of green wingback chairs. Charlotte sat on the edge of one, warming her hands and feet. She almost asked Will to seat her at a table, but knowing him, he wouldn't hear of it.

Charlotte only waited a few minutes, watching the other diners and the staff, before James came in. He removed his hat and searched the dining room. Seeing her as she got to her feet, he smiled. "Sorry I'm late."

"You aren't."

James had slicked back his hair, but hadn't shaved.

"Are you growing a beard, deputy?"

He ran his palm over his cheek. "Thinking about it. Gets damn cold here sometimes. Why? Don't you like beards?"

Charlotte shrugged. "If they're well kept. Michael's growing one too, to match his mustache. It makes him look older."

"Not always a bad thing, especially in his profession."

He unbuttoned his coat, revealing he had changed clothes as well, but wasn't wearing the more formal attire he'd had on for their first dinner together either. Of course he was wearing his gun, as dictated by his position. Will came to take James's coat and show them to a table. After going over the special for the evening, which they ordered, he promised to bring them some tea.

"How's the investigation going?" Charlotte asked when Will had departed. She kept her voice quiet to prevent the other diners from overhearing.

"Well enough, I guess. Parker and I went over the scene. Fire may have started near the register, where Fiske was found. The explosions we heard were paint thinner and other solvents on the shelves under the counter. It looks like the killer poured something over Fiske, set the fire—"

"To cover the knife wound," she said.

"Yes. Then spread more solvent and lit it. Inventory on the shelves heated, then blew when the vapors ignited."

"Michael had said the body wasn't as burned as he'd feared." Charlotte was once again grateful she hadn't attended the autopsy.

James nodded. "The explosion of cans may have blown out the flames and covered Fiske with debris from the shelves, preserving the body. Whoever did this hadn't considered that."

"I doubt he was considering anything but hiding his tracks. But it makes me think that perhaps this wasn't the work of the arsonist." Charlotte grinned when he quirked an eyebrow. "You and Parker don't think so either."

"No," he said. "What brought *you* to that conclusion?"

"An arsonist knows his materials. The fires he's set so far haven't been so careless and out of control. If he wanted to set a fire with the intent to destroy evidence of Fiske's murder, it would have been done properly, even in haste."

James crossed his arms and leaned back in his seat. He inclined his head in acknowledgement. "Well done, Miss Brody."

She shrugged, ignoring the little thrill that ran through her. "I try."

A waiter came down the aisle between tables and set their teacups and a teapot before them. He turned to leave, nodding to the well-dressed woman who had come up behind him before he eased around her. Charlotte expected her to sit at the next table, where she'd noticed two men and another woman taking their seats. Instead, the woman strode up to James, grinning.

"Fancy seeing you here, Jimmy."

James's eyes widened. He shot a glance at Charlotte before rising, like the gentleman he was. "What are you doing here?"

The tall brunette, in a stunning red dress, rolled her eyes at him, still smiling. Was she the woman from earlier that day?

"Having dinner, silly." She stuck her right hand out to Charlotte. "I'm Stella Eddington."

"How do you do?" Charlotte automatically shook her hand as the name made its way through her brain. "Eddington?"

James didn't have any sisters. A cousin, perhaps?

"Yep. I'm Jimmy's wife."

Chapter 6

W ife?

Charlotte's heart lurched. This was the woman she'd seen earlier, the one kissing James on the cheek in front of the federal building. She stared at Stella Eddington, imagining all manner of matrimonial interactions between her and the deputy.

"Damn it, Stella, that isn't funny." James turned to Charlotte. "Ex-wife."

It took another few moments to believe him, to convince herself he was telling the truth. To remember that James was a forthright sort of man.

So why hadn't he said anything about a wife or ex-wife in the last few months?

"Such a stickler," Stella said, laughing. "I know the ink's barely dry on the divorce papers, and it's not official until I file them with the judge, but you can't expect me to add the 'ex' so soon, can you?"

He wasn't quite divorced yet either. Damnation.

Charlotte clutched the napkin in her fist on her lap, her expression as neutral as possible and her brain flooded with questions. He'd never told her about Stella. How long had

they been married? How long had he been in Cordova without her?

"I expect you to behave yourself and not give Charlotte the
wrong impression," he said, his brow furrowed but his voice
low and civilized.

Stella pouted prettily. "Aw, don't be like that, Jimmy. I just
wanted to stop and say good-bye. I head back to Juneau on the
morning steamer." She met Charlotte's eyes. "Don't get the
wrong idea about him, honey. We've been separated for almost
a year. I've just been terrible about getting up here with the paperwork, is all. I'll leave you to your dinner. It's been fun,
Jimmy. Come down and see me some time." She grasped
James's hand, pecked him on the check, then leaned forward to
whisper in his ear.

Charlotte couldn't hear what she said, but whatever it was
turned James's face bright red. Gentle hands on his ex-wife's
shoulders, he separated himself from her.

"Good-bye, Stella. Give your mother my regards."

Smiling, Stella waggled her fingers at them and joined her
three companions, who had been watching the encounter with
curious amusement.

Stiffly, James settled into his chair again, looking ready to
snap in two. She knew how he felt. She silently willed him to
explain why he'd never told her he was married, never mentioned he was in the process of divorcing. Never said a damn
thing about any of this.

Ask him, Charlotte prodded herself, but she couldn't do that.
He had his reasons for not telling her. Everyone deserved their
privacy, didn't they? She surely wouldn't want him giving her
the third degree about her past.

What should have been friendly, pre-dinner banter between
them was replaced with tense silence and nervous fiddling with
silverware.

"James," she began quietly, "it's not a big deal."

Liar. It was. It felt like a giant cloud hanging over them, and by the tightness of his jaw and the tension of his body, he felt the same. So why hadn't he said anything?

He straightened his forks and knife, then met her gaze. "It's something I wanted to tell you in my own time, in my own way. It's hard for a man to admit failure."

She covered his hand with hers. "You didn't fail, James, your marriage did. There's a difference."

"You don't know the details," he said, shaking his head. "And when you hear them, you won't believe that it wasn't my fault, trust me."

They stared at each other for several moments, neither moving or speaking. There was guilt in his blue eyes. What did he mean? What had he done or thought he'd done? She didn't think he was infallible, but James Eddington truly seemed like the straight-shooter he appeared to be. Had he reacted to something the way Richard had to Charlotte's news? What was he hiding?

Everyone has their secrets, that little voice inside reminded her.

"Not here," he said, when she opened her mouth to ask. "Sorry. I'm not particularly hungry anymore."

Neither was she, but she didn't want to end the evening like this either.

"Come to my place. I'll make us some tea and sandwiches and we can talk, if you want."

A number of emotions crossed James's face. Surprise. Relief. Wariness. He laid his napkin on the table, accompanied by a few coins to cover the tea and the waiter's troubles. He rose, his hand grasping hers, strong and warm.

Charlotte stood as well, and they walked to the front of the restaurant without the slightest glance at Stella, her companions, or anyone else. Upon meeting a puzzled Will, James apologized for their unexpected departure and requested their coats. Will retrieved the garments, helped Charlotte with hers, and bade them good night.

Outside, the snow and wind had kicked up again. James took her upper arm to help support her as they walked the few blocks to her home.

"Deputy!"

Stopping beneath the streetlight, she and James both turned toward the man who had shouted out. Bundled in an overcoat, fur hat, and heavy boots, the stout figure hurried to them as fast as his legs and the slick ground would allow.

"Glad I ran into you. Evening, Miss Brody." Marv Johnson, the owner of the Mirage Club, breathed heavily, hands on hips as he spoke to James again. "Just got a call from my manager. Jack Pettigrew came in sauced to the gills and started in with Ken Harper. Harry settled them down, but Jack refuses to leave. I was just on my way down and saw you. I was hoping you could give me a hand."

Charlotte and James exchanged looks. She withdrew her arm from his. "Go, I can make it home fine from here."

"No, let me walk you to the door." He turned to Johnson. "Won't take a minute."

Without waiting for Johnson to respond, James took her arm again and guided her to her door. "I'm sorry about this, Charlotte."

He did look sorry, but relieved too.

"Another time," she said, smiling. Maybe she was more relieved than she'd care to admit too. Having him tell her what was behind his divorce from Stella meant opening themselves up to a deeper relationship than she was ready for.

James hesitated, as if unsure of what to do by way of departure. After their first dinner together, he had kissed her at her door. It had been one of the best kisses she'd ever experienced.

Charlotte rose up on her toes and pecked him on the cheek. "Good night, deputy."

Looking less unsure, and with the hint of a smile, James tugged the brim of his hat. "Good night, Miss Brody."

He waited for her to go inside, then thudded down the stairs to where Johnson waited. She hung her coat in the hall closet and removed her boots. Padding into the kitchen in stocking feet, she added coal to the stove and set the kettle to boil. Cheese from the back porch—where it was cool enough to keep—bread from the bread box, and a can of soup would suffice for dinner.

Charlotte toasted her sandwich while she waited for the soup to heat. She would use the time she had this evening to write more of her Alaska women series for Kit. And not think about James and Stella Eddington.

Charlotte spent the next morning at the *Times* office. Luckily, there was plenty coming over the teletype about the miners' strike down in the States and events around the world to fill out the pages quickly. And keep her mind off the previous night. Mostly.

Someone from the school had left a page with their activities in the drop box, neatly written but requiring her to type it into the Linotype herself. By the time the last line was cooling in the form, Michael appeared at the door to pick her up for Lyle's visitation.

He wore his black suit and good coat and shoes. His hair had been recently cut, and his mustache was neatly trimmed, though his beard was in that in-between untamable stage.

"Are you seriously going to keep that on your face?" Charlotte asked as he helped her with her coat.

"Why not?" He stroked the whiskers, sounding hurt. A few hairs sprang back, pointing every which way. "It's coming along, I think."

"The mustache was surprising enough. I'll hardly recognize you in a month."

"You're just jealous. My face will be warmer than yours this winter."

Charlotte cocked an eyebrow at him. "Jealous of the warmth, maybe, but not how you achieve it."

She locked the door and they headed up the street to the Fiske home. Several business owners along Main Street were doing the same. Charlotte and Michael greeted them, exchanged sympathies for Caroline and the terrible manner of Lyle's death, and let the conversation wane as they negotiated the slippery hill.

As they approached the Fiskes' home, Charlotte noticed Ben Derenov standing by the gate leading to the side yard. He leaned on the post, smoking a cigarette and eyeing the visitors. When Charlotte met his gaze, he frowned and disappeared back into the yard.

Mrs. Munson, the housekeeper, greeted everyone with a solemn nod as she took their coats and hats and handed them to a woman to deposit in another room. She quietly directed mourners to the parlor. Charlotte and Michael joined the others, who stood in small groups as they waited to express their condolences to Caroline. Men smoked pipes or cigars, their low voices rumbling through the room. Several women stood together, though a few protectively flanked Caroline where she sat in a wingback chair in the corner near the fireplace. Everyone was dressed in somber finery.

Caroline nodded and smiled wanly at an older gentleman who held her hand, shaking it with each word he spoke. His balding head glinted above a band of white hair, and his thick, white eyebrows were furrowed.

"Who's that?" Charlotte quietly asked Michael.

Michael watched the man for a few moments. "Bob Dexter. He lives out past the Eyaks' village, some six or seven miles from town. Has a little homestead. Doesn't get into town much."

Charlotte and Michael joined the wife, son, and daughter-in-law of the banker, who spoke with another group of men. Charlotte half listened to the conversation while studying the mourners. She recognized most of the business owners, having seen them at some point or another after she began working for the *Times*. A trio of men around Michael's age stood off to one side. Two of the men were engaged in a quiet, yet intense, conversation, but the third kept glancing down at his feet or up at Caroline.

Charlotte waited for the banker's family to make their way toward the new widow, then asked Michael, "Who are those three men?"

He looked over to where she indicated. "The man in the green suit is Jilt Harris. The larger man with the beard is Otto Kenner. The other is Otto's brother Adam."

So that was Otto Kenner. Now she had a face to go with the name. He certainly looked strong enough to wield hammers and such all day. Adam Kenner was a few years younger and wiry. Definitely more of the accountant in him.

Adam's frequent eyeing of Caroline made Charlotte wonder about them, but the name of the man in green filtered through her study of the pair. "Jilt?"

"His real name's Norman or Norbert. Something like that. He has a bit of a reputation for lovin' then leavin'. Please don't tell me you're interested in him."

"Not in the least." She'd had her fill of that sort. Charlotte gave Michael a discrete nudge as she watched Adam and Caroline. "And give me some credit. I'm not one to look for men at a wake."

Adam and Caroline didn't stare at each other, but each time their gazes met, Adam's brow wrinkled and he glanced away. Caroline was unreadable, allowing no reaction to mar her expression of grief.

Either Adam Kenner was a sensitive young man, sharing the widow's emotions, or he was Caroline's concerned lover. Or wanted to be.

"What do you know about Adam Kenner?" Charlotte asked Michael.

He sipped a glass of punch he'd picked up from the sideboard. "He and his brother came up from Portland to work on the railroad. Otto's a carpenter, but laid track. Adam did too, even though that isn't his profession. Once the railroad was finished, they went into business for themselves."

"Are they particularly friendly with the Fiskes?"

"Not that I'm aware of. I'm sure Otto did business with Lyle. It's possible Adam was his accountant, but don't quote me on that. Why?"

"I think Adam fancies Caroline." Perhaps more than fancies if they were already together.

Michael looked at Adam and Caroline, turning his head as if trying to catch the two of them blatantly winking and flirting. Charlotte grabbed his arm. "Stop that!" she whispered fiercely. "You're terrible at surreptitious observation."

He imitated her volume and tone. "Damn it, Charlotte, I'm a doctor, not a spy. Why are you interested in Adam Kenner and Caroline Fiske?"

Charlotte kept her voice down, well aware of the people in the room. She would bet most of them knew of or suspected Caroline's extramarital affairs, but it wasn't up to Charlotte to fuel rumors. "If Adam is Caroline's lover, could he have been confronted by Lyle? Or act against Lyle?"

Michael's eyes widened. He started to turn his head to look at Adam, but caught himself. Still whispering, he said, "Ridiculous. Adam isn't the type."

"Isn't the type to sleep with another man's wife, or to kill him?" she asked.

"Neither."

Charlotte glanced at the younger Kenner brother. He did appear to be less physical or physically intimidating than his brother. Maybe he wasn't the type to attack another man. But love and jealousy did strange things to even the mildest of souls.

She needed to know for sure that Adam and Caroline were together. Would there be any proof other than the blatant puppy dog stares? Letters, perhaps?

"Come on," Michael said, touching her arm. "It's our turn."

The two women flanking Caroline smiled thinly when they approached. Caroline looked up, reaching toward Michael's outstretched hand.

"So sorry for your loss," he said, bowing slightly.

Caroline nodded, then turned to Charlotte. Her sad smile faltered. "I understand you came by the other day, Charlotte. I'm sorry I wasn't able to see you."

There was a knowing glint in her eyes. Caroline was well aware that Charlotte had stopped by after the incident in the burnt-out store, while Caroline was on her way to somewhere other than her home. Was she waiting for Charlotte to bring it up?

"Absolutely understandable, Caroline." Charlotte gathered the widow's hand in hers, patting it reassuringly. "If there's anything I can do for you—anything at all—please let me know."

The other woman said nothing for a few moments. Hopefully she would see Charlotte as someone to be trusted, but it was difficult to tell.

Caroline thanked them for coming, then eased her hand from Charlotte's.

Politely dismissed, Charlotte and Michael joined the others again. With everyone down in the parlor, it was the perfect opportunity for her to slip away.

"Excuse me, Michael, I need to use the bathroom before we leave."

As if sensing she was up to something, Michael gave her a warning glare just before a fellow member of the city council drew him into a conversation.

Charlotte made her way out of the parlor and into the entry. No one was about. She hurried up the stairs, keeping her footsteps as light as possible to not announce her route. At the top, the hallway ran the length of the house, with several rooms on this floor. Doors were ajar but none completely closed.

She poked her head in the first open door. A sewing room. The black Singer on its walnut table dominated the small space. A dressmaker's mannequin modeled the majority of a deep purple dress, its unattached sleeves draped over the back of a chair. Baskets and boxes were stacked along the walls. Did Caroline sew her own clothes, or was it the work of Mrs. Munson?

The two bedrooms on the second floor were of good size, each with a wardrobe and vanity. The larger was obviously the Fiskes' room, and Charlotte assumed the smaller one, separated by the lavatory, was a guest room. With half an ear focused on the stairway, she quickly searched the vanity in the Fiskes' room. Nothing jumped out at her indicating who Caroline was seeing. Didn't lovers usually write to each other? If not detailed letters, at least a cryptic note or two? There were a few pieces of correspondence, all from what appeared to be friends and relatives in the States.

Caroline may have hidden any notes from her lover, but Charlotte didn't have time to search every nook and cranny.

Listening for anyone coming up, and confident all remained downstairs, Charlotte dashed to the room at the end of the hall. An office and library, with neat shelves lining the walls and smelling of cigars and old books. A pair of thickly padded, red-and-gold-brocade-covered chairs sat on either side of a tall lamp with a tasseled shade. The desk wasn't as massive as the one in Lyle Fiske's store office, though its squat, black shape seemed about to drop through to the first floor of the house. She could imagine the difficulty of getting the thing up the stairs.

Charlotte rounded the desk. The credenza against the wall there had a tray of crystal tumblers and a decanter of some sort of scotch or whiskey. Personal alcohol use didn't necessarily interest the marshals who enforced Alaska's dry laws, but Charlotte had to wonder where their supply came from. Did everyone bring a bottle or two back when they visited the States?

Pushing the thought aside, she tugged the handles on each of the three deep drawers on either side of the center desk drawer, as well as the center drawer. All were locked.

Damnation.

She doubted anything of Caroline's was in the desk, but perhaps there was something in Lyle's records that might hint at troubles brewing within his business circle. Or perhaps this was where he'd moved the mysterious black box. But wouldn't Caroline have searched here?

The locks didn't appear to be too formidable. A gal she knew in college used to get herself back into the locked dormitory using a hairpin. Charlotte had once asked how she worked the makeshift picks. Helen happily showed her. It had been a few years; could she remember the proper technique?

Charlotte eased two pins out from behind her ear, bent them the way she recalled being instructed, and knelt on the floor. Half listening for footfalls, she inserted the pins inside the lock of the center drawer. The thin metal scraped on the mechanism, caught on something, then clicked.

Surprised, Charlotte carefully twisted the pin. The lock turned. "Ah!"

She opened the drawer. Neat piles of papers and envelopes were stacked alongside engraved silver pens. Nothing useful or screaming "I'm cheating customers" to be found.

Charlotte repeated the picking process with one of the side drawers, one that might be deep enough to hold a black box. The lock refused to yield, and one of the hairpins bent.

"Damnation."

"Miss Brody, what are you doing in here?"

Crouched behind the desk, Charlotte jerked back and fell on her bottom, smacking into the sideboard. The tumblers and decanter rattled. She scrambled to her feet.

The housekeeper stood in the doorway, arms crossed and lips pressed together.

"Mrs. Munson, you startled me."

That was an understatement. Charlotte's heart hammered. Her ears throbbed with her racing heartbeat, and her face burned.

"I'd imagine so," Mrs. Munson said, one eyebrow cocked. "Were you looking for something in particular?"

Charlotte held up her hairpin. "Just dropped my pin while admiring this lovely desk set. I've been looking for something similar for my brother for Christmas. I caught a glimpse of the desk when I came up to use the washroom and wanted to sneak a peek." Would Mrs. Munson remember the office door had been mostly closed? Charlotte hoped not, but the skeptical look on her face indicated she might. "And the books. I love to see what people are reading. I hope I haven't intruded."

Good Lord, what a liar.

She palmed the bent pins.

"I'm sure Mrs. Fiske would be happy to discuss books with you another time." Mrs. Munson held the edge of the heavy oak door and inclined her head slightly. A clear indication that it was time for Charlotte to leave.

"Of course. Some other time."

She walked purposely out of the office, smiling at the housekeeper as she passed. Rushing might imply guilt. Charlotte descended the stairs in the same manner. Michael waited at the bottom, wearing his coat and holding hers. The expression on his face changed from vaguely aware she was joining him to mild suspicion as he looked past her to Mrs. Munson coming down behind her.

Holding her gaze, he readied her coat. "Shall we, dear sister?"

Her back to the housekeeper, Charlotte stuck her tongue out at him. "Yes, thank you. I'm ready to go."

Mrs. Munson watched them both as Charlotte buttoned her coat and put on her hat. She dropped the bent pins into her pocket. Did Mrs. Munson think Charlotte was going to bolt back up the stairs?

"Good-bye, Mrs. Munson."

"Good-bye, Miss Brody. Doctor."

Michael tipped his hat to her and let Charlotte precede him through the front door.

"Did you find whatever you were looking for?" he asked when they started down the street.

Charlotte considered telling him she hadn't been snooping, but why bother? "No. I would very much like to know who Caroline is seeing."

Confirm it, really, as she was pretty sure Adam Kenner was her lover.

"Why does it matter?"

"It could be important in learning who killed Lyle."

"Maybe," Michael said, "or it could just be your busybody tendencies getting the better of you."

"I'm a journalist, trained to look into questionable cases."

"Which is a natural outlet for your innate busybodiness."

She couldn't completely deny that, but it still stung that sometimes he didn't take her career seriously. "Well, I'm no doctor or anything fancy like that, but I like to think at least some of my work has merit."

Michael took her arm and stopped. "Don't be like that, Charlotte. You know I've admired your articles from the beginning. You're passionate about important subjects, stand by your convictions, and care for the people you write about. It's impressive and interesting."

That made her feel better.

"As long as I don't ruffle feathers."

He grinned. "You've never been one not to do something because it ruffles feathers." The grin faltered. "I know you want to figure out who killed Lyle. So do I. But you have to tread carefully. Snooping in a dead man's house isn't considered acceptable behavior in too many circles."

Of course he had a point. "I'll be careful."

With a peck on her cheek, Michael left Charlotte at the *Times* office and continued on to attend appointments.

Charlotte hung up her coat and changed out of her boots, then set the kettle on the stove and went to work. She wrote up a short piece on Lyle Fiske's visitation, noting a few of the other attendees and including the time and place of his burial in two days.

"As long as the ground isn't frozen." She didn't include that in the article. While it was certainly cold, she suspected strong backs and shovels would be available to inter Mr. Fiske. If not, the newly completed morgue was said to have adequate facilities to hold the dearly departed until the spring thaw.

To steer her thoughts away from images of dead bodies, Charlotte picked up an article received over the teletype on protests against the Volstead Act and counterprotests by chapters of the Women's Temperance League. She was just getting to the list of cities where gatherings would be held, and wondering if she could organize a debate in Cordova, when the bell over the door sounded.

Charlotte looked up and smiled at her visitors. Brigit and Della slipped in with a gust of cold, wet wind. "Hello, ladies. What brings you here on such a day?"

The women removed their hats and opened their coats in the warm office.

"Something I thought you ought to see," Brigit said. She gently nudged Della forward. "Go on, she won't bite."

Charlotte didn't know Della well, having met her only in passing whenever she visited Brigit at the house, but they'd been nodding acquaintances. What could be going on that Brigit thought it was important to bring the young woman here?

Hat in hand, Della crossed to the desk and sat when Charlotte motioned for her to take one of the chairs. Brigit stayed back, removing her coat and hanging it on one of the pegs. So she planned on staying for a bit, but Della didn't. Interesting.

"Brigit s-said I oughta c-come sh-show you this if I weren't gonna go to the m-marshal." Her stutter wasn't due to nervousness, Charlotte knew. Brigit had told her of Della's speech patterns, and had been quite surprised when the young woman completely lost the stutter if she sang. She was often called upon to entertain the visitors at Brigit's house.

Della reached into her coat pocket and withdrew a gold necklace with a cross dangling from it. She draped it on top of the papers on the desk and hesitated before moving her hand away, as if reluctant to let it go.

"Very nice," Charlotte said, looking at but not touching the piece. "Where did you get it?"

Della glanced up at Brigit as she sat in the other chair. "Tell her."

The younger woman started to speak, but now nervousness did make her stutter worse. She took a deep breath and said what she needed to say in a semi-singing lilt. She had a lovely voice. "It's mine, but I haven't seen it for a year."

Charlotte cocked her head. "Had it been lost? Stolen?"

Della shook her head. "I'd pawned it when I first got here, before I met Brigit, but the man I pawned it to was asking for more money than I could afford to get it back. I mostly didn't think about it. Until this morning."

"What happened this morning?"

Della and Brigit exchanged looks again, and Brigit nodded for Della to continue. "Found it on the porch in a plain paper packet with my name on it."

"Tell her who you'd pawned it to," Brigit said.

"L-Lyle F-Fiske."

Surprise lifted Charlotte's eyebrows. "Lyle? Was he a registered pawnbroker?"

Brigit snorted a laugh. "Not hardly. Mr. Fiske loaned money to our less than prestigious citizens. The interest rates he charged were near criminal."

That certainly wasn't a shock. Most legitimate loan rates were near criminal, in Charlotte's opinion. Is that what Brigit meant when she said the Fiskes lived above their obvious

means? How could income as an illegal pawnbroker to less affluent Cordovans be that lucrative?

"If Mr. Fiske's dead, and I didn't pay off the loan, how do I
explain getting the necklace back?" Though she sang the words,
Della's blue eyes were wide with worry.

"Considering what Lyle was doing was illegal to begin with,
I don't think you'll be implicated," Charlotte said, hoping to
assure the poor woman. "Someone else knew about his side
business and was wiping the slate clean, so to speak. A sort of
Robin Hood."

The question was, who would have done it? Caroline? If she
was an equal partner in the hardware store, why not in Fiske's
loan business as well? But then, why return a pawned item
rather than keep that endeavor going? Guilt?

"Was anyone else with you when you visited Mr. Fiske,
Della? Did anyone else know? Can you tell me about it?"
Charlotte asked.

"I'd heard from one of the other girls that I could get money
from him, so I went to the store. He took me into his office,"
Della said, "just the two of us. Thought for a minute he was
gonna ask me to . . . you know . . . service him at his desk, but
instead he had me sit in a chair, all businesslike."

At least Lyle hadn't been that despicable.

"Then what?"

"We talked about terms and such. He took a black box from
his safe, opened it up and counted out the cash, then put my
necklace in the box. I left right after that."

The black box Caroline was searching for, most likely, but
she'd been insistent about other sorts of papers. Whoever killed
Fiske had the papers and probably more pawned pieces.

"I wonder if other things are being returned."

But why go through the trouble?

"The girl who told me about Mr. Fiske pawned her mother's
pearl earrings," Della added. "She's gone though. Moved to
Anchorage last May."

"I'm sure Fiske had more than a few customers," Brigit said. "We'll let you know if we hear of anything." She turned to Della. "Why don't you head back to the house? I'll be along shortly."

Della nodded, then her gaze fell on the necklace. Poor thing. It meant something to her, but she was obviously torn about keeping it. Charlotte handed the necklace to her.

"I don't think anyone will come looking for it, Della. Take it, and keep it safe."

Della gave her a grateful smile, shoved the necklace into her pocket, and hurried out of the office.

When she was gone, Brigit leaned back in her chair and sighed. "Thank you. She wanted to help, though she has no feelings either way toward the Fiskes, but didn't want to go to the marshal's office for fear they'd take the necklace as evidence. Or even accuse her of killing him."

Charlotte rose and poured them each some tea. "I thought you and the girls were a little more trusting of James lately."

Brigit wrapped her hands around the delicate cup. "I am, but Della has had a few run-ins with lawmen that have left her wary."

"Has she broken the law?" Charlotte asked, then gave Brigit a crooked grin. "Other than the obvious, I mean."

Brigit smiled back. Charlotte was grateful they could tease each other about their jobs and not feel offended. "Trouble in California that prompted her to move here. I don't know the details, but she's been on the up-and-up since I've hired her."

"Even if Fiske's pawn business is related to his death, I don't think her keeping the necklace will be an issue, since she has no idea who returned it to her. Though James might want to ask Della some questions about the transaction."

"Like what?" Brigit asked then sipped her tea. "She learned Fiske made loans when no bank would give a girl like her a dime. James probably knows all about it."

Why hadn't he told Charlotte? "He's pretty damn good at keeping things to himself when he wants to, isn't he?"

"Most people are," Brigit said. She gave Charlotte a pained look. "I heard about last night."

Charlotte tried to act nonchalant, but it wasn't easy. "What do you mean?"

"That your date with James was interrupted by his wife."

The back of her neck tightened for no discernable reason. Or at least no reason she'd care to admit out loud. "Ex-wife, and it wasn't a date. How did you know about it anyway?"

"Two of my regulars were there. Saw and heard the whole thing before they came by the house. Idle pillow talk and gossip at the faro tables reveals a lot of information."

Heat rose on Charlotte's cheeks. Good lord, did everyone in this town know everyone else's business? "So much for discretion."

Charlotte wanted to snatch the words back as soon as she said them. The hurt look on Brigit's face confirmed that the dig against the madam's assertion of privacy within her house was petty and mean.

"I'm sorry, Brigit," she said earnestly. "I know you keep a lid on what you and the girls hear and see. We were in a public place, and I shouldn't be surprised people talked. Forgive me?"

Brigit didn't say anything for a few moments, and Charlotte feared she'd damaged their friendship. Finally, Brigit lost the tense, wounded look on her face. "It's all right. I shouldn't have made light of it. I'm sure finding out he was married was a shock."

That was an understatement.

"Did you know?" Charlotte asked, trying to keep the lingering ache from her voice. It wasn't the fact he was married or in the process of divorcing that rankled, but that he hadn't told her.

Brigit's expression softened. "No. I don't think anyone did. James Eddington is one of the most private men I've met. You get what you see with him, but only what he lets you see."

"That's true."

He wasn't being deceptive, just more reserved than Charlotte had expected. She was sure that reticence served him well at the marshal's office, but it was a hard pill to swallow in a personal relationship.

Then again, he wasn't the only one holding things back, was he? Did a lie of omission count as a lie?

"It really doesn't matter," Charlotte said, waving off the subject. "It's none of my business."

Brigit's eyebrows rose in surprise. "Isn't it?"

"Of course not. Why would it be?" The sideways glance Brigit gave said she was assuming a situation Charlotte wanted to avoid considering. "We're just friends."

"But you'd like there to be more."

The thought had crossed her mind upon occasion over the last three months. She and James definitely had some sort of connection, and they'd shared a kiss or two, but anything beyond that? It was too much to contemplate.

"I can't, Brigit, not right now." Charlotte rose and made herself busy setting her teacup on the credenza beside the stove. "It's better if we just stay friends."

"Don't hold this against him, Charlotte."

She turned to face her friend. "I won't. It's . . . it's not him or his marital status. There are things we need to sort out. That *I* need to sort out. This just isn't a good time."

"It rarely is." Brigit came around the desk and laid her hand on Charlotte's arm, a sad smile on her face. "You've had something on your mind since the other day, when the letter about Camille arrived. Talking to you helped me. I'd like to offer the same shoulder. Let me know if I can do anything for you. Friends, remember?"

Charlotte's throat tightened. "I will."

"I have to get back. See you soon." She bussed Charlotte's cheeks, then got her coat and hat. Brigit waved to her, and the bell over the door jingled gently as it closed behind the madam.

Charlotte sat at the desk, staring at the pages before her but not really seeing them. What a mess. Try as she might to put her past aside, there was no way she could completely eradicate the emotions that came out from time to time. Guilt from not feeling guilty about what she'd done, yet there was the shame and stigma attached to having had an abortion. Guilt from surviving the procedure when so many women had been injured or died. And so much relief that she hadn't been one of them, or hadn't needed to tell her parents what she'd done.

She couldn't possibly find the words to tell anyone else. Kit knew. Michael knew. She might be able to confide in Brigit, eventually, but to tell James? Not likely. Wade into a protest over women's rights to get a story? No problem. Confess her stupidity with Richard and what had followed? That required more guts than she had.

Admitting she'd been blinded by his charms and let herself be swayed by his well-played lies was just too damn embarrassing, to say the least. She'd have to explain what Richard had said and done to get her into his bed, which wasn't much more than convince Charlotte he was in full agreement with her on equality and voting rights for women. Truth be told, she'd enjoyed the intimacy with him and didn't deny the feeling of freedom in choosing to go to bed with him. But finally realizing he'd fooled her made her feel idiotic and naïve.

Charlotte had essentially sworn off men for the past fifteen months, and she'd been happy. Now there was James, who ignited feelings she hadn't realized she missed.

Brigit saw that she liked James. So did Michael. James probably saw it as well. Hell, *she* even knew it when she stopped pretending otherwise. But what she'd said to Brigit was true. She needed time to sort out her feelings, to figure out if she was ready to let someone get close again.

Charlotte knew herself too well to be sure anything more than friendship with James would remain as chaste as she needed it to be. There was no way she'd get herself into the same predicament twice in just over a year. She'd opt for life-long celibacy first.

That would certainly alleviate problems, even if resulted in complete frustration.

Before going home for the evening, Charlotte stopped in at McGruder's grocery and perused the aisles, hoping for something to strike her fancy for dinner that night. The clerk, one of McGruder's sons who was older than Charlotte by a good ten years, had asked if he could be of help, but then left her to decide on her own as he stacked items behind the counter. While she considered her desire for tomato versus vegetable soup, the front door rattled open.

"Just stop for a little while, for God's sake," a gruff male voice said. His anger and frustration were loud and clear. "It won't kill either of you to have a little restraint and respect."

Charlotte peeked around the display of canned vegetables at the end of the aisle. Otto and Adam Kenner stood at the counter. She saw only the back of Otto's head, and Adam stood in profile to her, a pinched, worried look on his face.

"We do have respect," Adam said, much more softly than his brother as he eyed the clerk at the other end of the store. "But this is rough for her. She needs a shoulder to cry on."

Otto snorted. "I'm sure you're giving her more than that."

The clerk came over and Otto ordered five pounds of ground coffee and a wedge of hard cheese. Adam shook his head and started to turn her way. Charlotte quickly ducked back into the aisle. Not that she was doing anything wrong; she was just shopping, after all. Staring at the Kenners, however, might be mistaken for eavesdropping or being the busybody Michael accused her of being.

Charlotte waited for the Kenners to make their purchase and leave before she grabbed a can of soup and went to the counter.

"That it for you, Miss Brody?"

"Some cheddar cheese too, if you please," she said, craning her neck to watch the Kenners walk up the street. Probably headed home.

"That Otto Kenner sure has a way about him, don't he?" the clerk asked.

Charlotte brought her attention to the McGruder man. "Do you know him or Adam?"

He shrugged. "Well enough, I guess. They're hardworking. Keep to themselves mostly, though Otto's been known to start a ruckus or two at the Mirage Club."

"Is he the violent sort?"

The clerk made a face. "Not unless you make him mad. Saw him deck a guy who cheated at poker, over a dollar pot. Wasn't the money, Otto said, the guy lyin' there with his nose broken, but the principle. I make sure I'm very careful when I count out his change."

Charlotte could see the elder Kenner brother flying off the handle and reacting in such a way. "I don't blame you. Honesty and fair play are important, especially in business."

"Absolutely," McGruder said. "Otto has no problem calling out business owners for not being on the up-and-up. They don't like it one bit, either being accused of cheating or getting caught at it."

"Did he ever have words with Lyle Fiske?"

McGruder didn't hesitate. "They had a real roof-raiser at the Businessmen's Association Dinner 'bout four, five months back. Didn't come to blows or nothing, but Otto's face was so red I thought steam was about to shoot from his ears."

Brigit had mentioned the same tussle between the men.

"Sounds serious. What was it about?"

"Same thing Otto always goes on about: price gouging. He accused Lyle of trying to take advantage of being the only hardware store in town and charging whatever the hell he felt like charging. Pardon my French."

"That would be irritating, to say the least," Charlotte said, considering the relationships between all the Fiskes and Kenners. "Thank you, Mr. McGruder."

The man grinned at her. "Have a good evening, Miss Brody, and remember, we'll deliver so you don't have to go out in this mess. Just give a call."

She smiled back and slid her purchases into her satchel. On her way to her house, Charlotte mulled the conversation between the brothers and the one she'd had with McGruder. One Fiske-Kenner relationship seemed to be vastly different from the other, but both put Lyle Fiske in the middle of passionate situations. Was he an instigator or a victim? Given his desire for financial gain, she could see that being a factor in his death; money was a strong motivator. Or was it the lovers who'd decided Lyle was in the way?

Otto Kenner's beef with Lyle seemed awfully intense. It was obvious from his conversation at the grocery store with Adam that Otto didn't think much of his brother's affair with Caroline. That might be a residual effect of his dislike for Lyle, though Charlotte would have expected Otto to support anything that could irritate his nemesis.

As she ascended the stairs to the green house, Charlotte grasped the bannister for support. It wobbled some, reminding her she needed to get it fixed. Someone like Otto Kenner would be the man to call on. She should see if he was available.

And see if there's any evidence behind Otto and Lyle's adversarial relationship.

Perhaps a visit to Otto Kenner's home, where he ran his contractor business, was in order.

Chapter 7

The next morning, just after eight, Charlotte pocketed a flashlight and purposely walked past the Kenner house on her way to the office, though it was well off her usual route. The house appeared dark and empty. Adam had an office in town, and from his advertisements Charlotte found in the newspaper, Otto based his business out of the home they shared. It seemed both men were out and working already.

Taking her chances, Charlotte strode up to the front door and knocked. There wasn't a peep from inside, as she'd anticipated. She knocked louder, just in case. No one called out or came to the door.

Checking the late November, still dark street for passersby and finding herself alone, Charlotte made her way to the rear of the house. She pulled out her flashlight, turned it on, then passed through a double gate that could be opened wide enough to allow an automobile or cart. Within the yard, a tarp-covered stack of lumber stood beside a large, windowless shed. A padlock on the door meant she wouldn't get a peek inside. That was unfortunate. She hoped that what she wanted—whatever it might be—was in the house.

She climbed the wide covered porch, noting more wood and tools, and knocked on the back door. Cupping her hand around the head of the flashlight, she pointed it through the uncurtained window. A small, neat kitchen with two chairs, a rectangular table, an icebox, a coal stove, and a deep sink. A doorway led to a dark hall.

Keeping her light low, Charlotte turned the doorknob. The latch clicked open.

Her heart raced like a car on Mr. Vanderbilt's Motor Parkway. Snooping inside Lyle Fiske's desk was one thing, but she'd never broken into a home before. Though it wasn't exactly breaking in if the door was unlocked, was it? Besides, if one of the Kenners was involved with Lyle's death, there might be evidence or something to implicate them

Or there might not, a little voice said in her head. And illegal entry negated anything James could use.

"But it could at least get him pointed in the right direction."

Justification made, flimsy as it was, Charlotte opened the door and stepped into the Kenner home.

The aroma of coffee from breakfast hung in the air, the dishes washed and stacked beside the sink. A narrow hall led to a small bathroom under the staircase on the right, and a parlor straight ahead. Charlotte stood at the bottom of the stairs, listening for any indication of someone on the second floor. Hearing nothing but the beat of her own heart in her ears, she went to a closed door on the left.

She pressed her ear against the cool wood, her hand on the brass knob. Again, no sounds from within. She turned the knob slowly. The click of the latching mechanism sounded terribly loud in the still air and she winced. She pushed the door in, slowly easing it open enough to see the room was dark. Charlotte slipped inside and swept her flashlight beam in front of her, no higher than her knees to keep it from being seen through the window. Two filing cabinets of the same dark wood were against the left-hand wall.

A large wood desk with a leather chair occupied the far end of the room, with a slanted-top table at a ninety degree angle to the right of the desk. Corner to corner, the two work areas made a squat L-shape. The drafting table—at least that's what it looked like to Charlotte—benefitted from the natural light coming in from the window behind it. Perhaps Otto Kenner wasn't just a repairman and carpenter, but an architect or designer of some sort as well.

Charlotte glanced at the papers on the drafting table. The drawings appeared to be of a cabinet from several views. The notations on the paper were too small for her to read quickly, and she didn't have time or interest in Otto Kenner's work in progress at the moment.

She moved to the desk and sat. The leather chair was old and well worn. Opening the top drawer, she found typical office bric-a-brac, a few personal letters to Adam Kenner from people in Oregon, California, and New York. Nothing to or from Caroline Fiske, and none of the drawers held the mysterious black box. Not that Charlotte was expecting to find it there. If Adam had the box—and she doubted that was the case—he'd probably be smart enough to hide it in a more personal space like his bedroom.

A man's desk isn't personal? the little voice chided. If she considered a home office more "public," Charlotte didn't feel as guilty about looking inside. It was ridiculous, of course, but for the moment it rationalized what she was doing.

Finding nothing pertinent to either of the Fiskes in the desk, Charlotte got up and started looking through the filing cabinets. There was a drawer of client files, mostly Cordovans, but a few from other Alaska towns. Another drawer held what looked like Otto Kenner's materials orders and invoices for jobs he'd taken.

Odd, some of the orders were through Fiske's Hardware, but many were directly from a supplier in Seattle. Was Kenner getting a better price by buying directly? A closer look showed recent orders of large quantities of nails, screws, paints, solvents, and other materials. Why would a single-man operation require six cases of paint thinner or three hundred pounds of ten-penny nails? It's like he was opening his own business in competition with Fiske.

Charlotte stared down at the bills in her hand. The excessive order was dated a few months ago, not long after Mr. Mc-Gruder said Lyle and Otto had gotten into an argument at the Businessmen's dinner.

If Lyle thought Otto was offering the same goods to Cordova and trying to undercut his profits, tempers would flare, given the history between the men. Was that what happened the night of Lyle's murder?

But what would Otto care or know about the black box? How did it play into this, if it did at all? The box was fast becoming an important missing piece of the puzzle.

Charlotte returned the paperwork to their neat file folders in the drawers and considered going upstairs to check the bedrooms.

"In for a penny, in for a pound, right?" She wiped her sweat-slick hands on her coat.

And what if she did find something? What if she found the black box? How would she explain it to James? It was bad enough she'd have to make excuses for rifling through the Kenners' office. He'd never forgive her if she went further.

No, this was bad enough. Anything more was too much to risk.

Charlotte made her way back to the kitchen, again keeping her light low to allow her to see where she was placing her feet. Making sure no muck was left behind from her boots, she checked the yard and eased the kitchen door open.

Safely back on the porch, she gently closed the door.

"Hey! What the hell are you doing there?"

Charlotte spun, heart hammering and feet frozen to the floorboards. Otto Kenner strode across the yard through the open gate, his flashlight beam bouncing enough to show the snarl of anger on his face.

"I was just—"

"You were in my house," he growled, heavy boots thudding up the porch steps. His free hand was balled in a fist. For half a second, Charlotte thought he was going to strike her. "I saw you coming out."

Her back against the door, Charlotte's mind whirled. "I was looking to talk to you about a job. The door was unlocked and I—"

Otto grabbed her arm and tugged her toward the stairs. "Doesn't mean you can go inside uninvited. Let's go."

Charlotte set her heels best she could on the wet porch, but Otto was stronger and determined. "Get your hands off me. What do you think you're doing?"

He didn't release her. "Taking you to the marshal."

A jolt of trepidation shot through her. Damnation. James was going to kill her. But better she face James than the new constables. Charlotte didn't know them all that well and was sure they'd give her little to nothing as far as consideration. Lucky for her, most Cordovans were apt to still call on the marshal's office. Or perhaps not so lucky, depending on how angry James became.

"Mr. Kenner, I assure you, all I did was poke my head in to see if anyone was home." Thank goodness she hadn't gone upstairs. Charlotte barely managed to keep her footing on the slick, half-frozen road. "Please let go of my arm."

Otto's grip tightened. "I don't believe you. I'm bringing you to the marshal, then coming back to make sure you didn't take anything."

"Of course I didn't take anything. This is all a misunderstanding." At least as far as her being a thief was concerned.

Otto didn't care about misunderstandings. He half dragged her down Main Street. People opening their shops or on their way to work stopped and stared at the two of them. Charlotte's face heated as she tried to make it look like she and Otto were going along together, but the scowl on his face clearly said otherwise.

They reached the marshal's office. Otto yanked open the door. He didn't quite shove her inside, but he wasn't all that gentle either.

James rose from his chair, his expression one of curiosity mixed with irritation and concern. He came around the desk, fists clenched. "Easy there, Kenner. I'll not have you manhandling a woman in my presence."

"She broke into my house," Otto said by way of explanation. "Saw her coming out the kitchen door when I went back for some tools I needed on a job."

James glared at him. "That's no excuse for treating Miss Brody in such a manner." He met her gaze and the heat of embarrassment spread to her chest. "Miss Brody?"

"I was there to ask Mr. Kenner about fixing the steps of my house." They needed repairing, and James knew it. It made her stomach ache to lie to him.

"A misunderstanding then," James offered.

Relief eased some of the tension in her gut, but she was still lying to him and that wasn't right. She'd have to come clean eventually. "That's what I told him."

"To hell with that," Otto said, his face bright red under the office lights. "She had no business being in my house. I want her locked up. Now."

Surely James could see that Otto was overreacting. It was obvious she hadn't taken anything. Was he afraid she'd seen something she shouldn't have? Charlotte wasn't about to admit to poking her nose into his business, since he was right on that account, but an innocent, rational man didn't demand someone get locked up for appearing to have entered their kitchen.

James rubbed his hands over his face, clearly unhappy with the entire situation. He strode over to her and gently took her upper arm. "Come on."

Charlotte's jaw dropped. "You can't be serious."

Her feet moved when he drew her toward the door marked "Jail," but she was still unable to believe he was doing what he was doing.

Glancing over his shoulder at Otto, James said, "I'll be back in a minute to take your statement."

He opened the door and led her down a short hallway that opened to a dingy white room. The two iron-barred cells, each with a single cot, an enameled sink, and a covered bucket, were empty. Thank goodness for small mercies.

"This is ridiculous," Charlotte said.

James removed a ring of keys from a hook above the chair resting against the wall across from the cells. "I agree, but the law's the law. If Kenner wants to file a complaint and press charges, it's his right." He led her to one of the cells and released her arm. "I'll try talking to him, but for now you're under arrest."

It wasn't the first time Charlotte had heard those words, but coming from him, they stung. "Do you have to put me in a cell? I promise to sit here quietly until you come back."

He held the metal frame of the door, not saying a word. His expression was cool, professional neutrality, but Charlotte felt his disappointment.

"Fine." She entered the cell. Sure, he was just doing his job; he was also putting her in here to make a point.

"Sit tight," he said, "and I'll be back as soon as I can."

He swung the door closed with a gentle clang.

Charlotte grasped the cold bars. "I have a good reason for going inside his house."

Despite his demeanor, he laughed. "I'm sure you do."

James retreated down the hall. The door rattled closed.

Charlotte sat on the cot. Surely he'd convince the carpenter she was innocent. Well, of theft of any sort, anyway. Once Otto saw nothing was amiss, the worst she'd be in trouble for was illegal entry. The hard part would be persuading James that he needed to look closer at the Kenners and their interactions with Lyle Fiske without incriminating herself. Something was definitely fishy there.

She set her elbows on her knees and rested her chin in her hands as she waited for James to return. No, he wouldn't appreciate her actions at all, because it was dishonest at the very least, and James was an honest man. But even his feelings for her, whatever they might be, wouldn't keep him from doing what was right.

The latch on the door leading to the marshal's office clicked. Hinges squealed. Charlotte sat up, rubbing her eyes. She'd lay down after a while, waiting for James to return, but hadn't fallen asleep. Checking the time on her pendant watch, she saw she'd been in the cell for nearly an hour.

James's heavy boot steps clomped down the short hall. He grabbed the back of the wooden chair, swung it around in front of Charlotte's cell, and straddled the seat. Arms crossed on the back, his blue eyes held hers. No nonsense here, they said.

"What's your side of things?"

Charlotte took a deep breath. She'd been rehearsing her case since he'd left her. It was pathetic, she knew, but at least she could offer him the truth now. "It's not what Otto Kenner believes. I did go into the house while they weren't there, but not to steal anything."

"I didn't think so, but you realize you just confessed to illegal entry, right?" James shook his head, resignation clear on his face. "Just tell me what you were doing in there."

"Is he pressing charges?" Being held was one thing. Actually having a criminal record beyond the unlawful assembly charges out of New York was another.

He held her gaze for several moments, and Charlotte feared he was about to tell her she was getting her steamer ticket out of Alaska that night. "I managed to talk him out of it."

Relief swept through her alongside an upwelling of appreciation for his support, even when he thought she was crossing the line. "Thank you."

"Don't thank me yet," he said. What was that supposed to mean? "Why were you in the house?"

"Caroline Fiske has likely been having an affair with Adam Kenner. Otto and Lyle had run-ins before over business dealings. I figured one or the other could have led to his murder."

"You were looking for evidence of infidelity or something? What would that prove?"

He had a point, but Charlotte had more.

"Caroline is desperate to find the black box Lyle kept in his safe. I was looking to see if the Kenners had it. If it was there, then I'd guess that Otto or Adam Kenner killed Lyle."

James stared at her, eyes narrowed as he contemplated her suspicions. "Adam kills Lyle, Caroline collects the insurance, they live happily ever after. Wouldn't be the first time that happened."

"No, but Caroline doesn't have the box, and I doubt Adam would keep it from her. But Otto might."

His grunt implied something between acknowledgement and disbelief.

"Did you break into the Fiskes' house too?" he asked in a half horrified way, frowning. How dreadful did he think she was?

"Of course not. I took a look-see in their home office during the visitation the other day."

"Good God, Charlotte, the woman's in mourning."

Apparently he thought she was pretty damn dreadful.

A sick feeling churned in her stomach. "I just did a quick search. It's not like I ransacked the place. Besides, even though Caroline had some sort of feelings toward her husband, she could have very well arranged for his death."

His expression said she had a point, but she wasn't feeling terribly triumphant at the moment. "Fine. So nothing at the Fiskes' and nothing at the Kenners' home."

"Something at the Kenners' home," she corrected, "just not the box."

He arched an eyebrow. "What? Not that anything you saw could be admissible in court."

She ignored that fact for a minute. "I found shipping records and invoices for tools and solvents and nails. Stuff like that."

"Shocking for a carpenter and builder."

She resisted the urge to stick her tongue out at him. "But does a one-man operation need cases of paint thinner and three hundred pounds of nails? Kenner's shed doesn't seem large enough to hold all the things he's ordered in the last few months. Why order so much as winter sets in?"

James scratched his chin. "That does seem odd. I think Kenner has a warehouse someplace for larger projects. He could be doing extra inside work, or has contracted a number of furniture orders. Still, that's a lot of hardware." He met her eyes again. "But you didn't know this before you went in."

"No," Charlotte admitted. "I'd heard Otto and Lyle were at odds. With that and the relationship between Adam and Caroline, I thought one or the other might be reason enough to kill Lyle."

James rose and returned the chair to its spot against the wall. "And you figured you'd steer the investigation that way, even if I can't use what you found or how you found it."

"I knew that if I gave you a hint you'd be able to pick it up and gather the proof you need." She rose, anxious to get out of the cell and on with her day.

"The only problem with that, Miss Brody, is if anyone learns how I got my lead."

"Mum's the word, right, deputy?" She gave him her most charming smile and was tickled when the corner of his mouth twitched as he tried not to smile back.

He shook his head, but didn't reach for the ring of keys hanging on the wall.

Her smile faltered as her joy sank. "You're not letting me out."

"Kenner might not be pressing charges, but I need you to understand one thing, Charlotte. You shouldn't break the law in order to obtain information, no matter how critical it is to a case."

She grasped the bars. Irritation warred with indignation. "I understand. Honest, I do."

"I'm not so sure." He turned and walked down the short hall.

"James! This isn't funny!"

"I'm not laughing," he called back to her, but she had a feeling he was. At least a little.

"Come back here and let me out."

"Later, after you've had a little time to think things over." The door latch clicked.

"James!" She tried shaking the bars, but they didn't move. Not that she expected them to.

"Or tomorrow. We'll see." The door rattled shut.

Charlotte stood there, thinking he'd be back any minute after giving her a good dose of reality. But he didn't return after a slow count to sixty, or one hundred twenty, or three hundred.

"Damnation."

She threw herself back down on the cot, arms folded. He was being ridiculous and using his position inappropriately. It was completely unlike him.

And for some reason, that made her laugh.

James returned two hours later. Charlotte had gone from angry to amused to perturbed while she cooled her heels waiting for his little lesson to be over. Now she was behind in her work. If Mr. Toliver heard about what she'd done she might have to look for another job. Though maybe a jailbird assistant wouldn't bother the newspaper man all that much.

James snatched the ring of keys off the hook and opened the cell door.

Charlotte swept past him. Being released from jail always brought a sense of relief, no matter how minor or ludicrous the charges.

He touched her arm as she started toward the hall. Charlotte stopped and looked up at him, trying to appear more angry than she was. She'd lost time at the office, and her pride had been wounded, but she knew she'd been lucky Otto Kenner hadn't pressed charges. She was mad at James, but at herself as well.

"I didn't want to do this." James's brow furrowed, his lips pressed into a thin line.

Charlotte busied herself buttoning her coat. "Of course you did. You want me to consider the ramification of my actions." She met his gaze again. "I do, believe it or not. I know what I'm risking when I set out to investigate a story. But knowing there's risk won't stop me from doing my job, and it shouldn't stop you from doing yours. I don't expect special treatment."

That wasn't completely true. Having a friend on the local police force was to a journalist's benefit, and often to the policeman's benefit. Mutual back-scratching and all that.

Charlotte started toward the door again, but James took hold of her sleeve. "Are you mad that I locked you up or because I never told you about Stella?"

She'd been hoping to forget about his soon-to-be ex-wife, but the prickling along the nape of her neck made it clear that wasn't happening in the near future.

"I resent that you assume my anger is about your ex-wife," she said. "But if you must know, yes, I am upset you never told me about her."

James's eyes widened at her response. Maybe he wasn't expecting her honesty. She hadn't expected it either, truth be told.

Charlotte took a deep breath and let it out slowly in an effort to calm herself. "I understand why you did what you did in both situations, but it doesn't mean I have to like it. Can I go now? I have to make up time at the paper."

He released her sleeve.

Charlotte walked through the main room, grateful Marshal Blaine was either gone or shut within his private office. James followed her as far as his desk, silent as she went out the front door. She refused to look at him, and closed the door firmly behind her.

A wet snow was falling, filling the street with a new layer of white. Charlotte set her hat on her head, ignored the rumble in her stomach, and set off to work. The clomp-sploosh of her boots on the walkway and slow, even breathing helped clear her head and cool her ire.

He was just doing his job, protecting himself as well as protecting her. Who could fault him for that?

Chapter 8

A long night at the paper, where she and Mr. Toliver worked side by side at the Linotype and printing press to get the paper ready, meant less sleep than usual for Charlotte. She didn't explain to him why she was behind when he came in at eight that evening, and thankfully Toliver was more concerned about getting the *Times* out than excuses.

Tossing and turning when she finally did get to bed, alternately angry with James and berating herself for her own antics, made the night that much shorter, and now her morning would be that much more of a challenge. The headache pulsing against her temples wasn't appreciated either.

Having her thoughts devolve into wondering why James kept his marital status to himself, and the stress of her own secret-keeping, didn't help matters. Everyone deserved privacy, but Charlotte irrationally thought he should have told her about Stella. On the other hand, she wasn't about to share her most intimate past activities with him.

Now that his secret was out, was she obligated to tell him about Richard? About the pregnancy? About—

Charlotte flung the covers off and got out of bed. The cold

floor shocked her brain back on the right track. No, she wouldn't tell him. Not yet. Maybe not ever. James neglecting to tell her, and likely others, he was married was one thing. Admitting she'd been foolish by being with Richard, believing lies, then putting herself at risk and breaking laws was another.

She dressed quickly and washed up, too agitated to even consider going back to sleep though it was barely six in the morning. She'd work on her *Modern Woman* serial while breakfasting on a cup of coffee and some toast. Maybe she'd surprise Michael by doing a bit of filing or transcribing patient notes. He'd said Mary wasn't working full-time for him yet, and she probably couldn't read Charlotte's shorthand.

After an hour of typing, her back and shoulders tight and a few too many pages corrected or crumpled in the wastebasket, she decided it was time for some fresh air to help clear her head.

One slippery step on the porch told her the temperature had dropped considerably overnight, freezing the slush to a hard, uneven surface. She turned back to dig a pair of crampons out of a bin near the entry. The Gibbinses had warned her they might come in handy.

After buckling the spikes to her boots, Charlotte turned on her flashlight and made her way down the dark, quiet streets to Michael's office. It was black as pitch on the road and eerily silent at such an early hour. A few distant clanks and clatters assured her she wasn't the only human being awake in Cordova.

Once she reached Main Street, the streetlights were sufficient to make her way without tripping over the edge of the walk or slipping on a patch of ice. She used her copy of Michael's key to open the outer door of his office. Charlotte found the switch on the wall and turned it. The office was cold and the exam room door was ajar, though dark within. She'd expect Michael to be up soon to open the door to his private quarters and allow some warmth from his stove to seep in. In the meantime, she'd keep her coat on.

Charlotte closed the outer door quietly, removed her spike-clad boots, and crossed to the desk. She turned on the lamp, the additional light brightening the small, chilled space. As suspected, a pile of patient files was stacked on the corner of the desk awaiting some organization. Settling on the cushioned chair, she pulled the top file and got to work.

She was halfway through the files an hour later when she heard Michael moving about in his room. The aroma of coffee drifted through the gap around the door.

"Pour me a cup, would you?" she called loudly.

Something clattered and fell, and a muffled curse made her grin. Michael's door flew open and he stumbled out, barefooted, shirt open at the throat, hair mussed.

"Christ, Charlotte. You nearly gave me a heart attack."

She rose and stretched, unable to hide her amusement. "Sorry. I got up early and decided to make up for neglecting you."

He ran a hand through his hair, smoothing down the blond strands only to have a few fall over his forehead. "Thanks, but warn a guy next time, if you please."

"I'll see what I can do." She sat again and straightened papers. "I didn't want your new girl to get thrown into a mess. When will she be starting full time?"

"Soon, I hope," he said. "We're still working out a schedule. I may be taking an office in another building, probably over the drugstore. It's too damn cold in here."

Charlotte rubbed her hands together. "Agreed. And how civilized of you to have an office separate from your house."

"It's convenient here though, when someone comes in the dead of night with an emergency. I don't have to get completely dressed to see them." He slipped his suspenders over his shoulders. "Since you're here, come on back and have some coffee."

The outer door squeaked open and a quiet, young voice drifted into the room. "It's okay, Esther. Doctor Brody's a nice man. He'll help."

Michael and Charlotte exchanged curious glances. He obviously wasn't expecting patients at this hour.

Two girls of twelve or thirteen, covered head to toe in wool caps, coats, and sturdy boots, came in, stopping suddenly when they saw Michael and Charlotte. One, taller than her friend, dropped her gaze to her feet. The other shut the door and looked directly at Michael.

"Rebecca, what's the matter?" he asked. "What are you doing here so early?"

"Saw your lights on and figured you were open," the bolder of the two girls said. "This is my friend Esther. She needs your help."

Both Rebecca and Esther had dark hair and the complexion of Alaska Natives. A rosy undertone to Rebecca's skin showed in her cold-reddened cheeks. It was difficult to see Esther's face with her head down. Rebecca, however, had no trouble meeting the eyes of either adult in the room. Maybe familiarity with Michael helped that, but Charlotte got the impression she was a leader among her peers.

"What's the problem, Esther?" Michael asked gently. He was very good at putting people at ease, understanding that coming to his office was often a stressful situation. "Are you hurt or sick?"

Esther flicked a glance up at him. "My mother and brother," she said so softly Charlotte barely heard the words.

Rebecca took her hand. "She's shy. Was all I could do to get her to come see you. Her mother and little brother have had a bad cough for a couple weeks. Right, Esther?" Esther nodded. "A village woman gave them some medicine, but they aren't getting better. She thinks it might be the same sickness from last year."

A jolt of concern went through Charlotte. The flu pandemic had finally waned after killing millions around the world, and only since the previous spring in Alaska. Entire villages in the territory had been wiped out, either directly or indirectly, as people succumbed to the disease or starved or froze to death when family members who hunted and tended fires passed away. The idea of another wave of influenza striking would panic the town.

"I told Esther you were a big help when my mother was sick," Rebecca continued, "and that you did everything you could for her."

Michael's expression turned sad as he met Charlotte's eyes. "Mrs. Derenov," he said by way of explanation.

Charlotte considered the young woman before her. Rebecca Derenov wasn't just a bold girl speaking up for her friend, but one who understood that sometimes people died despite all efforts. She didn't hold Michael responsible for the death of her mother, an indication of a level of maturity even some adults lacked.

"I'd be happy to stop in and see them," Michael said to Esther. "I doubt it's the same sickness as last year, but I want to make sure. Where do you live?"

Esther and Rebecca consulted in whispered words, half in English and half in the Eyak language, from what Charlotte could tell.

"Out along the lake. Not too far to walk. Can you come with us after school?" Rebecca finally said. Her dark eyes were full of hope and determination. "I'll just have to let my brother know where I'm going."

"That sounds like a good plan," Michael said, giving them a friendly smile. Though Esther probably hadn't noticed with her head down. "Come get me when classes are over and we'll go together."

Rebecca nodded and took her friend's arm. "We'll be here. Come on, Esther, we don't want to be late."

Esther glanced up at Michael, gave him a fleeting smile, then hurried out into the cold and dark with Rebecca.

"She's quite the go-getter," Charlotte said. "Seems older than her years."

"Yeah, Rebecca was the sole caregiver when her mother fell ill." He started back toward his living quarters. Charlotte followed, enticed by the promise of coffee and learning more about the girl. "Mr. Derenov had died a couple of years before, and their boy, Ben, was down in the States. Well, not a boy, a young man. He's a good nine or ten years older than Rebecca."

"No local friends or family?" Charlotte knew the Native community in the Cordova area was tight-knit, helping each other in numerous ways.

"Mrs. Derenov didn't have any family here," he said. "A few folks helped when she became ill, but there were some bad feelings between Ben Senior and his family. Marrying a white woman might have had something to do with it, I'm not sure. There may have been a falling out before that. A number of the white folks here had less than positive opinions as well, unfortunately."

"Not just here," Charlotte said. The blatant racism across the country made her cringe. Even within her own cause, which was supposed to be fighting for equality for all.

Michael shook his head as he poured them each a cup of coffee. "Attitudes are a little better now, but not by much, and the kids suffer from the adults' prejudices. Ben Junior had a real rough time of it, from what Mrs. Derenov told me. Lots of fights at school, then later when he was working. He decided to leave town and start over down south."

Funny how some came to Alaska to start again and others left for the same reason.

"That must have been hard on everyone." Charlotte sat at his rickety little table and stirred sugar into her coffee. "Did Ben get back up here before his mother passed?"

"Barely," Michael said. He picked up his pocket watch from the top of the dresser, wound it, then put it to his ear, grimacing as he shook the timepiece and wound it some more. "She was gone within the week he returned. It's been just him and Rebecca ever since."

"How sad." She couldn't imagine the heartache of traveling

so far just to watch your mother die. And for Rebecca to lose both parents so young? It happened all too frequently, and kids usually turned out fine, but Charlotte knew there were hardships and difficulties the Derenov children would face.

She pushed aside the thought of her own parents back in New York. They were both in good health. No reason to worry herself.

"Rebecca's a good kid, smart as can be," Michael said, tying his tie. "Be a shame if she had to quit school."

"Why would she have to do that?"

"I hear Ben's still having a tough time. Other than the occasional odd job, like for the Fiskes, I don't know that he has a regular income. Unfortunately, his reputation as a troublemaker hasn't faded from memory." He came to the table and sat with her to don his wool socks. "With little to no income, it'll be very difficult for them to survive up here."

The idea of sacrificing Rebecca's education piqued Charlotte's passions. "That's not right. The best thing for a young woman—for anyone—is to get as complete an education as possible. It's the key to equality."

Michael smoothed down his pant leg. "I agree, and I hope it doesn't come to that. But the graduation rate is iffy, more so for Native kids. If they make it to the eighth grade they're doing well. A number of families—white and Native—need the income from as many hands as possible."

"And that income would be higher the longer they're able to stay in school, and better if they can go beyond a high school education." She was gripping the coffee mug tightly with both hands. "Children like Rebecca Derenov and her friend Esther need to go to school."

"Maybe, if she and Ben stay here, she'll be able to keep going." He didn't sound hopeful. "If they head back to the States, it may be as tough or tougher on them."

"We can't let that happen," Charlotte said. The idea of such a bright and caring young woman missing the opportunity for an education because of basic financial need made her sick to her stomach.

"It's not up to us," Michael said. "They have to do what they can to survive."

"Someone has to convince them, convince Ben, that keeping his sister in school is critical." She considered the Derenovs' situation. "Can't you see if there's anyone who can give him a good enough job to allow them to stay?"

"People aren't keen on others butting into their business, you know."

"I know, Michael, but this girl's well-being is at stake, don't you think? And as her doctor..." She was playing into his sense of dedication to his patients' entire health, but she felt no guilt in doing so.

"Okay, I'll ask, but there are no guarantees." He rose, rinsed his coffee cup in the sink, then gave her a peck on the cheek. "I have rounds at the hospital, then a few homebound patients to tend."

Charlotte followed him to the outer office. "We need to do something, Michael."

He shrugged into his coat and donned his boots. Grabbing his black bag from behind the desk, he said, "We're outsiders, Charlotte. Ben Derenov is his sister's closest family and he's an adult. He makes the final decisions for her. We can advocate, but browbeating isn't going to work. Lock up when you leave, please. Bye, Sis."

Charlotte returned to the seat at the desk, her mind only half on the task at hand as she considered Ben and Rebecca Derenov. The situation wasn't right, it wasn't fair, and it was, unfortunately, not unique. But how to make it better?

Another hour of seeing to the files and Charlotte was ready for a real breakfast, the coffee and toast at home having tided her over longer than she'd expected. After a quick bite at the café, she was on her way to the *Times* office when Mr. Hanson, owner of one of the two jewelry stores in town, caught her eye as he swept muck from the walkway in front of his store. He smiled and waved, then went back to sweeping. An elaborate sign in the window stated a holiday sale on everything in stock.

Good gravy. Christmas was almost upon them and she'd hardly given a thought of what to get Michael. Maybe a new watch, if the price was right. With a month to go, it was unlikely she'd have time to order anything up from the States. Charlotte crossed the frozen mud of Main Street.

"Good morning, Mr. Hanson."

Hanson looked up from his sweeping and smiled at her again. A wool cap covered his silvery hair, and a heavy coat protected his dapper suit. The unbuckled boots on his feet would likely be changed into more appropriate footwear to tend customers.

"Good morning, Miss Brody. How are you today?"

"Very well, thank you." Charlotte gestured toward the window. "Is your sale still going on?"

"It certainly is! Go on in and have a look while I finish up here. Won't be but a few minutes." He held the door open for her, grinning.

Charlotte went inside, loosening the scarf at her throat and removing the mittens she'd just put on. Three glass cases of rings, earrings, necklaces, and watches, and a wall of clocks sparkled under the delicate shades of overhead lamps hanging throughout the store. Signs advertising a number of manufacturers also adorned the walls, as did one declaring "Repairs Made on Premises."

She barely glanced at the other offerings as she headed to the watches, their gold and silver cases gleaming, the crystals reflecting the bright light. Many of the metal cases were smooth and plain; a good number were etched with decorative designs or images of animals and scenery. Other than how they worked and how fancy the cases might be, Charlotte knew next to nothing about watches. Her father had a silver one he'd inherited from his father, and as a child she'd been allowed to wind it for him. Michael had had his watch since medical school, but it wasn't as durable as their father's. It was also possible Michael hadn't been as meticulous in caring for his as Father.

With a jingle from the bells over the door, Mr. Hanson came in. He removed his hat and coat, stashed them in the back office, then returned to the counter. "What can I help you with today, Miss Brody?" he asked as he finger-combed his thick hair and smiled.

"Michael needs a new watch," she said, "and I was thinking of getting him one for Christmas." She looked down at the display again. "I'm not sure which would be a good value."

There were no prices on the pieces, but she figured a decent watch would run about ten to fifteen dollars. She could save up a week's salary or work out a payment plan with Mr. Hanson.

"I guarantee the best prices in town," he said as he fished a pair of wire-rimmed spectacles from his inside jacket pocket and hooked the earpieces into place. "We have a number of makers, Elgin, Ingersoll, Waltham." He opened the case and withdrew a gold-cased watch. "This is a 992 Hamilton. It's a size sixteen case, has twenty-one jewel movement, and is yellow-gold filled."

"Beautiful," Charlotte said, reaching out with one finger to stroke the luxurious case.

"It retails for sixty, but with the sale it's fifty-five dollars," Mr. Hanson said.

She snatched her hand back as if merely touching the watch would cause her to break it, and therefore have to buy it.

"Fifty-five?" A month's salary. She loved her brother and wanted to get him a nice gift, but she didn't have that amount of cash on hand. "Do you have anything else?"

Mr. Hanson smiled graciously and slipped the Hamilton back into its place under the glass. "We have several others that might fit your budget, and we do offer a payment plan. How about this Elgin? It's fifteen."

Breathing a little easier, Charlotte listened as he gave her the details of a silver watch down the line from the majority of his inventory and compared it to several others on display.

The bell over the door chimed. Mr. Hanson glanced up. His congenial smile turned into a flattened expression of disapproval. Curious to see who could have caused such a reaction, Charlotte turned.

Ben Derenov stood just inside the door, hands shoved in his pockets, shoulders hunched. There was a scowl on his face as well. He looked decidedly uncomfortable.

"What do you want?" Mr. Hanson asked.

His gruffness startled Charlotte. All Ben had done was walk into the store.

"I got something to sell." Ben pulled his hands out of his pockets. The right one was closed into a fist. The left clenched and unclenched. "You buy jewelry, don't ya?"

Mr. Hanson narrowed his eyes at the younger man. "I'm with a customer. You'll have to come back later."

"It's fine, Mr. Hanson," Charlotte said. "I want to look at these two pieces a little more closely before I decide. Please, take care of Mr. Derenov."

Ben glared at both of them, a hint of suspicion in his eyes.

Hanson mumbled something, then strode toward Ben, keeping the glass display cases between them. "Make it quick. What do you have?"

Ben stepped closer and opened his hand. Charlotte couldn't tell what he held, but it wasn't a large item. Hanson held his hand out, palm up, just under Ben's. Ben dumped the jewelry into the other man's hand, and Charlotte caught a glimpse of gold.

"Real gold and pearls," Ben said as Hanson held a teardrop-shaped earring up to the light.

"I'll tell you if it's real or not, boy." Hanson removed his spectacles and fitted the jeweler's loupe that hung on a chain around his neck to his right eye. His scowl never wavered. He peered at it for several long moments, then exchanged the one for the other, giving it the same close inspection. He handed both back to Ben and removed the loupe from his eye. "Where'd you get them?"

"They were my mother's," Ben said flatly.

Charlotte inwardly winced, her heart aching for Ben and Rebecca. It had to be difficult for them to sell her things, but if Ben wasn't working a regular job, what choice did they have?

"I'll give you a dollar," Hanson said.

Ben's jaw dropped open. "A dollar? That's it? They're real, worth at least ten."

"Says who?" Hanson challenged, chin up.

"That's what—That's what my father paid for them."

"Then your father got cheated," Hanson said unkindly. "These are worth no more than five. The pearls are real, but not great quality, and the gold is just plate, not solid."

"Then how about five for them?"

Hanson shook his head. "No. A dollar and a half."

Ben's face darkened. "Three."

The jeweler folded his arms. "Dollar and a half."

"I can get that much for them at a poker game." Ben's voice cracked with disbelief.

Hanson shrugged. "Off with you then."

Ben closed his hand around the earrings, shot Charlotte an embarrassed glare, then stormed out of the store, the bell tinkling wildly.

Hanson watched as the younger man disappeared past the corner of the building. He took a breath, visibly calming himself, and came back over to Charlotte. "I apologize for the interruption, Miss Brody. I try to run a respectable establishment."

Charlotte tilted her head. "What was not respectable about what happened, Mr. Hanson? It appeared to me that Mr.

Derenov was merely mistaken about the value of his mother's earrings."

She felt bad for Ben, thinking he'd be able to sell the jewelry for almost a week's pay.

Hanson sneered. "*If* those were his mother's."

The implication caught her by surprise. "What do you mean? Do you honestly think he stole them?"

He held out both hands in a "who's to say?" shrug. "I wouldn't put it past the likes of him. Ben Derenov was a bad seed from the time he was a kid. Got into all manner of trouble, nicked candy and baubles from the drugstore. He grew up to be a no-good adult. No one was sorry to see him go when he left town."

Charlotte immediately felt defensive of Ben, though she had no other reason than because Mr. Hanson was so damn hard on him. "I'm sure his mother and sister missed him terribly." Hanson had the courtesy to look embarrassed. "He did return when he heard his mother was ill, and he's trying to make an honest living to take care of Rebecca now. That deserves some credit, don't you think?"

"Maybe so," Hanson conceded, "but it'll take time for people here to get over the things he's done. Actions speak louder than words, and right now Ben Derenov is still needing to prove himself."

Charlotte had the feeling it would take Ben Derenov years of near-perfect behavior before the likes of Mr. Hanson considered him redeemed. Was Hanson's opinion of Ben typical of the town? No wonder he was having such a hard time finding a job.

"Can I show you anything else, Miss Brody?" The jeweler gestured toward another display. "We have some cigarette cases and lighters that your brother might enjoy."

"He doesn't smoke. I think the Elgin will be just fine," she said without really knowing if having seventeen or twenty-one jewels really made much difference to Michael. "I have a little money on me right now and can come back later with the balance."

Hanson scooped up the silver watch, the pleasant smile back on his face. "Of course. We're happy to work out a plan that's satisfactory. Step over here, if you would."

As she made the arrangements with Mr. Hanson, Charlotte couldn't help but compare her experience with the jeweler to Ben's. What a vast difference. If Hanson had known of her own run-ins with the authorities or her stance on women's rights or her indiscretions, would he have refused to sell to her? Proprietors often discriminated against people due to race, creed, color, or reputation.

That gave more credence to Lyle Fiske's backroom pawn operation. He was willing to do business with anyone needing cash and charged everyone horrible interest.

"How terribly evenhanded of him," she muttered.

"Pardon me, Miss Brody? Did you say something?" Mr. Hanson was holding out her receipt for the three dollars she'd given as a down payment.

"Nothing, Mr. Hanson. Thank you. I'll be back later."

She left the store, agitation still prickling at the back of her neck. Hanson's attitude rubbed her the wrong way. Surely not everyone in town felt that way toward Ben Derenov. His difficulty finding work, however, made her think he might have burned some bridges in Cordova. No wonder he was considering moving away.

She had no say in how Ben Derenov lived his life, or what he decided was going to be best for himself and his sister. But damnation, the idea of Rebecca losing out because of those decisions or some people's prejudices aggravated Charlotte to the bone.

Charlotte spent the day in the *Times* office, mostly at the Linotype, or designing a few simple advertisements and writing new announcements. With the holidays approaching, many of the businesses were having sales, and there seemed to be a dance or holiday party scheduled for every week, sometimes several, on top of the weekly gathering at the Prism Social Club. The Cordova Jazz Orchestra would be playing at the upcoming dance. The seven-piece band was quite good and Charlotte made a mental note to attend.

When she had everything ready for Mr. Toliver's night of printing, Charlotte tidied the desk, donned her winter gear, and stepped out onto the walkway. It was just after five in the afternoon and black as midnight. The electric streetlight glow was softened by the lazy spirals of snow. A scant covering on the walk and streets meant getting home wouldn't be too messy, but Charlotte had the feeling she'd be shoveling off the steps come morning.

Many of the shops were closing for the evening, but several still had their lights on. On the second floor of the building housing the laundry and the barber, the light was on in Adam Kenner's office.

Leave it be, Charlotte, she told herself. Yet there she was, crossing the street to the door sandwiched between the two other establishments. Painted in black script on the frosted glass was Adam's name, with "Accounting and Bookkeeping Services" below it.

She opened the door onto a narrow staircase and went in. Listening for any indication that Adam Kenner was with a client, and hearing nothing over the sounds of the launderer coming through the wall, Charlotte started up the stairs. Halfway to the top, the office door flung open, in toward the office, and hit the wall with a rattling thunk. Charlotte froze.

"I don't know why you care what happened to Fiske." Otto Kenner came out onto the landing but had half turned to look back into the office. "We both get what we want now. Give it a rest."

He faced the stairs, large fists clenched at his sides and face flushed with anger. His thick eyebrows met in a scowl when he saw Charlotte. Otto headed down, his broad shoulders practically touching the walls of the narrow stairwell. His heavy boots thundered on the wood, sending vibrations up through her legs.

She pressed her back against the wall to allow him to pass. When he reached the same step, Otto glared at her. "Keep your nose out of our business, lady," he growled.

His tone was low and menacing, and Charlotte was sure Adam hadn't heard it upstairs.

Indignation vied with wariness, keeping her nerves on edge. She'd expected him to be curt, angry even, but threatening?

"Finding the truth *is* my business, Mr. Kenner. That's what journalists do."

He leaned closer, his beard and mustache unable to cover his sneer. Whatever he'd had for lunch had had copious amounts of garlic. "Stay out of my way."

Charlotte swallowed hard but refused to avert her gaze.

Otto continued down the stairs, yanked open the door, then slammed it closed behind him. The glass rattled hard enough she feared it would shatter.

Charlotte pressed her palm to her chest, over her racing heart. She hadn't considered Otto getting physical with her, but he was certainly intimidating when he wanted to be. Avoiding him sounded like the most prudent course for now.

Allowing herself to calm down, Charlotte straightened her dress and smoothed her hair before continuing up to Adam Kenner's office. She peeked around the frame. Adam was at his cherrywood desk, his back to the window. One hand threaded through his hair, elbow on the desk, as he shuffled papers and compared them to the entries in a ledger. More papers and files were piled off to the side.

Three mismatched wood cabinets took up most of the space left in the small office. An adding machine and typewriter were on a roll-away cart behind the desk, and additional ledgers were stacked on the cabinets. A single straight-backed chair was in front of the desk. There was just enough floor space to open the door without hitting anything.

Charlotte knocked lightly on the door. "Mr. Kenner?"

Adam lifted his head. He was a good-looking man, with dark eyes framed by long, black lashes. There was intelligence and sensitivity in those eyes, a gentleness in his fine-boned face that was missing from his raw-hewn brother. Though even with all the differences, you could see the Kenners were related.

"Miss Brody." He stood and smoothed back his black, curly hair. "Did we have an appointment?"

She stepped into the office. "No, I wanted to ask you a few things, if you have a moment."

Curiosity flickered in his eyes. "Please, have a seat."

She sat on the edge of the offered chair. Adam waited for her to get comfortable, then took his seat. "Please excuse the disorganization. I'm still getting settled."

"You were working out of your home for some time, is that right?"

A shadow of irritation crossed his face. Otto must have told him about finding Charlotte at their house.

Not wanting to admit any more, she quickly added, "Your advertisement in the newspaper always listed your home address."

He relaxed a little. "Oh, yes. I still keep a home office. Mostly for Otto's business. I mean, our business. We're partners. But I wanted a separate space for other work."

Charlotte smiled. "That makes sense."

"What can I do for you, Miss Brody? Do you have some questions about investments or concerns of a financial nature?"

Obvious reasons to come to an accountant, though her salary from the *Times* and the small payments from *Modern Woman* didn't amount to enough to require assistance. Her savings had been pretty well spent to fund the trip to Alaska, and a small trust fund from her grandparents was under her parents' financial control until she married or turned thirty. Grandmother and Grandfather had been a bit old-fashioned requiring that stipulation.

"I'm not exactly rolling in cash, Mr. Kenner."

The flicker of light in anticipation of income faded in his eyes. "I could still help you with a budget. Sometimes *not* having much is more difficult to manage."

Her immediate instinct to lie to him about needing his services caught in her throat. She didn't think Adam Kenner had the personality to intentionally harm anyone, even his lover's husband. Of course, anything was possible, and he might be guilty as sin. Then again, he might not. But either way, Charlotte had the inkling Adam knew something.

"I didn't come here seeking financial advice, Mr. Kenner. I came about the Fiskes."

The worst he could do was throw her out, right?

Adam cocked his head, bemused, then understanding dawned. "You want to know if I had anything to do with Lyle's death."

Charlotte blinked at him, surprised he'd cut to the heart of the matter like that. Adam may have been the quieter, kinder of the Kenner brothers, but he wasn't one to dance around either. "It crossed my mind."

"Is that why you were in our house, Miss Brody? Looking for evidence?"

She squirmed a little under the very rightful accusation. Avoiding the question, she asked, "What were your feelings toward Lyle?"

Adam Kenner stared at her for several moments, his warm brown eyes never leaving hers. "I hated him."

The admission should have surprised her, but it didn't. Though Adam Kenner didn't seem like the sort to hate anyone, your lover's husband was probably a good candidate. And if you were Lyle Fiske, the reverse was probably true as well. Lots of potential for emotions getting out of control and someone doing something unfortunate.

"Any particular reason?"

Anger hardened Adam's gaze. "For all the pretense Lyle and Caroline showed in public, their relationship was difficult."

That seemed obvious, given that Caroline took a lover and Lyle visited the local brothels. But Charlotte didn't think that was what Adam referred to. She held her tongue—no easy task—and waited for him to continue.

"Lyle was a mean-spirited little man," Adam said. "Out in public and at parties, he was friendly enough, showed Caroline a certain amount of affection, if not love." His eyebrows came together. "But in private, he was abusive."

"He hurt her?" It wouldn't be unusual for a supposedly quiet, affectionate man to use his fists behind closed doors. Charlotte had seen it more than a few times reporting on marital disturbances when she was first starting out. Caroline had never sported a telltale black eye, as far as Charlotte knew, but that meant little.

Adam shook his head. "No, not physically. Despite their mutual agreement to live separate lives, he treated her like one of his children, maybe even with less consideration. Caroline's smart, a savvy business woman, but Lyle ignored almost all of her suggestions or called her stupid for trying to be more than the pretty thing on his arm when it suited. He threatened to cut her off, financially, more than once when she challenged him."

Everyone Charlotte had spoken to, including Caroline, had implied Caroline was an equal partner in the marriage, and close to that when it came to the hardware store. Wishful thinking? A delusion that was formed and manipulated by Lyle, then perpetuated to make their relationship more amiable than it really was? Another pattern of marital abuse.

"Caroline must have been upset by the charade," she said.

"She put up with his behavior for years." Adam shrugged, but was it in resignation or understanding that women were compelled to do such things? "She kept telling me it was fine, that she could handle him. That her patience—our patience—

would be rewarded. But I saw how it wore on her. Every day, she seemed to fade a little more."

His expression shifted when he spoke of Caroline, softening with concern. Charlotte wasn't sure how Caroline felt about him, but she'd bet her bottom dollar that Adam Kenner was head over heels, deeply in love with Caroline Fiske.

Could that love, combined with his hatred of Lyle, overcome Adam's seemingly gentle nature? People did crazy things over matters of the heart.

But was he the instigator, or could Caroline have purposely set him on Lyle by talking up her husband's abuses? Did she convince Adam that getting rid of Lyle was the only way they'd be happy together?

"Lyle's death must have been somewhat a relief for her." Charlotte knew she was taking a risk by questioning his lover's emotions, but it had to be done.

"You'd think," he said, looking puzzled, "but she's been devastated. The loss of that damn box and the papers inside means she doesn't have the latest copy of Lyle's will. If their lawyer down in Seattle doesn't have a copy, it could mean Lyle's children from his first marriage are his sole beneficiaries. But more than that, she's been truly saddened by his death." Adam shook his head again, saddened and confused. "I just don't understand."

Neither did Charlotte, considering how Adam described the Fiskes. Though she certainly understood how people lied to themselves about relationships.

Adam fell into a thoughtful silence, but Charlotte had a few more questions to explore.

"On my way up, I couldn't help but overhear your conversation with Otto." Well, Otto's end of the conversation, but that was neither here nor there. "What did he mean by you're both getting what you want now that Lyle's gone?"

The color on Adam's cheeks deepened, though from anger or embarrassment, Charlotte couldn't tell. "He didn't mean anything by it," Adam said. "Just that with Lyle gone, Caroline and I will be able to have a more public relationship. After an appropriate mourning period, of course."

"Of course. But what does Otto gain by Lyle's death?"

Charlotte had an idea, but would Adam confirm it?

"Nothing to gain or lose," he said. "The relationship was purely business. Otto and Lyle were not friends, but their head-butting would never . . ." The words lost conviction momentarily, then Adam recovered, supporting his brother as brothers did. "No, Otto wasn't keen on Lyle Fiske, but he'd never do anything like that."

Adam stood abruptly, his chair scraping across the wood floor. "If you'll excuse me, Miss Brody, I have some work to do."

Charlotte rose, a pang of regret making her heart heavy. She hadn't wanted Adam to consider his brother or lover as suspects, but the possibility was there. The Kenners and Caroline Fiske had a lot to gain with Lyle out of the way.

"I appreciate you talking to me, Mr. Kenner. When Deputy Eddington deems it allowable, I'll make sure the truth is put into the newspaper. Leaving out your personal connection to Caroline, of course."

"I appreciate that. Good evening, Miss Brody."

Charlotte shook his offered hand and left the office.

On the way down the stairs, she considered Adam's claim that Otto wouldn't have hurt Lyle. She couldn't quite believe that herself, but siblings often had a skewed view of each other. And often a fierce sense of loyalty. Adam would probably cover for Otto, and Otto for Adam. Just as she and Michael would do for each other.

Chapter 9

It seemed to Charlotte she was spending all her time either at the café or the *Times* office. She really needed to expand her repertoire of locations. Perhaps she'd take in a matinee at the Empress or challenge Michael to a midday bowling match. In the meantime, however, hunger pangs drew her to the café that Saturday morning.

All the tables were full by the time she arrived at eight o'clock, the cold and dark bringing Cordovans together for a hot meal and lively discussion of the news of the day. It made her smile to see the *Times* laid out on tables while readers talked and gestured at a particular article. Love it or hate it, if a piece of writing stirred emotion, it was a good one.

At a table in the corner with three other men, his back to the wall, James Eddington looked up from his plate and their eyes met. Charlotte's heart gave a little jump. They hadn't spoken to each other since James had locked her up, and neither had made the effort to clear the air of that or allow him to explain Stella. Luckily, now wasn't the time either. She gave him a quick nod of recognition then sat at the counter.

Henry carried two plates in from the kitchen and delivered

them to a table. The four men there barely paused in their conversation. Seeing Charlotte as he scanned the dining area for anyone who needed him, Henry grinned. "Morning, Miss Brody. Be right with you."

"No hurry," she said, unbuttoning her coat. Beside her was Tom Gint, manager of one of the clam canneries, eating eggs and drinking coffee. "Good morning, Mr. Gint."

"Mornin'. How goes the newspaper business, Miss Brody?"

"Always something different. Otherwise it wouldn't be news, I guess. How's the cannery business?"

"Kinda stinky, but good. Interestin' bit you wrote on the Volstead Act the other day." From his casual tone, it was difficult to tell if Mr. Gint was in agreement with her or the Temperance League. He nodded then, leaning toward her, and winked. "It sure got those ladies all a-squawking, didn't it?"

Smiling, Charlotte whispered, "That's my job, now, isn't it, Mr. Gint? To get people squawking?"

She winked and straightened on her stool.

Mr. Gint laughed. "Sure as hell is." He tapped the folded copy of the paper beside his plate. "Says here them miners striking in the States are lookin' to unionize."

Charlotte glanced at the article. She remembered some of the details from reading it last night. "The idea is gaining traction. What's your opinion on the matter?"

Henry reappeared and set a cup of coffee, cream, and sugar in front of her. He didn't take her order right then, which was fine by Charlotte; she wasn't sure what she wanted yet.

"Well, I reckon a fair day's work deserves a fair day's pay," Mr. Gint said. "But no one likes to be bullied into doin' anything. Even if it's the right thing."

"That's true." Charlotte sipped her coffee. With the café being so busy, it was fresh and hot and strong. She added a little more sugar. "Though sometimes polite requests get ignored and people are forced to make their cases heard by any means available."

A man down the counter from Gint joined in with his two cents. "Them guys work in hellish conditions. Men and kids dyin' from greedy bastards not wantin' to part with a dollar or two for basic safety. Pardon the language, ma'am. We got it better up at Kennecott, but it still ain't easy."

"It's dangerous work, for sure, Bill," Gint said. "The owners need to pony up and make it right."

The copper miner supported his coal mining brethren while Gint explained to him how managers were caught in the middle. Charlotte and the two men engaged in a discussion on pay scale and unionization, interrupted only by Henry taking her order for scrambled eggs and toast.

As Charlotte ate, listening to them when her mouth was full, an unexpected figure coming out of the kitchen caught her eye. Rebecca Derenov carried a tray laden with clean cups, saucers, and silverware, arms straining to keep the tray level. Her black hair was tied back in a tail, covered with a kerchief, and she wore a white apron over her simple dress. Rebecca set the tray on the rear counter and started replacing the dish- and silverware that had been used through the busy morning.

"Rebecca," Charlotte said, getting the girl to look up and pause in her task. "I didn't know you worked here."

She gave Charlotte a quizzical look, then recognition dawned. She divided her attention between stacking and Charlotte. "Oh, hello, Miss Brody. Yeah, I just started this week. After school and on weekends."

"You'll still have time to study, won't you?" Remembering her conversation with Michael about how a number of students left school after the eighth grade, Charlotte hoped the answer was yes.

"Well," Rebecca said, drawing out the word and not meeting Charlotte's eye. "So far, it hasn't been a problem. I'm kinda beat when I get home, then there's chores to do. I've been doing well in school this year, so I don't need to study a whole lot."

"I hope your school work doesn't suffer," Charlotte said. "A young woman such as yourself can go far with a proper education."

A pained expression flickered across Rebecca's face. "I know, but with Ben only getting part-time work, we need the money." She fiddled with a ring on a string around her neck. Charlotte caught a flash of gold and red between her fingers. "I have to help where I can."

"I understand." Charlotte bit her lip to keep from pressing the girl. By the dark circles under her eyes, she was already losing sleep.

Rebecca rubbed the ring between her fingers for another few seconds, then slipped it under the neckline of her dress. "I better get back to work."

"Take care, Rebecca." Charlotte had never meant the sentiment more in her life.

Rebecca snatched up the tray and hurried into the kitchen as Henry came out.

Charlotte sighed with renewed dismay at the Derenov situation. Was Rebecca going to be able to stay in school? Not if Ben couldn't get a regular job. And if they moved out of Cordova, who's to say a larger city wouldn't require both of them to work in order to survive? Perhaps there was someone in town she could convince to give Ben a break. Mr. Gint, maybe?

Before she had the chance to ask, Gint and the other man rose, doffed their hats to bade her good day, and paid their bills. Charlotte didn't want to discuss Ben Derenov here in public anyway, and made a mental note to visit the cannery. It was very possible Ben had already applied and been turned down.

"Done with your breakfast, Miss Brody?" Henry's question pulled her from the depressing scenario involving the Derenovs.

"I am, thank you." She opened her purse and left enough to cover the food and a tip.

"Any other leads on that arsonist?" Henry glanced up at her

as he deposited the coins in the till, an odd expression of concern on his smooth face.

The question had come from left field. Charlotte hadn't written anything else about the arsonist since the fire. "Not really. Why, have you heard anything?"

Henry was a good source for tidbits. Usually nothing so earth-shattering, but local gossip was as good as it got some news days.

He shook his head and closed the till. "Nope. Just wondering. Have a good day, Miss Brody."

Something wasn't right. "Henry?"

The boy raised his head. His usually open and happy demeanor was shadowed by worry. And perhaps fear. What was going on?

"Come talk to me later," Charlotte said. "I'll be at the office or at home."

Without any indication he'd do as she asked, Henry turned on his heel and hurried into the kitchen.

Charlotte buttoned her coat as she walked to the door. Maybe she was a busybody, but her concern for the people in her life was real. Henry was obviously anxious about something to do with the arsonist, and as his friend, as well as his more-or-less superior at the newspaper, she was compelled to find out what was bothering him.

Before she could grab the handle, someone reached around her to pull open the door.

"Allow me, Miss Brody." James's drawl tickled her ear as he leaned forward.

She turned her head just enough to meet his eyes. "Thank you."

He smiled, showing that damn dimple.

Out on the walkway, under the electric streetlight, neither moved on.

James set his hat on his head and squinted up at the still-dark sky. "They say more snow's on its way."

"Are you fond of winter activities, deputy? Skiing? Sleigh rides? That sort of thing?"

"Snowball fights," he said, pantomiming tossing a snowball and winking.

She laughed, imagining him as a boy engaged in an all-out battle with his brothers and friends.

"Do you have a minute, Charlotte?" He was smiling, though there was a hint of apprehension in his eyes.

A flurry of excuses about getting to work or being cold ran through her brain, but Charlotte knew that at some point they'd need to talk. He'd been hesitant the other night, and her stint in his jail had overshadowed more personal concerns. She'd been more than willing to put off the inevitable out of fear of being expected to reciprocate. It was probably harder for him to get up the nerve to talk to her about Stella than it was for Charlotte to keep her own struggles bottled inside; she'd become quite good at showing a different face to those around her.

Besides, her curiosity about the reserved deputy's relationship with the flamboyant Stella got the better of her. "Of course."

James gestured for her to walk down the street toward his office. They passed a few people going in the opposite direction on their way to work or Saturday errands, greeting those folks but not speaking a word to each other. As they drew closer to the federal building, Charlotte was getting antsy. She preferred it when their conversation was light and easy, a friendly chat at one of their offices, or over a meal or a cup of tea. While she was sometimes at a loss for what to say to James, this awkward silence between them wasn't normal.

Charlotte angled toward the outer door of the building, but James touched her arm. "I'd like to walk a little, if that's all right."

She nodded and shoved her hands into her pockets. What did he need to say that he didn't want Marshal Blaine to hear?

They walked under the last electric light on Main Street. With just a hint of light from the sun peeking over the mountains and the lights from the scant houses set back from the road, Charlotte had to watch her footing along the frozen mud and pockets of slush.

"Blaine thinks looking into the relationship Otto Kenner had with Lyle Fiske could have some merit," James said.

Charlotte's head came up. Blaine's take on the murder was not the topic of conversation she'd expected, and it took her a moment to get into the right mindset. "Do you think Otto knows anything about Lyle's death?"

He shook his head. "Hard to say. I talked to Fiske's employees. The two got into it over material costs and such. Kenner thought Fiske was charging more than he needed to."

"I'm sure a lot of customers feel that way at times," she said, "especially here. That might explain why Otto was buying his own supplies directly."

"Maybe so, but from what you said about quantity, I can't understand how Kenner could afford to purchase so much. There's no way he was working enough jobs this time of year to cover those expenses." James's brow furrowed as it often did when he was mulling the facts of a case.

Charlotte didn't understand it either, though she had no inkling of how much material a builder needed for a bookcase, let alone a house. Hundreds of pounds of nails as they headed into winter did seem excessive. Even if Otto had motive to kill Lyle, what about opportunity?

"Where was Otto that night?" she asked. "For that matter, where was Adam?"

"Still considering the lover-husband quarrel angle? I don't know. I'll talk to them, but I'm willing to bet they'll have alibis for each other."

"I'm not taking a sucker's bet."

James laughed.

"Does Marshal Blaine know about Otto having me arrested?"

"You were never officially charged, just held."

"For most of the morning," she reminded him.

In the dimness of the new day, she could see James give her a sidelong glance. "Count yourself lucky Kenner didn't press for formal charges, or bring you to the constables' office for that matter. I didn't bother to log any of it in, so no, Blaine doesn't know anything about it."

She did count herself lucky, and she was grateful James had gone to bat for her. That he had also taken her suspicions seriously enough to consult with the marshal meant he trusted her instincts, even when she was being reckless. "Thank you. That means a lot."

He shrugged as if it was no big deal, but they both knew he'd taken a risk. "I saw no reason for Blaine to hear about *not* charging you."

"Treading a fine line there, deputy."

"Just saving us both a bit of trouble, Miss Brody."

Charlotte laughed. The exchange of banter was much better than the tension of the last few days. She hadn't realized just how much she'd missed it until now.

She would have been happy to have the conversation end at that, on a friendly note. But they walked on, without any indication that James was done with what he had to say. The bite of burning coal and the clatter of cars on rails grew stronger and louder. Men's voices carried on the chilled air, and shadowed figures hurried about the rail yard under bright lights.

"Is that all you wanted to tell me?" she asked.

James stopped, staring across the yard. Charlotte waited for him to collect his thoughts. She flipped up her collar and watched as well, not at all interested in the goings-on of the CR&NW railway. She doubted he was either.

Finally, he turned to her, half his face lit by the lights, the other half in shadow. "About the other night. With Stella."

"You don't have to tell me anything you don't want to, James." She was giving him an out, mostly so she wouldn't feel obligated to reciprocate. Ever.

"No, I want to tell you what happened." He stared down at his boots, took a breath, and blew it out in a slow, silvery stream. He looked up again, holding her gaze. "Stella and I met in Dawson City when we were barely more than kids. Her parents ran a hotel. Not too many kids our age around, so we were naturally drawn together."

Charlotte could imagine younger James being smitten by younger Stella. And vice versa. "Outgrew the fun of snowball fights, did you?"

He grinned. "Not completely. We lost track of each other when my family moved to Nome, following the gold. Then one day she showed up at an assayer's office, working as a secretary. We started keeping company."

Charlotte realized she was shivering and ran her hands over her arms. Her toes were getting numb.

"Come on," he said, "let's keep walking. This won't take long." James took her arm and gestured to a side road along the back of the rail yard. "Anyway, we got married."

"And?" She wanted to keep him talking, to get it over with. No need to draw out the discomfort for either of their sakes.

"And things were good for a while, though Stella enjoyed going out with friends more than I did. About three years in, I thought she was cheating on me. I confronted the guy."

Years later, in the semidarkness of a winter dawn, Charlotte saw he knew he'd been wrong. "What happened?"

"I beat the hell out of him. Put him in the hospital."

Charlotte's breath caught. She had seen James react violently only once, and that was in self-defense. The thought of him purposely hurting someone didn't fit with the man she knew. But jealousy, anger, and suspicion were powerful emotions. People didn't think clearly under those influences, they just re-acted. All that mattered was protecting what was yours.

He continued, his tone almost matter-of-fact, but quiet. Like he didn't want to be saying what he had to tell her, yet knew it had to come out. "Friends spoke up for me, told the police the guy started it. That wasn't quite true, but he never pushed to have me arrested. That makes me think he was guilty, but still."

James paused for a moment, shaking his head slightly, a look of disgust on his face. For the other man? Himself? Both? "Anyway, Stella and I left Nome as soon as we could. Settled in Juneau. It was never the same between us. I couldn't stop thinking about what I'd done, and she couldn't convince me of her innocence, or that I was more than the angry, foolish man I was, deep down."

Charlotte winced. "James, you know that isn't true. You're one of the most decent men I've ever met."

He gave a humorless laugh. "I was a jealous, short-fused son-of-a-bitch. And that man is still lurking inside me somewhere. I wanted to make sure you had the opportunity to decide if you still wanted to be . . . to stay friends or not."

She stopped, drawing him to a halt as well. Face-to-face, she saw who he was, and it wasn't the man he feared.

"You didn't have to tell me any of this. All you had to say was you'd been married and it was over," she said. He remained perfectly still. "That tells me the man you *think* is in here," she laid her hand flat on his chest, right over his heart, "isn't. The man in there is the good person I've come to know, and I want to stay friends with him."

He nodded slowly, allowing her words to sink in. Did he believe her?

After a few moments, a slight smile curved his mouth. "Thank you, because I want to stay friends with you too. I like you, Charlotte." He cupped her cold cheeks in his warm hands. "I like you a lot."

James held her still and bent to kiss her. Their breath mingled, creating a silvery cloud. Charlotte closed her eyes as their lips met. An electric pulse shot through her, and she clutched the front of his coat where her hand lingered over his heart.

She should have told him they needed to stop, but instead she flicked her tongue against the seam of his mouth. He responded as she'd hoped and feared, reciprocating and deepening the kiss. Need and desire welled inside her. Images flashed in her head of limbs and bodies lit by the soft glow of a bedside lamp, of searing kisses along bare skin.

Exactly what she wanted. Exactly what she couldn't handle. Not yet.

"Wait," she said, gently pushing him away while her heart pounded. Charlotte gulped a breath. "I'm sorry. I shouldn't. I can't."

His palms still on her cheeks and her hand still on his chest, James gazed down at her. Not angry, as Richard might have been, just trying to collect himself. "I understand."

No, he didn't. He probably thought she had never been with a man, let alone done what she'd done. He probably didn't realize the thoughts in her head were not those a "good girl" imagined when she kissed him. Not even close. But she wasn't ready for a confession. Someday, maybe, but not today.

He touched his lips to hers and lowered his hands. Charlotte stepped back and clasped her hands together.

"I don't want to push you into anything you aren't ready for, Charlotte."

She almost laughed. Let him assume she was protecting her virtue. She'd enjoyed being intimate with Richard, but most men weren't keen on the idea of learning they weren't first in line.

"Whenever you're ready to tell me what that bastard, whoever he is, did to you, I'm here. And if you decide to never to say a damn thing, that's okay too."

Charlotte blinked at him. How had he known? She'd never mentioned anything about having a relationship, failed or otherwise. Michael wouldn't have said anything either.

"There's nothing to tell." *Liar liar liar.*

"You've had an air about you since you arrived. Like you're trying to forget something or pretend it never happened. I've seen it a lot on people who come here. Hell, myself included." He gave her a fleeting, crooked grin, then the earnestness was back in his eyes. "But every time we get close, there's a tension that goes through you. You're like a taut wire about to snap."

"It's not you," she said, glancing away.

He tilted her chin up so their eyes met again. "Glad to hear that. I just want you to realize I'm not perfect—far from it—but I'm not him."

Her voice was low and rough when she said, "I know."

James smiled again. "Good. Let's get you to your office so you can warm up."

He looped her arm through his and they headed back to town.

Now what was she supposed to do?

The rest of the day was one distraction after another, from the ringing telephone to people dropping in. But the worst came from within Charlotte's own head, causing her to have to reset four different articles in the Linotype. She also burned her finger when she returned used slugs to the crucible to melt down, and smeared ink on the skirt of her favorite dress despite wearing an apron.

By the time she was headed home, all Charlotte wanted was a hot meal and a hotter bath. She trudged up the snowy road to the little green house, flashlight in hand, making a mental list of things she had to do over the next several days. Writing was always at the top of that one, though for the life of her she couldn't understand how sitting at her typewriter suddenly made her brain go blank. She also needed to get Christmas gifts out to Mother and Father. They'd likely be late, given the mail service from Alaska and her procrastination. Mother and Father wouldn't mind, though.

She smiled thinking of them, missing them, but at the same time glad to be out from under their scrutiny. Overall, they were good about letting her be who she was, yet there was always the need to get their approval. Or at least avoid stirring things up by blatantly misbehaving in their eyes. Charlotte had pushed the confines of propriety on numerous occasions, all without her parents' knowledge. At least she assumed they didn't know what she'd done. It was silly, really. She was a grown woman and shouldn't have to sneak behind her parents' backs. Yet she had.

"Miss Brody?"

The voice came from her porch. Charlotte shined the flashlight beam in that direction, catching poor Henry right in the eyes. "Sorry," she said, lowering the light. "You startled me. How long have you been waiting?"

"Not too long," he said as she climbed the rickety stairs. "You asked me to come see you, so I figured I'd come over tonight, if that's okay."

"Of course it is, Henry."

Told him to come see her was more like it, and she wasn't surprised he'd obeyed. Henry was a good kid who liked to please people. It made him a popular server at the café, and he garnered generous tips there as well as when he delivered newspapers.

His uneasiness over the last several days wasn't like him. As a friend and fellow employee at the *Times,* Charlotte wanted to see if she could help.

"Let's get inside and have some tea. Have you had supper yet?"

Henry shook his head, his dark hair falling into his eyes as he entered the house and pulled off his cap. Charlotte hung up her coat and unlaced her boots, watching him as he did the same. Good Lord, he was just a boy, wasn't he, all smooth-cheeked and wide-eyed as he looked around the parlor. His heavy sweater and trousers weren't new, but they were clean and neat. The result of someone taking care of him or a talent of his own?

"Let's go into the kitchen," she said, giving him a reassuring smile. "I'll get the stove started and it'll warm right up in there."

Henry followed her obediently and sat at the kitchen table. Charlotte set out the plate of cookies she kept on hand to have with her tea in the evenings. He hesitated, glancing up at her as if to ask permission.

"Have some. There are days when you have to eat dessert first." She winked at him and he smiled, more relaxed.

While he nibbled, Charlotte set about firing up the stove and taking ingredients out of the icebox. "I hope you like fish cakes."

"Love them," he said around a mouthful of cookie.

Henry being Henry, Charlotte was pretty sure he'd say he loved anything she offered, just to be nice.

"Do you know how to cook?" she asked. "I hear the top chefs are all men."

They discussed food while Charlotte puttered about in domesticity. She reined in her inclination to jump right on him about what was going on. Henry had readily come over when she'd asked, but he was nervous. Chatting about food and other neutral topics put him at ease.

Charlotte set two plates of fish cakes, green beans, and buttered bread on the table. She poured them each a cup of tea, then sat.

Henry bowed his head, murmuring grace before looking up at her, red-faced. "Sorry."

"Nothing to be sorry about," she said, laying her napkin in her lap. "My family was never terribly religious."

He picked up his fork and dug in like the still-growing young man he was. "Mine was. Grace at each meal. Prayers before bed. Church every Sunday."

"Was?" Charlotte asked gently.

Henry hesitated, a forkful of fish cake halfway to his mouth. He took the bite and nodded slowly while he chewed. Charlotte kept eating, encouraging him to go on with her silence.

"We lived in a small town in Kansas, me, my folks, my brothers and sisters. Loaded up the wagon every Sunday to go to church. Even if we could've afforded one, Pa didn't believe in automobiles. Said they were for people too worried about getting places without experiencing the journey."

Charlotte smiled. It sounded like something her own father would say. "Your pa sounds like a wise man."

"He was." Henry looked up from his plate, meeting her gaze for a moment before finding his green beans unusually interesting. "He and ma died when I was ten."

"Oh, Henry, I'm so sorry." Charlotte knew too many children who had lost their parents. She reminded herself how lucky she was to still have hers, even when they gave her a hard time.

He shrugged. "My brothers and sisters and I got sent to different families. I hated it. Ran away and came up here when I was thirteen."

Kids who'd lost parents often grew up too fast, requiring them to figure what was what in the world. It took a certain motivation—and a great deal of luck—for a thirteen-year-old boy to travel from Kansas to Alaska.

"How did you manage that?"

"Stowed away on a steamer." Henry raised his head, his dark eyes filled with sorrow, and something Charlotte couldn't quite place. "I had to get away from there, Miss Brody. Too many memories."

She laid her hand on his arm. "That's understandable, given the circumstances."

He shook his head, wincing. "No, you *don't* understand. My parents dying was my fault. And I couldn't stop doing it."

What could a ten-year-old have done that made him think he was responsible for his parents' death?

"Doing what?"

He started to speak, but the words seemed to catch in his throat. Tears trickled down his face. He trembled beneath Charlotte's hand. "It was an accident, I swear. I just liked to watch the flames."

Oh, Henry, no.

She knew where he was headed even before he continued, her heart breaking for him.

"One night, I was too close to the back of the barn. A spark flew up and caught the hay loft on fire. Ma and Pa ran in to save the animals and never came out." He was breathing fast now, his chest heaving and his voice rough. "Even after that. I couldn't stop doing it. I tried, I really did, but . . ."

He lowered his head, shoulders shaking as he cried.

Charlotte knelt on the floor beside his chair and wrapped her arms around him. At sixteen, he was almost a man, but right now he was a scared and hurt little boy.

"It was an accident, Henry. You didn't mean to hurt them." To be so young and have such a heavy burden of guilt, accident or not. But his obsession with fire, the jittery way he'd been acting lately, and his presence at Fiske's that night led to only one conclusion. Despite her sympathy for him, Charlotte knew she had to get him to speak the truth. "You're the one who's been setting the fires here the last couple of years."

He nodded, guilt and sadness etching years into his young face. Taking a deep breath, he let it out in a slow, shaky exhalation. Charlotte returned to her seat. After swallowing a few times and wiping his face on his sleeve, he seemed calmer, more in control of himself. "I've been able to stop doing it all the time, but near the anniversary of their death, I—I just have to get it out of my system. I've been real careful though."

It was true. None of the fires this year or last year posed any danger to anyone or damaged property. The arsonist had made sure the flames would go out on their own, as long as something like a brisk wind didn't spread them.

But she had the feeling Henry wasn't just there to confess his past crimes.

"What about the Fiske fire, Henry?"

His expression changed, his eyes widening with shock. "No, that wasn't me, I swear. I was looking to snatch a few pieces of dry wood from Fiske's stock alongside the store, but that was it. I didn't have anything to do with that." He swept an X over his chest with his forefinger. "Cross my heart, Miss Brody."

Charlotte welcomed the relief running through her. Though she and James suspected a thief had started the fire to cover Lyle's murder, she wanted to be certain of Henry's innocence.

"You were there that night," she said. "You came up and spoke to me while the fire was going." He nodded, scared and guilty all at once. "I believe you didn't set that fire, Henry, but you saw something."

He nodded again and swallowed hard. "Just as I was getting close to Fiske's, I saw someone run out the front door. He left it open. I was going to go in, to check it out, then I saw the flames."

He closed his eyes and the tension seemed to fade. Was he seeing the fire again in his mind? What sort of obsession did he have? Charlotte had to give him some credit for self-control, considering he'd managed to contain his activities to a few instances in a year, all around the time of his parents' deaths. Not that it meant he was okay. Henry needed some help to get over his guilt. But that was a conversation for another time.

"Who did you see running from the store?"

He blinked a few times. "I-I don't know. A man, for sure. It was dark, and I was hiding behind Mr. Fiske's truck, off to the side."

"Was he a big man?" If one of the Kenner brothers were involved, Henry's description could help narrow it down.

"Not tall, but kind of wide shoulders. Dark hair. No hat. He was carrying something."

The black box, most likely.

"Which way did he run?" Not that it mattered. Most of Cordova was up the street and away from Fiske's.

"Into town, but he didn't pass under the streetlamp at the corner. He kept going straight up, then I lost sight of him." Henry's face scrunched in dismay. "Sorry, Miss Brody. I know that isn't much help."

She patted his arm. "It's plenty of help, Henry."

"You see why I couldn't tell Deputy Eddington what I saw, right?"

Charlotte nodded. "I understand. But why are you telling me?"

He seemed startled by the question. "You and me, we're friends, right?"

"Well, yes, but I'm not a priest or a lawyer, Henry. If you'd been involved in Mr. Fiske's death, I would have been obligated to tell Deputy Eddington, or at least strongly encourage you to confess."

He hung his head again, looking up at her through his lashes. "I know, and I'm hoping this isn't something you need to tell."

Charlotte considered his request. The earlier fires had been a problem, but no real harm had been done. The marshal's office and the public were more concerned about the fires spreading or the arsonist going after occupied buildings than any damage that had been done so far. "No, I won't tell him about that, but we'll need to do something to help you, all right?"

Maybe Michael would have some ideas. He wasn't a psychologist, but he might know someone Henry could talk to.

Relief smoothed the stress lines on his face. "Thank you, Miss Brody."

"I'll tell Deputy Eddington what you told me about the night of the Fiske fire, but I'll cite you as an anonymous source." He nodded again, more at ease than Charlotte had seen him in the past week. "Okay. Finish your dinner and have another cookie."

Chapter 10

I hope James gets back soon, Charlotte thought as she fought with the key in the frozen office door late Monday afternoon. She'd gone to his cabin the day before to talk to him about what she'd learned from Henry, but he wasn't there. A note on the marshal's office door said he had traveled out the rail line and would be back late Sunday or early Monday. But he hadn't returned by lunch Monday.

Worry gnawed at Charlotte's gut, along with anticipation of talking to James about the case. Surely he was fine, and just delayed by weather or people bending his ear.

"Miss Brody?"

Glancing up, Charlotte saw Rebecca Derenov come toward her. "Hello, Rebecca," she said, removing the key and rubbing it between her mittened hands. "How was school today?"

Bundled head to toe, her cheeks red with the cold, the girl smiled. "Great. I got one hundred percent on my math test."

"Good for you!" Math wasn't Charlotte's strong suit, and she admired anyone who could do well in the subject.

Rebecca reached under her coat and drew out a wrinkled

piece of paper. "I have this week's School Happenings for the *Times*."

Charlotte breathed on the key then inserted it into the lock. After a bit more rattling, it clicked open. Finally! She'd leave the door unlocked if Toliver wasn't so worried about vandals and mischief-makers. "Thank you for bringing it by," she said, pushing the door open. "I'll make sure it gets into tomorrow's edition."

She held her hand out for the paper, but Rebecca didn't relinquish it. She looked up at Charlotte, nervous but determined. "Can I watch you?"

They stepped into the small entry of the office. Charlotte shut the door and removed her coat. "You want to watch me set the Linotype?"

Working the Linotype was one thing, but watching someone do it sounded boring to Charlotte. Then again, if you'd never seen the thing in action maybe it seemed exciting enough.

Rebecca smiled, her eyes glinting with anticipation. "Oh, yes, please! I promise to stay out of the way and just watch. I won't bug you by talking or asking questions or anything."

Her enthusiasm was catching and Charlotte found herself excited to show the girl how she spent much of her day. "I'd be terribly disappointed if you *didn't* ask me questions. Hang up your coat and come on back."

Rebecca gave her the lined, handwritten page and quickly doffed her coat, hat, and scarf. She followed Charlotte deeper into the office, slowing as she read the framed front pages along the walls. While Rebecca perused those, Charlotte stoked the coal stove. She waited for Rebecca at the desk, sorting through the articles she wanted to set for the next edition.

"Ready?" she called to Rebecca.

The girl hurried to meet Charlotte at the door of the Linotype and printing room. Rebecca stared at the machines, her mouth open in an O of wonder.

"Wow."

Charlotte had seen the metal mammoth almost every day for the past three months and had become used to its size; at seven feet tall and six feet deep, it took up the corner of the room. But it was the intricate connections of the shuttles, elevators, keyboard, and magazine of letters that she was seeing again as if for the first time through Rebecca's eyes. Waiting silently, it was a thing of engineering beauty, and the Linotype wasn't even running yet. She couldn't wait to see Rebecca's expression once she got it going.

Charlotte donned a printer's apron, passed one to Rebecca, and secured her sleeves with an old pair of garters. "We don't want to get lead bits or ink on our clothes," she said.

Rebecca tied the apron strings as she followed Charlotte to the stool in front of the Linotype. "It's warm over here."

"A bucket of molten metal will stay hot for some time." Charlotte pointed out the crucible of lead and the thick leather gloves used to open the lid when adding old slugs to be reliquefied. She gave the girl a quick rundown of how the Linotype worked. "The keyboard is used to type in the lines of the article. Each keystroke releases a letter, number, or punctuation mold from the magazines up here." She pointed to the encased rack of molds held in place at the top of the machine, then to a floor-to-ceiling cabinet against the far wall. "Those magazines over there hold different fonts and point sizes. The molds, called matrices, or mats, drop down, spacers get inserted, creating a line of type, and are infused with the hot lead. Here, let me show you. It's going to be a bit loud."

Charlotte flipped the switch for the electric motor that ran the gears and chains. The growl filled the room. She typed Rebecca's full name. As she pressed the keys, the letter matrices dropped into place with a clatter. Another lever filled the molds with lead, giving off a whiff of hot metal. The lead slug dropped into the rack to her left.

From the corner of her eye, Charlotte watched Rebecca gaze

in awe as the machine worked. It was rather amazing, she thought. Mergenthaler's innovation had revolutionized printing, making it possible for a one- or two-person operation to put out a daily eight-page newspaper rather than a weekly one. Not since Guttenberg's printing press had the industry been so completely transformed.

While the piece cooled for a few seconds, she operated another lever to return the matrices to the magazine that held hundreds of the letter, number, and punctuation molds.

Plucking the slug off the rack, Charlotte juggled it a little to help cool it down. "Still quite warm. Be careful."

She handed the thin line of lead to Rebecca. The girl read it. A wide smile curved her mouth.

"Want to try?" Charlotte asked. She could hardly move off of the stool fast enough for Rebecca.

It took nearly an hour for them to set the type for the school activities section of the newspaper, three times longer than it would have taken Charlotte to do it herself. But she didn't mind the fact she'd have to stay later than usual that evening to finish her work. Rebecca was an enthusiastic student, asking many questions, some of which Charlotte couldn't answer. She'd have to remember to pass the girl's queries on to Mr. Toliver.

After the school piece was finished, Charlotte showed her how to place the lines in the printing frame, double-check alignment, and run a test print with a hand-rolled layer of ink and a piece of paper. Satisfied that all was ready, it was time to type up another article for that page.

"But first," Charlotte said, "a cup of tea and some cookies."

Rebecca grinned, the smudge of ink on her cheek making her look like a professional already. Charlotte led the way back into the office and closed the door. It didn't take long to prepare the tea, as the kettle on the coal stove was hot. Rebecca sat on the other side of the desk. Charlotte put a plate of cookies she'd brought in earlier in front of her.

With a sigh of satisfaction, she sat down and relaxed.

After several sips of tea and nibbles of cookie, Rebecca asked, "Did you always want to be a reporter, Miss Brody?"

"Ever since I read Nellie Bly's *Ten Days in a Mad-House.* Though I confess, what she went through scared the jeepers out of me."

Bly's 1887 exposé of the horrendous treatment of patients at the Women's Lunatic Asylum on Blackwell's Island, New York, had made the young woman's journalistic career. Her investigation—at the risk of being permanently remanded—had resulted in calls for better care and assessment of the seriously ill. Charlotte admired Bly's bravery and determination, and strived to fight a similar, if not as extreme, fight for justice and basic human rights. Nellie Bly had been one of her heroes growing up.

"Oh, I loved reading about her race around the world." Rebecca sat at the edge of the chair and gave Charlotte an enthusiastic version of the thirty-year-old competition between Nellie Bly and Elizabeth Bisland.

Charlotte had read the account numerous times years ago, and let Rebecca describe the story to her without interruption. She listened to the girl's use of words and phrasing, how she was able to create dramatic tension. Rebecca had a knack for storytelling.

When she was finished with her breathless rendition, Rebecca sank back in the chair, a smile on her face.

"I don't think I've ever heard that told with quite the same gusto," Charlotte said. "Even from Miss Bly herself."

Rebecca's mouth dropped open. "You've met her?"

"I have. I attended a lecture she gave about the trip, then got a chance to talk to her for a few minutes afterward." Charlotte smiled at the girl's look of awe. It *was* pretty amazing to have met the woman who had spurred her own career. "She can weave a fine tale, that's for sure."

"I love adventure stories, real ones or made up ones. It

doesn't matter." Rebecca ate a cookie in two bites. "Miss Atkins—that's my teacher—says I'm a good writer."

"I'm not surprised." Charlotte sipped her tea. "Are you thinking about a writing career of some sort when you're older?"

She'd almost said "grown up," but Rebecca's manner and intelligence made her practically an adult to Charlotte.

"If I can," Rebecca said. The air seemed to go out of her, like a flat tire. "You need to go to school for that, don't you? College or something?"

"Well, it depends." Charlotte was a proponent of higher education for all who could get it, despite having dropped out of journalism school herself. "It would definitely benefit you to go as far as you can."

Rebecca's gaze dropped to her lap. She grasped the gold and ruby ring strung around her neck, stroking it as if it brought some sort of comfort. "I don't think that'll be very far."

Charlotte wasn't surprised the girl understood her current circumstances. Rather than go into a rant about the importance of education—Rebecca had that one figured out already—Charlotte changed the subject to something she hoped was more pleasant.

"That's a beautiful ring."

Rebecca looked up, smiling. "My mother's. I thought we'd gone through all of her stuff and sold everything, but then Ben found this. He said I had to keep it, no matter what."

"I'm glad you have that to remember her by," Charlotte said.

Rebecca's smile turned sad. "Me too. She didn't wear any other jewelry except this and her wedding ring."

No other jewelry? Just because she didn't wear other pieces didn't mean Mrs. Derenov didn't own others. Before Charlotte had the chance to ask her about the earrings Ben had tried to sell the other day, the outer door whooshed open.

"There you are," Ben Derenov said, slamming the door behind him. Snow dusted his hat and coat, clumps of slush slid off his boots. "What the hell are you doing here? Went all the way to school and Miss Atkins said you were dropping something off here. You shoulda been home an hour ago."

Charlotte and Rebecca got to their feet.

"I was bringing Miss Brody the school news, and I asked her to show me the Linotype. You should see it, Ben. It clicks and clacks, and gears and chains move to make the letters fall into place so Miss Brody and Mr. Toliver can put out the newspaper every day. And look." Rebecca dug into the pocket of her apron to retrieve the lead slug Charlotte had made her. "My name."

Ben glared at the bit of metal, then at Charlotte. "She was supposed to be home."

Charlotte came around the desk to stand beside Rebecca. "That's my fault, Mr. Derenov. I should have made sure it was all right for her to stay here so late. I'm sure Rebecca will square it with you next time—"

"Get your coat," he said to his sister. "Dinner's nearly ready, and you've got chores to do."

Rebecca gave Charlotte an apologetic glance, then removed the apron. Handing it to Charlotte, she went over to the rack to don her coat, hat, and scarf. When she was bundled up, she smiled at Charlotte. "Thank you for showing me everything, Miss Brody. I had a wonderful time."

Charlotte returned the smile. "So did I. Come back whenever you can. And I'd love to read the stories you've written, if you're willing to show me."

Rebecca's brown eyes shined. "Oh, I would. I'll bring something by soon. Good night."

"Good night, Rebecca." Charlotte met Ben's hard gaze. "Good night, Mr. Derenov. Again, my apologies."

Ben yanked the door open and ushered his sister out. Before it closed, Charlotte heard him start lecturing Rebecca on worrying about work and chores rather than writing.

Disappointment replaced the joy Charlotte had felt while

visiting with Rebecca. Her brother didn't encourage the girl's aspiration of being a writer. Charlotte understood the need for practicality when it came to financial straits, but was it necessary for him to flat-out toss her dream aside?

Poor kid.

She sat down at the desk to finish her tea. Looking over the next articles she'd set, Charlotte decided something else along with the mental calculation of where lines would fall: She would support Rebecca Derenov's goal of becoming a writer any way she could manage.

And she hoped she could get Ben Derenov to see it was important for dreams to be fostered even during tough times. Perhaps especially during those times.

Before heading home for a quick supper, with plans to return to the *Times* to finish setting the paper afterward, Charlotte walked to the marshal's office. The sinking sun cast pink alpine glow on the mountains to the southeast. The sky had cleared and there was a colder bite to the air. The weather in these parts sure was changeable.

Charlotte pulled open the door to the office. James wasn't at his desk, and the door to Marshal Blaine's private office was closed. The low rumble of male voices came from behind the frosted glass. She stopped at the door and listened. Not to eavesdrop, really, but to ascertain the tone of the conversation. If it sounded like James and the marshal were having a heated argument, Charlotte would come back another time. No yelling or raised tones.

Were they discussing the Fiske case?

She made herself as comfortable as she could on the straight-back chair before James's desk. There were papers and files open for all to see, and it was too tempting not to look.

A quick glance told her the pages had nothing to do with the Fiske case. Uninterested in Mr. Vero's complaint against Mr. Harris for busting his fence, she shifted on the chair and settled in. She didn't have to wait long. The marshal's door opened and James came out, a scowl on his face.

Uh-oh. Maybe she shouldn't have stayed after all. The conversation with the marshal may have been in civil tones, but whatever was said had irritated the deputy.

When he saw her sitting at his desk, James's frown softened to a smile. Charlotte's heart made an off-rhythm twitch. The memory of their kisses—the first in the rain outside Sullivan's rooming house in August, the one two days ago behind the rail yard—came rushing back in a warm wave.

Behind him, Marshal Blaine stood at his door. He gave Charlotte a curt nod. She and the marshal were friendly enough, though certainly not bosom buddies. He was tolerant of her questions, which she appreciated. Charlotte nodded back, smiling. He closed his door.

"Miss Brody. How are you today?" James asked as he came around the desk.

"Good evening, deputy. I'm well. How are you? How was your jaunt out the rail line?"

Since their walk and kiss, things had gone back to normal between them, yet there was still an underlying tension. At least on her part. She wasn't sure what to do about her feelings about him. Or what, exactly, those feelings were. Just friends? More? Kissing him sure made if difficult not to think of the potential for more. It was all a big muddle in her head. His patience while she figured it out was nearly that of a saint compared to other men she knew.

"Bob Dexter thinks someone's stealing his chickens, and Sarah Paine threatened her husband with a shotgun." He sat down. "Nothing too unusual. What can I do for you?"

Charlotte was grateful he was able to set aside their pesky personal issues and get to the point. It was something she needed to work on. "I want to talk to you about a couple of things."

"Related to the Fiske case, I reckon?"

"Yes, though I'm not sure what you already know or what might be useful."

"Won't know until you tell me," he said, grinning.

"True. First off, did you know about Fiske's illegal pawn operation?"

The pleasant look on his face turned sour. "I did, though we never had anyone come right out and accuse him of anything we could nail him on. Mostly rumors and the like. Folks are pretty tight-lipped over illegal doings around here."

Charlotte stared at him, a glimmer of hurt in her chest. "You knew? Why didn't you tell me? What if the robbery and murder were related to that and not just random chance?"

"Because I can't share everything I know about every case, Charlotte. I wouldn't be doing my job if I spilled all my inside knowledge, now, would I?"

He had a point, but it still rankled a bit that he'd held back.

"The question is," he said, "how do *you* know about it?"

She smiled sweetly at him. "Now, James, I can't share anonymous sources, can I? My job relies upon a certain amount of trust and discretion."

His lips pressed together and he narrowed his eyes. "Funny. So what do you know about Fiske's side business?"

"Probably not as much as you do, but what I do know is that someone is returning things that Fiske was holding." The surprised look on his face made her feel better about their little information game.

"Why do that? And how?"

Charlotte shrugged. "I have no idea about the why. Guilt? Sympathy for people being under Fiske's thumb? As for the how, that would have to do with the notebook Fiske kept."

"Notebook? I'm guessing he kept it in the same box Caroline was looking for." James rubbed his palm over the new beard on his chin. "Makes sense that Fiske kept some sort of record. The thief takes this box with some small items people pawned, the notebook, and the legal papers. Maybe some money too. But he doesn't want everything in the box. Papers might be kept or thrown out. As for the pawned goods, may be hard to sell them here."

"Or he feels guilty, or wants Lyle's customers to get their things back without paying," she reminded him.

"Right. So how did your source get their item back?"

Being careful not to use specific pronouns, she said, "They found it on their porch in a plain package."

"And came to you. Why?"

"Because they wanted to remain anonymous, of course." It seemed simple and reasonable to her, but the perturbed look on his face told her James didn't quite feel the same way. "Honestly, James, telling the marshal's office might be more trouble for them, don't you think?"

"What I think is this person might have been the killer. Maybe they were lying about how they 'found' their pawned item and came to you to appear to be innocent. Did you consider that?"

Of course she hadn't, because she knew Della wouldn't have done such a thing. Well, probably not. But she definitely wasn't the perpetrator in this case. "My source doesn't fit the description of someone seen at the fire."

"What?" He sat up straighter, if that was possible, eyes bright. "You have information? A witness?"

She had promised Henry she wouldn't snitch, and she'd keep that promise. "I do. Well, in a manner of speaking."

James's forehead furrowed, then he quirked an eyebrow at her. "Will I ever get a straight answer from you?"

Charlotte smiled, but her stomach quivered for some reason. *Probably not.* "I will when I can, or if it's dire. You know that."

He stared at her for a moment, then shook his head slightly. "So what do you have that you *can* tell me?"

She took a deep breath. "The arsonist wasn't responsible for the Fiske fire."

"And you know this how?"

"Another reliable anonymous source." That was true. She trusted Henry despite his admission.

"You mean the arsonist." James leaned forward, forearms on the desk, his eyes hard and intense. "You spoke to him."

"I did, and he promised no more fires." Charlotte hoped Henry was finished, for the year at least. Whether he'd feel the need to set more next year on the anniversary of his parents' death remained to be seen. "But there's something he told me you should know."

Obviously frustrated with her or the arsonist, he raked his fingers through his hair and sat back. "He was at Fiske's that night. What—"

She held up a hand to forestall his asking the questions she knew were popping into his head. "Near, but not responsible for the fire. He saw someone coming out of the front door right before flames erupted."

"Who?"

"He couldn't tell me. The man he saw was turned away from him. All he saw was dark hair and a strong build, and something in the man's hands. Likely the box."

"Clothing? Where was the arsonist when he saw this? What time had he been there? Did he hear any arguing? See anyone else? Damn it, Charlotte—"

"Slow down. I'll tell you all I know." She relayed Henry's description and what had happened and what he saw, though it wasn't as detailed as James probably wanted. There was no confirmed identification or any indication Fiske and his killer had exchanged words.

James took notes, his lips pressed together. When she finished, he tapped his pen on the desk. "It's not much."

"No, but it's more than you had."

He held her gaze. "And you're sure your arsonist wasn't involved."

"He's not my arsonist, just a source. He didn't have to come to me at all, you know."

The deputy laid the pen down and sighed. "I know, but he trusted you for some reason. So did your pawn client. Why?"

Charlotte shrugged. She couldn't say much more without betraying Henry or Della. "I'm a trustworthy soul?"

The corner of James's mouth ticked upward. "That must be it."

She blew a raspberry at him, and he chuckled. "Maybe because I'm less intimidating that a certain lawman. Seriously, James, while the man's face might not have been seen, it sounds like he was too broad in the shoulders to be Adam Kenner."

"If not Adam—"

"Otto." Charlotte had been leaning toward the elder Kenner.

"Maybe," James said emphatically. "Or it was someone completely different. There's no evidence Otto is responsible or has motive, other than he and Fiske didn't get along."

"If that personality clash meant Otto felt his business was being threatened, he had strong motivation and opportunity. Who else would want Lyle dead, accidentally or otherwise? Surely the man didn't have that many mortal enemies."

"Another pawn customer? Someone who felt cheated by Fiske?"

She had to agree that it was possible. But who? How many were there? "There has to be more than a few. Without the notebook, there's no way to find out." Charlotte stood, buttoning her coat. "There isn't much in the way of tangible evidence, is there?"

"Find the box and we find the notebook." James rose and followed her to the door. "I can look closer at Otto Kenner, but not at the expense of wearing blinders to other possibilities. I'll talk to him again, see if I can trip him up over his alibi. He leases a warehouse near the canneries from Squint Bauer. That might have something in it."

The thrill of the hunt for evidence went through her. "Are you going out there?"

"Me, yes. You, no." Warning and concern filled his eyes.

"I'm serious, Charlotte. Otto's ready to blame you for anything and everything that happens to him. Don't give him reason to charge you with harassment or do something worse than
haul you into my office. If he catches you anywhere near him
and I'm not around, I'm afraid I'd have to charge him with
some terrible crime." He lifted her chin slightly and stared into
her eyes. "If I don't kill him first."

"You wouldn't." His confession and guilt over the man he'd
hurt when he suspected Stella of cheating on him had made
Charlotte believe James would never do such a thing again.
"You promised."

"I promised to not beat a man in a jealous rage. I make no
such promises when it comes to protecting you."

James touched his lips to hers and Charlotte closed her eyes.
She placed her palm on his chest to steady herself. God help
her, she shouldn't let him do things like this.

*Stop fooling yourself. You aren't "letting" him do anything
you don't want.*

True. Too true.

Pushing herself away from him, she took an extra half step
back and said, "Let's hope it doesn't come to anything that
drastic."

He lowered his hand. "It won't. But it's better if you wait for
me to give you information rather than poke around on your
own."

"You would think I was coming down with something if I
ever did that." She set her hat on her head, grinning, trying to
pretend her lips weren't still tingling.

James opened the door. "That's the truth. Have a good evening, Miss Brody."

"You too, deputy."

Charlotte left the federal building. Standing on the walk, she
drew in a long, slow breath. The cold cleared her head some,
but it didn't erase the sensation of his mouth on hers.

Damnation.

Chapter 11

On Tuesday morning, Charlotte stood in the middle of the post office, fishing in her satchel for the key Mr. Toliver had given her. The damn thing always seemed to make its way into the corner of her bag, often hiding until she dumped the contents out.

Ah! There it was. She extracted the key and fit it into the lock of box number 502. Inside were several subscription payments and a bill for Mr. Toliver from Lerner & Sons Menswear in Seattle.

Charlotte tucked the mail into her satchel and closed the brass door.

"Miss Brody, do you have a minute?"

Caroline Fiske, dressed in widow's black, stood with her gloved hands grasping a small purse. Her makeup, little that Charlotte could detect, didn't quite cover the bruise-colored circles under her eyes, and her pale complexion attested to restless nights.

"Of course, Mrs. Fiske. What can I do for you?"

Caroline glanced over at the mail clerk standing behind the counter, making no pretense that she wasn't listening. She grinned at the two women.

"Perhaps we can take a walk, if you're not in a hurry," Caroline suggested.

"I'm not."

Caroline led the way to the post office door and held it for Charlotte. Charlotte preceded her down the stairs, ready to grasp the bannister should she slip or—

Don't be ridiculous.

Caroline Fiske wasn't about to shove her down the stairs. Even if she had masterminded her husband's murder, surely she wouldn't try to kill Charlotte literally in front of the marshal's office on the ground floor.

When she reached the bottom, Charlotte tried to ignore the fact that James was likely on the other side of the door. He was a different risk altogether.

Caroline joined her and the two continued onto the walk. The noon whistle at the rail yard had blown less than an hour before and the sun peeked through fat white clouds. The snow had abated for the time being, giving everyone the chance to shovel walks.

Up the street, the man from the Brite-White Laundry secured a bundle of clothes on a sled. The six-dog team yipped and yapped, dancing in place. The man stepped onto the back of the sled, jerked the snow hook from the ground, and grasped the handlebar.

"Hike!" he yelled, and the dogs bolted, yapping excitedly. "Hike," he called again, and the dogs ran faster.

Like a scene from *The Call of the Wild*—minus the laundry bags—the sled zipped down the snowy street, heading east out of town, the man encouraging his team all the way. Though Charlotte knew the delivery man worked long, hard hours, it sure looked like he was having a good time. The dogs certainly were.

"Are you headed to your office?" Caroline asked.

"I am. What did you want to talk to me about?"

They started walking, but Caroline didn't speak until they

passed a pair of men standing outside the cigar store beside the federal building.

"You spoke to Adam the other night," she said. It was a simple statement, with no inflection of accusation or concern. No emotion of any sort that Charlotte could detect.

"I did."

"And he told you about my marriage." She flicked a glance at Charlotte, but nothing more.

"He did."

Caroline nodded. Was she only after confirmation? Not likely.

"Do you truly think Adam killed Lyle?"

The abruptness of Caroline's question surprised Charlotte. Subtlety was not on the table this afternoon.

"Do you?" Charlotte asked. From Henry's description of the man he saw at Fiske's Hardware that night, she figured Otto for the murder. Could the brothers have schemed together?

Caroline didn't hesitate. "No. Adam is a good man. He has a kind heart. He wouldn't do something like that."

"Even if you asked him to?"

She stopped in the middle of the walk and stared at Charlotte. There was no vehement reaction of denial. No demand that Charlotte take back such a terrible accusation. Was Caroline concerned that Adam could have taken matters into his own hands after hearing about the humiliation and abuse she suffered at Lyle's? If he had, would Adam withhold the papers he knew she was so desperate to find? To what end? Even if Adam didn't want to present them to her himself, he could find a way to have the papers delivered anonymously.

Caroline rubbed a tic that flickered at the corner of her left eye. After a moment, she resumed walking. Charlotte kept pace with her.

"No. And I wouldn't have asked him to kill Lyle, even if I thought he'd do it. Lyle and I had our problems, and I'll admit he could be brutal at times, but I didn't hate him enough to have anyone kill him."

But perhaps, given time, she would have? Or would have done it herself? No sense in speculating about a crime that would never happen.

"What about Otto?" Charlotte asked.

Caroline sighed and shook her head. Not in denial, more like resignation. "Otto. He and Lyle had a few run-ins."

"I understand they were at odds over your late husband's business practices." That was all the detail Charlotte had, but maybe implying she knew more would get Caroline to expand on the subject.

"They were, and rightfully so," she said, skirting a pile of dirty snow on the walkway. "Lyle enjoyed being the king of Cordova hardware. Otto threatened to start a boycott and bring in his own materials."

From what Charlotte had seen of his inventory list, it seemed he'd more than threatened. But eliminating a business rival would defeat Otto's free market ideals. Unless something got out of hand.

"Do you think Otto had the wherewithal to kill him?"

Caroline barely hesitated. "Given the proper circumstances, I think he's capable of all sorts of acts. Otto is a volatile man. He sticks to his guns and is hard to move."

"So you think he could have done it," Charlotte said.

"I think it's possible." Caroline emphasized the last word, clearly unwilling to make blatant accusations. Knowing Otto Kenner's temper, Charlotte couldn't blame her.

They were almost to the *Times* office, and Charlotte had a question she wanted cleared up. "Caroline, what happens if you don't retrieve the papers in the box?"

The widow's brow furrowed. "Lyle has grown children from his first marriage, down in Seattle. They hardly ever contacted him after we moved here, but they are happy to take his money.

Despite his actions with me, he always tried to do right by them financially."

"And without the papers in the box they get everything?"

Caroline smiled, but it was brittle and forced. "Almost everything. I'd have the house here. They'd get all the business and life insurance if the old copies of his will and insurance policies on file down there are the most recent ones. He told me he'd made a new will and took out new policies with different lawyers and a different insurance company, but never gave me details."

"But you were his wife."

"Indeed. It's something he'd been holding over me for years. If I stayed married to him, played my part, and kept my affairs quiet and discrete, I'd inherit." She let out a humorless laugh. "I asked myself every day if it's been worth it."

Adam had said Caroline was truly devastated by Lyle's death. She didn't sound devastated to Charlotte. "So having Lyle dead works in your favor."

They stopped outside the *Times* office. Caroline turned to her, dark eyes hard. "Not if I don't have what I need. With him dead and the papers missing, I'm at the mercy of lawyers and his children." She took a long slow breath. "That's the point I want to make, Charlotte. Lyle's death wasn't in my best interest. I didn't do it, obviously, and I didn't have Adam do it. I'd appreciate it if you'd stop pursuing that line of thought."

"The truth, whatever it is, will come out one way or another, Caroline." Charlotte sympathized with the woman and wanted to believe Adam was innocent, but claims of innocence to mislead an investigation weren't new tricks. "If there's any proof that Adam had a hand in this, the marshal's office will find it. If Adam's innocent, then the best thing he—and you—can do is be honest and cooperative."

"And do what, admit to the entire town I've been sleeping with another man? Tell them my husband was a horrible human being? That will do more harm than good." Caroline

pulled her gloves on in short, quick movements. "We are innocent, and I'd greatly appreciate it if you'd leave us alone."

She continued down the walk, arms swinging stiffly at her
sides.

Charlotte watched until Caroline turned the corner, presumably headed back to her home. Did the lady protest too much?
Did she know more than she was letting on? If not, why come
to Charlotte? To plant the seeds of innocence? Caroline had de-
fended herself and Adam, but she implied Otto was capable of
killing Lyle.

What, exactly, had been going on between the two men?
More than disagreements over the price of nails and hammers,
Charlotte would wager.

Charlotte turned around and made her way toward City
Hall. All she needed was a quick look at the public records,
specifically land holdings, to find the location of Squint Bauer's
warehouse.

The night couldn't fall fast enough for Charlotte. Even
though it was dark by six in the evening, she waited another
hour to reduce the chances of being seen by someone heading
home for dinner. It was, perhaps, the longest hour ever, as she
talked herself into and out of her plan a dozen times, knowing
it was potentially dangerous. Otto Kenner couldn't do anything if she was on public property or property owned by
someone else. Not legally do anything himself, anyway. But
knowing his temper, and his attitude toward her, he might not
care if she wasn't breaking the law this time.

Dressed in a pair of her brother's old trousers, a thick shirt,
an old coat Mr. Gibbins had left behind, and her heavy winter
boots, Charlotte tucked her hair up under her hat, wrapped her
scarf around her face, and set out toward the row of ware-
houses down on the road to the canneries. She was able to use
the streetlights for a short part of the journey, but once she got
to the burned ruins of Fiske's Hardware, she had to rely upon

the full moon. There was a flashlight in her coat pocket that she'd turn on if and when she was sure no one was about.

According to the city records, Bauer's lot was roughly a block and a half past Fiske's. He owned three good-sized buildings, leasing two of them to locals. One was Kenner's, of course, and the other, she'd learned, was storage for Clive Wilkes's transportation operation. Clive used his Studebaker Touring Car as a taxi, but also owned an open-bed truck, tarps, straps, and other equipment required for large, heavy loads. The other Bauer building was used by the Bauers themselves for their plumbing and heating business.

It was the building at the back of the property, tucked into the shadows, that Charlotte sought. A few dozen feet from the nearest neighbor, the warehouse Otto Kenner used was far enough away to allow him to work on carpentry projects without interruption by or interruption to his neighbors. With its main doors facing away from the others, it allowed a certain amount of privacy as well.

Charlotte followed the frozen, rutted footpath around the first two buildings, avoiding the road on the other side of the buildings and staying in the shadows where she could. If anyone came along, she had little option but to dash behind a scraggly, ice-rimed bush.

As she drew closer to Kenner's building, she stopped for a moment to catch her breath and listen. Nothing from the buildings she'd passed. Nothing coming along the path or the road that she could see or hear. Focusing on the structure ahead of her, Charlotte thought she heard voices. There were no windows on this side, just weathered planks and snow drifts.

Before reaching the corner at the front, Charlotte moved off the packed snow of the path and pressed her left shoulder to the wall. Anyone checking would see her boot prints in the untouched snow, but maybe they'd think it was a kid or something. Better to have them see her prints later than risk being seen right in front of Kenner's business. Creeping along, her boots crunching softly in the snow, she listened for others, especially wary of hearing Otto's gruff voice. She reached the corner of the building.

There. Low voices and the sound of wood scraping on wood from inside.

Charlotte removed her hat and crouched down. Slowly, she eased forward to peek around the corner. The front of the warehouse was open, with a wide door slid aside to allow a dark green truck with an enclosed bed to have backed in. A regular-sized door was closer to her, no more than ten feet away. The vehicle's engine was off, as were its headlights, and a dim light glowed from deeper within the building. There was no way to see what was inside because of the truck and her viewing angle.

"Five hundred, just as we agreed," an unfamiliar male voice said. Charlotte could vaguely make out a figure near the driver's door.

"The next shipment might take a bit," Otto Kenner replied. He had to be standing right near the man, but she couldn't see him. "I'll let you know when it comes in."

"Sounds good."

The man climbed into the truck and started the engine. He didn't turn on the lights as he pulled away, and Otto had the warehouse door almost closed by the time the rear of the truck cleared the opening.

Damnation.

What were Otto and the man doing there after typical business hours? What shipment was coming in?

If she could only get inside and see what Otto kept there.

Charlotte started to rise. A strong hand clamped down on the lower half of her face. A thick arm wrapped around her chest, grasping her too-large coat and yanking her backwards. She would have screamed if she could have drawn a breath, but she could only gasp into the heavy leather glove over her mouth.

Chapter 12

Charlotte threw herself back, hoping to surprise her assailant and break loose. She landed on top of him. He grunted, but didn't release her. She twisted in his arms, or tried to. He was strong and held fast.

"Charlotte, it's me," James said in a fierce whisper. "Stop thrashing about."

Breathing hard through her nose, she stilled. James?

Slowly, he released her, removing his hand from her mouth. She started to turn over. He grabbed her shoulders, stopping her. "Be still and quiet," he whispered again. "He might be coming out."

Charlotte froze. Sure enough, the door no more than ten feet from them squealed open. It shut hard. Keys rattled.

Would Otto turn this way to head home?

Boots crunched on frozen mud and snow, heading in the opposite direction. A motor wheezed, then roared to life. Not a car, by the sound of the engine. A motorcycle? In this weather? The roar faded away as Otto returned to town.

Charlotte sat up, kneeling in the snow, and turned toward James. She could barely make out his face in the shadows, and despite the fact they were likely alone, she kept her voice to a whisper. "You scared the hell out of me."

He lifted his upper body and rested on his elbows. Responding in the same low tones, he said, "You're lucky it was me who saw you and not Kenner. That blond hair of yours shined like a beacon when you took off your hat. What are you doing here, skulking about?"

"What are *you* doing here, skulking about?"

She could imagine the glare he was giving her. "I'm supposed to be here, considering it's my duty to investigate. Been watching Kenner the past two nights. You, Miss Brody, have no excuse."

Charlotte snatched her hat off the snowy ground and got to her feet. She reached out to help him up. "I have an excuse for skulking then, since I'm not supposed to be here."

He grabbed her forearm. She braced her feet and yanked, fully aware she had little to do with helping him to his feet. He didn't release her, but instead drew her closer. With his face inches from hers, she could now make out the frown he wore. "Yet here you are. I could arrest you for trespassing."

"I haven't even attempted to get inside."

"You're still on private property without permission."

"That's splitting some fine hairs, deputy." Why was he being like this? Did he think she needed another lesson in consequences?

"Maybe. Maybe I should write in my report that I was making my rounds and thought I saw someone skulking about near Kenner's warehouse."

Charlotte stared at him in the darkness. Was he trying to set her up? To scare her again for making a rash move in the investigation? "You wouldn't—"

No, he wouldn't, not like that. Having her sit in his jail cell was one thing. He was getting at something here. Charlotte took a chance she was reading him correctly and said, "Maybe you need to check on a possible skulker."

He rubbed his chin. "Maybe, and if I scared off what I

thought might be a thief, I'd need to look inside Otto Kenner's warehouse, to make sure everything was jake."

"You'd just be doing your duty." She cocked her head at him. "What happened to not breaking the law to gather evidence? A bit hypocritical, isn't it?"

"I did say that, didn't I?" James picked his hat up from the ground and slapped it against his leg to get rid of some snow, but went no further in his explanation or excuse. He set his hat on his head, hands on hips. Charlotte could practically feel the conflict rolling through him. "Too bad the door's locked."

"Maybe if the door was ajar, you'd have cause to go inside to double-check." Charlotte removed her gloves, shoved them in her coat pocket, and pulled a couple of loose pins from her hair. They sure as hell weren't doing much to keep her hair in place after she and James fell to the ground. She started to hand them over, but stopped. "Do you know how to use these?"

"Yep." He hesitated. "Why? Do *you*?"

She smiled at the suspicion in his voice. "I'd rather not answer that question, deputy."

"I bet. Play lookout, would you? It would be embarrassing to be caught like this."

"Not just embarrassing, you'd lose your job," she said. "We don't want that. Why don't you stay here and keep an eye out while I check the door? The worse that could happen is you have to arrest me if someone happens by."

Without waiting for him to agree, Charlotte made sure no one was in the area, went to the door, then knelt down and fiddled with the pins and lock.

"Don't leave fingerprints on the door or knob," James said, just loud enough for her to hear.

"I'll be careful," she replied at the same volume. "Besides, no one has my prints on file."

"That's good to know. Do you need some light?"

"Nope." A faint scraping and clicking later, she stood, pocketed the pins, and in a whispered, damsel-in-distress voice called out, "Deputy! Deputy! I do believe someone has been skulking about Mr. Kenner's warehouse. Come quick!"

By the light of the moon, she saw him shaking his head as he walked toward her. He opened the door slowly to minimize the squeal. The two of them slipped inside. He stopped her with a hand on her shoulder.

"You're not like most women, are you, Miss Brody?" There was more than a little wonder and, dare she suppose, affection in the question.

"Are you just figuring that out, deputy?"

His laugh came out as a small grunt. "Maybe you should stay near the door and listen for Kenner, in case he decides to come back. You'd be able to get away faster."

She understood why he was suggesting it, to keep Kenner from having a reason to be angry with her yet again, but there was no way she'd let him have all the fun of searching the warehouse. "We'll hear his motorcycle in plenty of time."

It was pitch-dark in the warehouse, so all she heard was James's sigh of resignation. "Fine. But let's be quick. Between these late-night dealings of his and a couple customers of Kenner's who've hinted about his inventory, we don't need more than a good reason to come back for an official search."

He turned on a flashlight. She put her gloves back on, retrieved her flashlight from her pocket, and turned it on as well.

A small table and a couple of chairs were near the person-sized door. Two shot glasses were on the table beside a hastily stacked deck of cards, and two unmarked bottles lay on the ground. James peeked inside an old metal barrel near the table and held his hand close to it.

"Burn barrel. Not used too recently. This afternoon, maybe, by the residual heat."

"A warm fire, a bottle of homebrew, and a deck of cards," Charlotte said. "Cozy."

"Simple pleasures," James replied. He aimed his flashlight deeper into the warehouse. "What do we have here?"

Charlotte followed his lead. Stacked along the back wall and at the far end were crates and barrels of all sizes. She couldn't see the marks stenciled on them, but she'd bet a good number were from the hardware suppliers down in the States.

There were also several pieces of furniture in various stages of assembly. Was one of these based on the drawing she saw in Kenner's office the other day? Charlotte walked up to the closest one, an open-front cabinet taller than she was. "He does beautiful work."

James moved past the furniture to the inventory at the far end. "Come on, we don't have a lot of time."

Charlotte joined him, their flashlight beams playing over the containers. Most of them were sealed tight, and a few were dusty. How long had Otto been stockpiling supplies?

James climbed over a crate with "Bremmer Lubricant and Solvents" stenciled on it to access the pieces in the back. "One of these looks like it's been opened, then nailed shut again."

"Do you need a crowbar or something?" Charlotte turned about to search for a helpful tool. Spotting one on top of a barrel, she started toward it. Her foot smacked into a small crate marked "saw blades." The crate moved and the contents rattled, the tinkling of glass-on-glass very unlike what she'd expect saw blades to sound like. "James?"

James's light swung toward her and the crate. "I heard. Go get that crowbar, will you?"

He climbed down and met her back at the crate. He handed her his flashlight and took the crowbar. Sliding the notched end between the lid and the base, where it looked like it had been opened before, James carefully pried up the lid. The nails barely squealed, giving as if they'd been loosened before. He lifted the lid and moved aside the straw packing material. Beneath it were a dozen bottles with black rubber stoppers. James pulled one out, and Charlotte fixed one of the flashlight beams on the black and cream label.

"This is some good stuff," he said, hefting the whiskey. "My da was partial to Jameson's, back in the day. He jokes that that's who I was named for."

Charlotte laughed and James winked at her. His demeanor sobered again when he considered the bottle and its mates.

"There's a tax stamp," she said. "At least Otto isn't breaking that law."

"No," James said, slipping the bottle back among the others, "but black market booze in a dry territory will get him a nice long stint in the Valdez jail. The man who was here just now was Ken Avery, owner of the Tidewater. He supposedly has a back room for special events."

"Very special, I bet." Charlotte swept her light beam across the other containers. "I wonder if Otto has other things here."

"Like what?" He set the lid crooked on the crate and placed the crowbar on the floor.

"I don't know," she said. "Whatever people feel they need that they can't get here. What are you doing?"

"Making it look like someone broke in." James took his flashlight back from her. "If I'm going to risk my job, I want to at least make it as realistic as possible. Once I get Blaine, we'll secure this stuff, then go arrest Kenner."

"I could stay here and watch the building."

He shook his head and gently turned her toward the jimmied door. "I don't want you anywhere near here now, Charlotte. We got what we need. I doubt Kenner will be back tonight. When I was watching last night, he did the deal, then went home to bed. We'll leave things as is. Even if Kenner returns, Blaine and I'll be here soon enough."

Charlotte recognized an order when she heard it, even if he said it so very nicely. Besides, now that she thought about it, should Otto return and catch her, it was possible he'd do something unpleasant. "All right."

James hesitated for a moment. "That was easy."

"I'm not foolhardy, deputy. Every now and again I consider consequences." Hadn't he asked her to do that very thing more often?

"Glad to hear it. Now let's get the hell out of here."

After making sure no one was around, she and James left the warehouse.

"If my story is going to hold water with Blaine, we'll have to leave the door unlocked," he said quietly. "Should be fine for the next hour or so. I guess I owe you some new pins."

Charlotte patted her pocket where she'd stashed the makeshift picks. "I think I can afford to sacrifice these for the cause."

He chuckled quietly, then gestured for her to head back up the path they'd come in on. "Let's avoid the road for now."

Charlotte led the way, again using the moonlight to keep her on the packed snow path, walking single file until they reached the wider road. "Do you think all of that stuff in Kenner's was contraband?"

"Doubt it. I'd guess you were right about him bringing in more supplies in order to do his own little hardware business on the side."

They were passing Fiske's burned building now, and Charlotte said, "I wonder if Lyle had known what Kenner was doing in the name of competition."

"It wouldn't surprise me," James said. "Probably got him pretty riled too."

"Do you think Lyle knew Otto was selling alcohol on the side?"

He shrugged. "Could be. Obviously Kenner has at least a few clients."

Had Brigit obtained her liquor from Otto or some other source? Not that she'd ask, but she'd make sure to tell Brigit certain supply lines were drying up—no pun intended—now that James was on to Kenner.

"I'll walk you home," James said as they passed Main Street.

"You don't have to."

"I want to. Besides, it's on the way to Blaine's place."

The next block was an icy slope that had no lights. Concentrating on their footing, they were about to turn the corner to Charlotte's house when James took her arm and drew her back into the deep shadow of a thick spruce tree.

"What—"

"Shh. Look."

He leaned forward and pointed own an alley between a double row of old cabins. A broad-shouldered man was peering into a window. After a moment, he headed their way.

James pulled her closer and around the trunk of the tree. Charlotte craned her neck to see. The man came out of the alley, looked up and down the snowy street. He moved away from them, checking behind as if he was afraid of being followed. Light from a house close to the street allowed her to see his face, and that he held something in his right hand.

"That's Ben Derenov," she whispered in James's ear.

"Wonder what he's up to?"

Ben disappeared down a side street.

"Come on." James turned on his flashlight and went into the alley.

Charlotte followed. Mucky, trampled snow and bits of debris were all that was there. He stopped at the window where Ben had looked in. It was a ramshackle little log cabin, the chinking mostly gone, the interior dark. James cupped his hands around his eyes and peered through the cracked glass, just as Ben had.

"Do you see anything?" she whispered.

He shook his head. "This was Kermit Farley's place. Don't think anyone lives here anymore."

"Where's Mr. Farley?" The name didn't sound familiar to her.

"Moved down to Sitka to be with his mother. He's an ancient sod, so I can imagine how old his ma might be." He said it with amused respect.

"I wonder what Ben wanted with him?"

James shrugged and shook his head. "No idea. Maybe he knew Kermit when he was a kid." He gestured for her to head back to the street. "He wasn't looking to be destructive or anything, so I have no cause to ask."

In a few minutes, they were on Charlotte's porch. James waited for her to unlock the door. She turned to him.

"Thank you for seeing me home, and for letting me help you search Kenner's place."

"I'm just glad I found you before Kenner did. You really shouldn't have been there at all." He was trying to admonish her, but the resigned look on his face made her think he wasn't too terribly upset.

"If I hadn't been there though, you would have had to make up some story about a potential thief. Besides, I had the right tools for the job." She patted her hair.

James laughed. "True enough."

"Be careful when you go to arrest Kenner," she said, serious now. "He has a temper."

"I will." He touched his fingertips to the brim of his hat. "Good night, Miss Brody."

"Good night, deputy."

Neither of them moved. Was he going to kiss her again? Was he waiting for her to kiss him? The idea wasn't unpleasant in the least, but it sent tremors through Charlotte's belly. One chaste kiss in a series of chaste kisses wouldn't be so bad, would it?

Charlotte raised up onto her toes and touched her lips to his. She lowered herself down, staring at him. No, that wasn't bad at all, in fact, it was rather nice.

A slow smile curved James's mouth. "Good night."

"Good night."

He bounded down the stairs, then turned up the street toward Marshal Blaine's home.

* * *

Charlotte worked all morning at the *Times* office, waiting for word that James or Marshal Blaine had arrested Otto Kenner and confiscated the contents of his warehouse. But nothing came her way.

Had he gotten wind of their intentions and eluded them? Was the marshal waiting to make the arrest for some reason?

Maybe she'd better go see what was happening.

She exchanged her shoes for her boots, donned her coat and hat, then locked up the office. The sun had decided to stick around, brightening the sky to a brilliant blue and reflecting off the snow-covered mountains. With the clear skies, however, had come a distinct drop in the temperature. Charlotte covered her cold nose and mouth with her scarf.

The laundry sled whooshed down the street toward her, returning from a delivery. Dogs yapped joyfully. The driver's face was a white mask of frost. He called them to a stop in front of the laundry as Charlotte reached the federal building. The dogs yipped some more, but they seemed sad now that the run was over.

Laundry via dog sled. That definitely had to go into one of her articles for *Modern Woman*.

The outer door to the building was open, but the inner door to the marshal's office was locked. Curious. Usually someone was there. Unless they were down at Kenner's *now* making the arrest. She was half tempted to go to the warehouse and check it out.

No, James would be upset by the distraction. Best if she just waited for him to tell her about the outcome. She hated to wait.

Out of the corner of her eye, Charlotte caught a glimpse of someone running. Young Charlie O'Brien dashed across the street, headed down the side road toward home. Maybe Charlotte could talk to Brigit, see if she'd heard about anyone else having pawned items returned. While she was at it, Charlotte might ask about the black market dealings in town.

She followed the path Charlie took and made her way to Brigit's front door.

Edie, the new girl, opened the door when Charlotte knocked. She was dressed to go out running errands, not for customers. "Oh. Hello."

"Hello, Edie. Settling in all right?"

"Well enough," she replied with an indifferent shrug.

Sensing Edie wasn't interested in small talk, Charlotte asked, "Is Brigit available?"

"She's getting Charlie some lunch. Go on back to the kitchen if you'd like." Edie sidled past her to the walk. "My turn to collect the mail and do some shopping. So long."

"Bye."

Charlotte closed the door behind her and unbuttoned her coat. Charlie's coat and boots were strewn across the entry in typical hurried child fashion. She hung up her own hat and coat in the closet and set her boots by the door. Wearing her thick wool socks, she padded into the parlor, then on through to the kitchen.

Charlie and Della sat at the table eating soup. Brigit was at the stove checking the contents of a pan. Both of the women wore simple skirts and blouses, quite unlike their typical evening attire. The aroma of toasted cheese and bread made Charlotte's stomach rumble.

All three looked over at her. Charlie went back to slurping soup without much change in his demeanor. Della nodded a greeting.

Brigit smiled at her. "What a nice surprise. Have a seat, Charlotte. I'll make you a sandwich, and there's plenty of soup."

She retrieved another bowl from the cupboard and set it by the pot on the stove.

"Thank you. It smells wonderful." Charlotte took one of the empty seats.

The kitchen wasn't large; the big butcher-block table and six chairs filled most of the space. The icebox and stove had seen better days, but everything was tidy and clean. Brigit ran a tight ship, no matter where things were happening in the house.

After setting a plate of sandwiches in the center of the table and a bowl of soup in front of Charlotte, Brigit sat down to join them. "What brings you here?"

Charlotte swallowed a bite of deliciously gooey toasted cheese and bread. "I wanted to ask you if you'd heard anything more about that situation we'd discussed at the office." She gave Della a significant look, drawing her into the conversation. "Word of another return, or anything like that."

Brigit and Della exchanged glances. Charlie ignored the women. Or seemed to be ignoring them. Best not to be too free with the topic around young ears. Though considering where he lived, Charlotte was sure he'd heard more questionable conversations than a typical ten-year-old.

Della shook her head.

"I haven't heard anything either," Brigit said. "Truth be told, I wasn't exactly asking questions."

"I hadn't expected you to." Charlotte smiled. "Just wondered if you'd heard anything in passing."

"Sorry."

"There's something else I wanted to talk to you about, Brigit, but it can wait until after lunch." The topic of Otto Kenner and his black market dealings were not for all to hear. Especially since there was no confirmation of his arrest.

Brigit's dark eyes held hers for a moment, then she smiled back. "Of course. We'll finish here, then go into my office."

When everyone had their fill of soup and sandwiches, Brigit hurried Charlie back to school. Charlotte stood with them in the entry as he put his winter gear on. He started to dash toward the door, but Brigit called him back. She bend down and pecked him on the cheek. He made a face, though Charlotte saw the happiness in his eyes. He loved his mother and she loved him.

"Have a good day, and remember to tell Miss Atkins I can make cookies for the party next week."

"Okay. Bye. Bye, Miss Charlotte." He was out the door before Charlotte could respond.

"That boy." Brigit chuckled quietly and shut the door. She was still smiling as she turned to Charlotte. "Come on in and make yourself comfortable."

She led the way into her office. Charlotte settled into one of the cushioned chairs before Brigit's desk. Brigit took the other. Papers and ledgers occupied the desktop and the chaise.

"Sorry for the mess," Brigit said, waving her hand absently. "I'm reorganizing my stock portfolio. My financial adviser in Ohio sent me some information on a few companies. Wading through that has been a challenge."

"I wouldn't have any idea of where to start."

Charlotte's father kept track of an investment account that was in her name, and she supposed an independent woman like herself should be in charge of her own finances. Truth be told, she wasn't interested in all of that. Besides, Father enjoyed "playing" with her money and was quite good at it. For now, she lived off what she made working and was doing well enough. At some point she'd get involved, but not yet.

"It can be a challenge," Brigit said. "But you aren't here for that. As I said, I haven't heard about anyone else having their pawned goods returned."

"I'd expect if anyone has they'd be much like Della, wanting to keep it quiet." Charlotte was sure the only reason Della came to her was because Brigit insisted. Few others would have cared to let her or the marshal's office know about the illegal operation. "I wonder if someone else will take Lyle's place?"

"I'm sure someone will, if they haven't already. It's amazing how quickly a niche is filled. People are keen to jump on opportunities." Brigit laughed. "Hell, the establishment of the entire Alaska Territory—this country—was based on grabbing an opportunity, wasn't it?"

Charlotte smiled. "It sure was. There's another niche that may be opening soon."

Brigit cocked a slender eyebrow. "Really?"

"When I was here the other day, I couldn't help but notice you served me some very fine whiskey." She kept any accusation out of her voice, because she wasn't accusing Brigit of anything. "Without naming names, could you tell me how you acquired it?"

Brigit didn't say anything for a few moments, but sat back, her legs and arms crossed. "You and I are friends, Charlotte, and I'd like us to stay that way."

"So would I." What was she getting at?

"Things we discuss here, they're between you and me, not to be shared casually."

Did Brigit think Charlotte gossiped or passed on information without agreeing to it first? "Of course not. Unless someone's in dire straits or under physical threat, we keep each other's confidences. Do you think I wouldn't?"

Brigit shook her head. "No, no, of course I trust you. But I know as a journalist you're obligated to get to the bottom of things."

"I'd never write or speak about anything involving you without your permission. If I do feel the need to tell the marshal's office anything, I'd clear that with you as well. And I'd never use your name or anyone else's, Brigit. I swear." As a reporter, her promise to keep anonymous sources anonymous was crucial. As a friend, breaking a confidence was completely unacceptable.

"I appreciate that." Brigit's shoulders relaxed and she smiled. "Not that I had doubt, but admitting to breaking several territorial statutes is difficult."

"The breaking or the admitting?" Charlotte asked, grinning.

Brigit laughed. "A bit of both. Despite being only two men, the marshal and the deputy are incorruptible and make engaging in criminal activity a challenge, which is a good thing, really. I recognize the fact that my continued operation is purely at their whim. Any hint that I'm involved in anything more will see me in a Valdez jail cell or on a steamer headed south."

"Michael says there's talk of adding more policemen in the next few years."

The local police consisted of two men as well, who mostly patrolled the main part of town. Even with four lawmen, they still had a hard time covering all of Cordova and the surrounding area.

Brigit nodded thoughtfully. "I guess I'd better be more careful. But you asked about my liquor supply. I'm assuming you want to know how I, and other places, get their booze when Alaska is a dry territory."

"I figured you might bring it in yourself, but smuggling a personal bottle or two on board a steamer won't satisfy your customers." Charlotte's former landlady, Mrs. Sullivan, had her sherry, and Charlotte was sure other people managed to either sneak in or make their own. Making, then selling, larger amounts of alcohol seemed to be the greater concern of the lawmen.

"I do have friends and visitors deliver what they can, but you're right," Brigit said. "My business requires more quantity and variety than that."

"A black market."

Brigit nodded but didn't say anything.

"Can you get more than alcohol?" Charlotte asked.

The madam tilted her head, an amused grin curving her lips. "Are you looking for something in particular?"

"Not me. I was merely curious. What other things might you find being offered?"

Brigit thought for a moment. "Certainly booze is the most popular, from what I hear. There's also cigars and cigarettes, loose tobacco. Condoms."

"Condoms? You buy those on the black market?"

The prophylactics were legal to use, but putting them in the hands of men who needed them had been a hassle for years. Some states outright forbade their advertisement, while others didn't allow them to be advertised as birth control, only as preventing sexually transmitted diseases. Whatever it took to get them used, Charlotte supposed.

"The drugstore usually orders some, but they're always running out. It's faster, easier, and actually cheaper for us to buy them from a . . . private supplier. We keep a small stock on hand here, as do most of the houses."

"That makes sense." Customers and girls alike stayed healthy that way. Her brother, Michael, who gave the girls regular exams, probably appreciated it too.

"But I'll have to find another source and renegotiate services now that Fiske is dead."

Surprise jerked Charlotte to the edge of her chair. "Fiske? He was your supplier?"

She had assumed it was Otto and had been prepared to warn Brigit of his pending arrest.

"I told you he was making more money than the store's books would show." Brigit pressed her lips together. "You can't let that get out, even though he's dead."

"I won't spill the beans, I promise," Charlotte said. "I guess pawning small items and jewelry wasn't all that profitable."

"Not if people couldn't afford to buy back their things. I'd imagine Fiske was selling some of what he kept to other people in town, or shipping items down to the States and getting money that way. It's the only way he'd make anything on them."

"But his black market business was doing well."

"Yes," Brigit said, sounding impressed. "It was quite the operation as I understand. He'd bring in the standard stuff— booze and the like—but was also able to get specialty items. A partner in the shipyard in Seattle repacked crates for him when he ordered for his store."

Was that how Otto Kenner ran his side business as well? Was the competition between the men for more than their legitimate business reasons? That would certainly add to Otto's motive for killing Lyle. If he killed Lyle, which it was looking to be more and more likely to Charlotte.

"I wonder if James knows about Fiske?" He'd been suspicious of Otto's over-ordering, but if they hadn't searched the warehouse and found the bottles of whiskey Otto could have explained the excess hardware goods away as starting his own store. Fiske already had his cover.

"Doubtful," Brigit said, "or he would have raided the store long ago. The marshal's office probably suspected a number of retailers here, but without complaint or evidence..." She shrugged and shook her head, indicating the marshal and James having had little to no chance at catching Fiske.

"Do you know if Lyle kept records?" Charlotte asked. If so, maybe those were in the black book as well.

"I have no idea. I'm sure he had inventory and purchase lists for the store, but those would cover for the other items he brought in. He telegraphed or telephoned his contact in Seattle to place orders."

"Slick as a whistle, wasn't he? Providing folks who were hard up with loans they couldn't pay back, but making money selling contraband and hard-to-get goods." Charlotte wasn't sure if she hated the man or admired his initiative. Though after learning how he treated Caroline, she was closer to hating him.

"I can appreciate his business acumen, but Lyle Fiske was only interested in looking out for Lyle Fiske," Brigit said, her dark eyes hard. "If he'd been backed into a corner, he would have ratted on all of us who used his services."

No love lost between Brigit and Lyle, that was obvious.

"Had he ever threatened to do anything of the sort?"

"Only if I complained about his high prices, and not in so many words." Brigit's mouth twitched into a wry grin. "But I didn't kill him, if that's what you're asking."

"Of course I'm not," she assured her friend. "I would think he could have threatened to do the same with a rival."

"I'm sure he was quite capable of making that threat. And following through."

Another reason, perhaps, for Otto to get into it with Fiske. But all Charlotte had was "supposes" and "what-ifs." She was itching to talk to James. He'd ask Otto all the right questions that might trip up the carpenter and get him to confess to the murder.

"Charlotte, while I have you here, can I ask you a favor?" Brigit sat on the edge of her chair, hands clasped in her lap, apprehension in her eyes.

Charlotte covered Brigit's hands with her own. "Anything. Except I won't work for you."

Brigit smiled slightly, though not with the same amusement she usually got from Charlotte's denial. Her asking Charlotte to join the house and Charlotte's refusal had become a playful exchange between them. "Never say never, but no, that's not it. I'm headed south for a month or so. Can you look in on the girls while I'm gone? Mr. Larsen will be here, but they'll talk to you if there's something they can't go to him about."

"Of course. I can do that." She'd miss having Brigit around for so long, but it wasn't worth it to travel to the States for anything less than a couple of weeks. "Can I ask where you're headed?"

"Tess, Charlie, and I are going to Cincinnati to visit Camille's grave and attend a memorial." She lifted her chin. Her eyes were hard behind the shine of unshed tears. "Then I'm going to look for the doctor who killed her and make the bastard pay."

Chapter 13

"Pay? How?" Charlotte couldn't believe Brigit would do anything drastic, but her anger and grief made it a possibility. Her hands turned ice cold. Numb, she grasped Brigit's fingers. "Brigit, no, you can't. What good would it do?"

As much as she hurt for her friend, she couldn't condone an act of vengeance like the one Brigit might be planning. Yes, the doctor who'd pushed Camille out of his office was responsible for her death. There was no denying that. But kill him?

"He deserves to die."

Brigit spoke in a low, reasonable tone. She wasn't hysterical. She wasn't beating her breast, shouting cries of anguish. There was sadness behind the determination in her eyes, and a coldness in her voice that scared the hell out of Charlotte.

"Camille trusted her life to that man, but he was more concerned with saving his own ass than keeping her alive. He had his money and didn't care that she would go home and quietly bleed to death. Too many women have to put their lives in the hands of men like that." Brigit closed her eyes, slowly shaking her head. "You don't understand, Charlotte."

"I do. I know exactly what's at stake." Charlotte's mouth

dried, her throat tight as if gripped by a fist. Getting Brigit to see that she did understand might be the only thing to keep her grieving friend from doing something foolish. "I know what women in Camille's position have to risk. What I risked."

Brigit stilled. She opened her eyes and stared at Charlotte as if seeing her for the first time. "You?"

"Over a year ago," Charlotte said. She moistened her chapped lips as best she could with her mouth like sand. "I—" A tremor went through her chest, stopping the words.

Brigit patted her hand and rose. She went over to a sideboard and opened the cabinet. Retrieving an elaborately etched bottle and two tumblers, she returned to where they were sitting. She pulled the stopper, poured them each a couple of fingers of amber liquid, and handed a glass to Charlotte. "The really good stuff I bring in for myself."

Charlotte attempted to smile but couldn't. She drank instead. The bourbon went down smoothly, warming her throat and belly. "Thank you."

Brigit sat, silently sipping her drink as Charlotte gathered her thoughts. Despite her assertions of being a "modern woman," there was so much stigma and shame attached to what she'd done. Even good friends and relatives had turned on women who'd made choices like hers. Only Kit and Michael knew her secret, and now Brigit.

What if Brigit felt like those others she'd heard about? She was angry at the doctor responsible for Camille's death, but how did she feel about Camille's decision? That was what scared Charlotte the most, especially since she didn't feel like she or Camille had done anything wrong, that it was no one else's business but their own. She didn't want to lose Brigit's friendship over this.

It was too late to turn back now. The words, the feelings, built up in her chest like floodwaters threatening to breach a dam.

"It's a long story," she began. Then she told Brigit everything. Everything about meeting Richard and attending lectures, about going to parties and dances with him, about being charmed by his wit and good looks. About enthusiastically going to his bed. "God, he was amazing."

Brigit smiled knowingly but didn't interrupt. Charlotte told her how Richard had agreed that women should be allowed to determine their own destinies, to make their own decisions about what their lives would be.

"Except he wasn't keen on the idea of *me* doing it if it impeded *his* destiny." She gave a harsh laugh and drank the last of the bourbon in her glass in a single gulp.

"He used you." Brigit said, pouring her another.

Charlotte shook her head. "No, he fooled me, and maybe I fooled myself, but he didn't use me. I was enjoying it as much as he was. I was looking for a doctor when I told Richard I was pregnant. He was adamant about my not having a child on my own or giving it up for adoption, and initially against termination."

Against it? He'd been brutal, calling anyone who had an abortion nothing short of a low-class whore. Having a bastard running around was only slightly less sordid in his eyes.

"Richard insisted that my family would be horribly disappointed in me if they found out. I'd been concerned about the same thing, of course. He almost convinced me to marry him. Almost. I was scared and confused. I don't know why I believed him."

Charlotte swallowed the lump in her throat. Admitting her gullibility when it came to Richard would never get easy. Neither would admitting what she'd done and why. "Then he said I'd have to quit working. That he'd have a proper wife to mother his children. That finally made me realize he was a lying, manipulative bastard. Anything he said served his own purpose, whether it was agreeing with my stand on equality to make it look like we were compatible, to proposing marriage. I turned him down and told him I was finding a doctor. He said if anyone found out what I'd done he would make life a living hell for me and my parents. That I did believe."

Brigit didn't say anything. Her mouth was pressed into a thin line, her hands wrapped around the tumbler. Nothing on her face showed her to be judging Charlotte, to be bitter because Charlotte had been lucky enough to have a doctor who performed the operation with care and concern while Camille had died at the hands of a selfish one.

Sometimes having the money to pay for a good doctor wasn't enough, and the thought of all the other women who were financially strapped, who didn't have a choice, ate at Charlotte on a daily basis.

"It's not always an easy decision," Brigit said quietly. "But I guess some women know right away what they're to do. Victoria wrote that Camille had thought it over some, because I'd had Charlie and made it work. But that was *my* decision. You made yours, and Camille made hers. No one should have to risk their lives for being honest with themselves. She wasn't ready for a baby either, but she shouldn't have died for that."

"No, she shouldn't have. No one should." Charlotte drank more bourbon. Her head was starting to feel muzzy, but she didn't care. She and Brigit wouldn't part ways over this and that was worth celebrating.

"Amen to that," Brigit said. She wiped her eyes with the cuff of her blouse.

Charlotte considered the woman across from her, how she'd reacted to Camille's death, how she'd made no judgment of Charlotte's decision or the reasons behind it. "You went through with your pregnancy. Not many women in your position have done that."

"More than you might think." Brigit stared down into her glass, then met Charlotte's eyes. "I could have found someone to perform the operation, and yes, probably died of it. Likely died of it. But I couldn't, and that was my choice. It wasn't any better or any worse than what you and Camille decided. That's what I felt was right for me, at that time in my life."

"Few think that way," Charlotte said.

Certainly too few publicly supported a woman's choice to feel comfortable speaking about it on a regular basis. Brigit was a rarity. An overwhelming surge of gratitude made Charlotte's eyes tear and her throat tight. How lucky had she been to befriend this woman?

"That's what all this women's equality and right to vote is for, isn't it?" Brigit said. "That's what those articles you write are for, to remind people we all deserve to make certain personal choices. Maybe someday women won't have this sort of conversation, or mourn our friends, or fear for our lives."

Charlotte tapped her glass against Brigit's. "Amen to *that*."

They both drank and sat with their own thoughts for a moment. Charlotte felt closer to Brigit, a closeness that came with trusting someone with your most intimate thoughts and feelings. It was a relief to reduce the weight of her secret that rested on her shoulders.

But the thoughts and feelings Brigit had for the doctor responsible for Camille was still a concern.

"Brigit, I know you're hurting, but please reconsider what you plan to do in Ohio."

Drawn back to the topic, Brigit's eyes hardened. "He needs to pay. He needs to understand that what he did was wrong. Other women are going to him. Who knows how many might die from his neglect?"

Charlotte leaned forward and laid a hand on her knee. "I know, and he has to be held accountable. But if you try to do something and get arrested, you would suffer and Charlie along with you. I know you don't want him to lose you."

Maybe it was a terrible thing, to use her son as emotional blackmail, but that didn't make the potential risk any less real.

Anger flared in Brigit's eyes as she realized what Charlotte was doing, but only for a moment. She closed her eyes and tears trickled down her cheeks. "I have to do something for her. I can't just let it go."

Charlotte set her glass on the table. She knelt on the floor beside Brigit's chair and drew her close. Brigit rested her head on Charlotte's shoulder. "I know, but not that. Find another way to get him, to protect other women. I'll give you the names of some reporters I know in the area. Maybe they can help."

Brigit breathed slow and deep, collecting herself. "Maybe I can get the police to arrest him, but not when he's in the middle of an operation."

"Yes, I bet you can." Charlotte eased away from Brigit, smiling. She wiped a tear off the madam's cheek with her thumb. "I think Camille would prefer you stay out of jail."

Brigit laughed and dashed away another tear. "Probably."

Charlotte sat back in her chair and poured them each another finger of bourbon. "Another toast, to clear thinking." They clinked glasses. "Though if I drink this, I won't be thinking all that clearly, and I still have to go back to work."

Brigit touched her glass again. "Makes for more interesting news that way."

Charlotte walked in a mostly straight path back up the road to the federal building. The cold air had helped clear her head some, but the world was pleasantly fuzzy around the edges. Hopefully she'd be able to speak to James in a sober manner.

Not likely, she thought, smiling.

At least she wouldn't smell drunk. Brigit had given her some water and a piece of mint candy to chew. She had a few more pieces in her pocket, just in case.

Good lord, when was the last time she'd had that much alcohol? And twice with Brigit in the span of a week.

"Miss Brody."

Charlotte stopped dead in her tracks. Her head swam at the sudden lack of movement.

"Mrs. Hillman," she whispered with dread as she turned to face the Women's Temperance League chapter president.

Mrs. Hillman strode up to her, having come down the side street Charlotte had just passed. "I'd like to speak to you, if you have a moment."

"I'm in a bit of a hurry," she said, awkwardly waving toward the *Times* office and the federal building. Her legs felt wobbly. Charlotte stiffened her spine and limbs to keep from stumbling.

"This won't take long," the woman said. She smiled, but it was not a natural look for her. "I wanted to thank you and Mr. Toliver for giving the Women's Temperance League equal space in the *Times*. We may have our differences, but—Are you all right, Miss Brody? You look a little green."

Despite her attempt to not waver, Charlotte felt as if she was standing on the deck of a ship. "I'm fine, Mrs. Hillman. A bit of a stomachache."

More like bottle flu.

She suppressed the giggle that bubbled up. "But please go on. You were saying?"

Mrs. Hillman narrowed her gaze. "I was saying that while we have our differences of opinion over the enactment of National Prohibition, I'm very pleased that all voices can be heard in Cordova."

Charlotte smiled sweetly. "Yet you still think I'm wrong." She patted Mrs. Hillman's arm. "That's all right. I think you're wrong too."

The older woman pressed her lips together. "Be that as it may, I'm sure next time—if there is a next time—Mr. Toliver will consider the ramifications of neglecting the prevailing mindset of his readership and present a more balanced edition right off."

"Ramifications?" Charlotte tilted her head. "What ramifications?"

Mrs. Hillman lifted her chin. "People will let him know quite clearly how they feel about certain . . . opinions, and take appropriate action."

"By appropriate action you mean . . . what, exactly?" When Mrs. Hillman and her friends had confronted Charlotte about her article, she had been afraid of this happening. "Did you threaten Mr. Toliver with some sort of boycott of the paper?"

"Don't be ridiculous." Mrs. Hillman's wide-eyed innocence might have been genuine, but Charlotte didn't buy it. "I simply reminded him that people bought newspapers to be informed, not to read the opinions of his staff who don't understand how things work here."

Be civil, said the voice in her head.

She ignored it.

"I think I know exactly how things work here, Mrs. Hillman."

The woman smiled triumphantly.

Charlotte stepped up to her, putting her face inches from Mrs. Hillman's. The smile faded into a frown. "But let me remind *you* of something. Alaska may do its own thing, in its own way and time, but it is still governed by the Constitution of the United States. The First Amendment is the law of the land."

Mrs. Hillman held her gaze. "As will be the Eighteenth Amendment come January. Good day, Miss Brody."

She turned on her heel and strode down the walk, head high.

The contents of Charlotte's stomach churned, bourbon, cheese, and soup roiling in anger. Damn that woman, thinking she ran the moral majority of this town. Not everyone agreed with her and the Women's Temperance League, and Charlotte was sure she could get that support.

"We'll see whose amendment prevails, Mrs. Hillman."

Charlotte turned abruptly and regretted it in an instant. Her stomach stayed facing the street for a long moment while she focused on the federal building. When it caught up to the direction she was facing, the remains of lunch tried to lurch up into her throat. She swallowed hard and fast to keep it down, sweat breaking out on her face and back.

That was close. She breathed slow and deep to steady her head and stomach. Reaching into her coat pocket, she found a piece of candy, unwrapped it, and popped it into her mouth. The mint cleared her head and settled her stomach some. She gave it another few moments; going to see James while in this condition would cause even more problems than with Mrs. Hillman.

When she was sure she wouldn't vomit on the walkway, Charlotte went in. She stopped just inside the door, leaning on the frame.

James sat at his desk, his back to the door while he typed with two fingers on some sort of form. The marshal's door was open, the office empty. Loud voices came from beyond the door marked "Jail."

"Is that Otto Kenner in there?" Charlotte asked.

James turned quickly, brows drawn together. "It is. He's claiming illegal procedure."

She couldn't help but grin. "Accusing you of not doing everything by the book? How dare he? He didn't believe you were only trying to keep some skulking thief from stealing his legitimately purchased nails and saw blades?"

There was no hint of their shared escapade in his eyes or on his face. "Blaine does."

Charlotte nodded. "Good enough."

She started toward the chair near his desk, her steps slow as she concentrated on not weaving off course.

"Charlotte, are you okay?"

"I'm fine." She didn't look up at him until she was seated. Why was it so warm in here? Charlotte opened her coat. "So he's putting up a bit of a fuss. Not surprising. Have you asked him about his rivalry with Fiske?"

"Kenner admits he was at odds with Fiske, that he was planning to establish a new store, but nothing else. He claims we planted the contraband in the warehouse." James shook his head in disbelief. He'd probably heard all sorts of excuses and explanations to cover wrongdoing in his time as a deputy.

"When you question him again about his black market business, ask him if he and Lyle were at odds there too."

James's eyebrows rose, but he wasn't as surprised as she'd expected him to be. "So that's who else was bringing things in. We knew there were at least two, possibly three, sources, but could never narrow it down enough to justify searches of inventory and ship manifests."

Charlotte blinked at him. "You used the information I found in Kenner's home to do that."

"That's why you came to me with it, isn't it? It gave us a good idea that he was doing something he shouldn't have been doing. We just had to get into the warehouse to confirm, and we did."

She smiled at him. "We make a good team."

He smiled back. "We do at that."

"Are you going to ask Otto if he killed Fiske?"

"No."

Charlotte straightened, startled by his surety. "They were rivals, both in legitimate and not so legitimate businesses. Lyle's prices probably dug into Otto's profit margin, and Lyle couldn't care less. That's plenty of motive to kill him, the way Otto felt about fair competition. And a witness saw someone who looked an awful lot like Otto leave the fire."

"All that's true," James said, nodding. "Except I checked his alibi. He was at the Mirage Club most of the night of the fire."

"Most of it. Where did he go when he wasn't there? With a large enough window of time, a man walking fast or on a motorcycle would have ample opportunity to leave the club, get to Fiske's, and get back."

"Except none of the witnesses seems to think he was gone all that long, and your arsonist didn't see the man leave on a motorcycle."

"Oh. Right." She'd forgotten that part.

James seemed as disappointed as she was. "At least we have him for the illegal booze and such."

Charlotte's stomach churned along with her thoughts. The bourbon wasn't sitting well with the anxiety of losing her main suspect.

"Are you going to be sick?"

She shook her head. "No, I'm fine."

He frowned. "You don't look fine. You look like you're about to spew your lunch all over my desk."

The very idea of "spewing" or "lunch" made her gut cramp, which made her head spin. Apparently the pleasant muzziness of bourbon went directly into a hangover for her. Charlotte slumped back in the chair, her head swimming. She closed her eyes. "Damnation."

"Why don't I take you home." His chair scraped back along the wood floor.

Charlotte opened her eyes and held up a hand, stopping him from getting to his feet. "I have to get back to the paper. I'll stop at the café for some coffee. I'll be fine."

"You sure? I don't mind seeing you home."

She gave him the best smile she could muster. It felt odd on her face. Then again, the alcohol had made everything feel rather odd. "I'm sure. I'll stop by later to get some quotes from you and the marshal."

Charlotte rose gingerly, careful not to jostle her stomach. She felt James's eyes on her as she reached the door. Turning, she smiled and waved to him. Back outside in the fresh air, the queasy feeling abated with a few slow, deep breaths. If she could make it to the café down the block without vomiting, she'd be grateful.

Chapter 14

There was still a good number of people in the café an hour past lunch, mostly pairs of women and older folks, chatting or reading the newspaper. Charlotte found a seat as far away from the kitchen as she could, as a precaution. Thankfully, the coffee and food aromas wafting through the dining area weren't as difficult to tolerate as she'd feared. Though now her head started to ache, and she was desperate for a nap.

Unfortunately, there was still work to be done, being the middle of the week and all. A number of Associated Press pieces had come in just before she'd left the office. Putting them off until after what she'd thought would be a quick visit to Brigit and James seemed foolish now.

"Coffee, Miss Brody?" Henry asked, pot and cup in hand. "I almost missed you sitting over here."

Charlotte nodded, stopped when the ache in her head became a pounding, and rubbed her temples instead. "Coffee. Yes. Please. And do keep it coming."

Henry poured her a cup, then dashed back behind the counter for cream, sugar, and a spoon. "Are you all right, Miss Brody?"

That seemed to be the question of the day.

She smiled at him best she could. "I'll be fine. Can I have a piece or two of dry toast as well?"

"Sure thing." He checked on the other patrons on his way to the kitchen.

Charlotte added cream to her coffee and sipped. Nice and strong. That should help get her through the afternoon. A year ago, a finger or two of liquor gave her the pleasant sensation she'd initially felt today and lasted longer before turning on her. Was it the time of day or her body that changed? Either way, she'd be much more cautious about visiting Brigit when they were both feeling anxious or melancholy.

Henry returned with a glass of water. He set it and two white tablets down beside the saucer. "Figured you might need these." She gave him a questioning look. He grinned and shrugged. "Just a hunch. We keep a bottle of Bayer in the back."

"Thanks, Henry." Charlotte took the aspirin and swallowed some water.

"Be right back with your toast."

As he returned to the kitchen, Rebecca Derenov came out carrying a small, white enameled tub. She wore an apron over her dress, her hair pulled back in a ponytail. The gold and ruby ring strung around her neck swung back and forth as she walked into the dining area.

Charlotte's heart sank. It was the middle of a school day. What was the girl doing here? After school and on weekends was one thing, but if Rebecca was working instead of attending school, things had gone from bad to worse for her and her brother.

Going from table to table, Rebecca collected dirty dishes from patrons. Some ignored her, but several smiled as they passed her their plates. She turned toward Charlotte and hesitated. Her cheeks darkened as she made her way to Charlotte's table.

"Good afternoon, Miss Brody. How are you today?"

At least she didn't comment on Charlotte's state.

"I'm doing well. How are *you*?"

Rebecca shrugged and looked down into the tub of dishes. "Okay, I guess."

She certainly didn't seem "okay." The poor kid. Just yesterday the two of them had discussed the importance of her staying in school. Rebecca wanted to continue her education, and at the same time knew she needed to have a job. Had Ben guilted his sister into going to work? Charlotte hoped not. What a terrible situation for the Derenovs.

Charlotte touched Rebecca's arm, drawing her attention from the dishes. "I'm sure it's only temporary. When you get the chance, I'd love to have you come by the office again."

Perhaps she could find something for Rebecca to do there for a small wage. A chat with Mr. Toliver was in order.

Rebecca's eyes lit with anticipation. "That would be wonderful, Miss Brody. I had a swell time learning about the newspaper business."

Charlotte smiled. "And I had a swell time showing it to you."

"Oh! I have something I need to ask." Rebecca set the tub on the floor and hurried into the kitchen. She was back in a few moments clutching lined pages. "I wrote a story and was hoping you'd take a look at it for me." Her cheeks pinkened again, but she was smiling this time. "When you get a chance."

"I'd love to," Charlotte said, taking the pages. She glanced through them quickly, her head in no condition to concentrate on Rebecca's small, neat writing. "Is it a fiction piece?"

Rebecca nodded enthusiastically. "About a girl and her dog lost in the wilds of Alaska." She frowned. "I've never had a dog, so I asked some friends about keeping one."

"Research is always a good idea. Try to be as accurate as possible, even in fiction. Though a little artistic license is allowable."

The girl beamed, and Charlotte smiled back, thrilled to give her a bit of praise.

"Rebecca," a man called from the kitchen, "get back in here and wash those dishes."

Rebecca glanced over her shoulder. "Yes, Mr. Conway." She hefted the tote and turned back to Charlotte. "I gotta go. Thanks a heap, Miss Brody."

"You're welcome. I'll read these tonight and make notes, if that's all right?"

"Sure thing! See ya!"

Despite the weight of the tub and dishes, Rebecca's step was light and quick as she hurried into the kitchen.

Henry held the swinging door open for her, a bemused expression on his face. He brought over a plate with two pieces of toast and refilled her cup from the coffeepot he held in his other hand. "Here you go, Miss Brody. Sorry it took so long."

"No problem." Charlotte set Rebecca's story aside. Before he could turn to go, she touched his arm, stopping him. "How are things with you, Henry?"

Understanding she was asking about how he felt now that he'd confessed, not just his general well-being, he glanced around the dining area to make sure no one was paying them any particular attention. They weren't. "I'm all right, I guess. Haven't felt like doing, well, you know. Did you, um, talk to . . ."

She nodded. "I think it'll be fine. The information was greatly appreciated."

Relief eased the worry lines furrowing his brow, making him look like his happy sixteen-year-old self again. "That's good. I hope it helps."

"If you need to talk or anything, Henry, I'm happy to lend an ear."

He smiled. "Thanks, Miss Brody. I'll keep that in mind. Better get back to work. Mr. Conway is hoping to close up early today, so he's pushing us a bit."

"We wouldn't want Mr. Conway getting angry," she said. "I'll talk to you soon."

Giving her a quick nod, he headed to another table where three women had just settled in and were discussing the selection of pies available.

Charlotte finished her toast and drank down the rest of the coffee. She considered asking for a third cup, but decided a cup of tea while she worked would be more productive than lingering at the café. She left enough money on the table to cover the food, drink, and a reasonable tip. Then she added another nickel; hopefully the staff split tips left by patrons.

She buttoned up her coat, picked up Rebecca's story, and made her way out onto the walk. Sure she could manage the rest of the day, Charlotte took a steadying breath and returned to the *Times* office.

Nothing thwarted the headache. Charlotte had spent two hours at the Linotype, her ears plugged with bits of paper and her scarf wrapped around her head to muffle the noise, before she finally gave up. There was no way to keep the motor, small as it was, from making her head feel like it was ready to explode.

No more bourbon in the middle of the day for her. Though between Prohibition and the reduction of black market booze, she was probably safe from that prospect.

Head thrumming, she sat at Toliver's desk writing a note to the man about where she'd left off. There wasn't much more to do for the next day's edition, so she didn't feel too terrible about going home "sick." More aspirin and a good night's sleep were all she needed to get back on her feet.

As she finished the note, Charlotte spied the pages of Rebecca's story. She'd promised the girl she'd read them, though she hadn't set a timeframe. But curiosity overcame her head's thumping and she started to read.

Within the first page or so, Charlotte saw Rebecca's talent for storytelling had translated nicely to the page. There were some misspellings, and a few grammatical issues, but overall the story was engaging and fun. Just what you'd expect a twelve- or thirteen-year-old to enjoy, yet with a higher degree of aptitude than her years suggested. Rebecca had potential as a writer, and it would be beyond a shame not to have it nurtured.

But working instead of going to school wouldn't help that at all.

Perhaps if she could mentor Rebecca, get Toliver to publish this story and others, Ben would see how much his sister's life could benefit. Maybe even his as well.

She had to talk to him.

Tomorrow, her aching head pleaded.

But Charlotte knew that if she spent the night thinking about it she'd never sleep and never get rid of the damn headache. Better to try to talk to them now, or at least ask Ben to sit down with her tomorrow so they could work out a way for Rebecca to keep writing and contributing to the family.

She packed Rebecca's pages into her satchel and got her hat, coat, and boots. It was just after dinner. Would Ben and Rebecca be home? She stopped short on the walk outside the office. But where did they live? Being Ben's employer, and having employed Mrs. Derenov, Caroline Fiske might know.

Flashlight in hand to avoid the iciest of areas as she trudged up the hill to the Fiske home, Charlotte was breaking all manner of social protocol by intruding on Caroline at the dinner hour. Oh, well. It wasn't her first breach of etiquette and wasn't likely to be her last. She knocked.

Mrs. Munson opened the door. "Good evening, Miss Brody. How nice to see you."

She didn't seem terribly pleased to see Charlotte, but that wasn't a surprise.

"Good evening, Mrs. Munson. I'm sorry to intrude, but was wondering if you or Mrs. Fiske could tell me where Ben and Rebecca Derenov live?"

Mrs. Munson's lips pursed. "I'm afraid I don't know, and Mrs. Fiske—"

"Mrs. Munson, do have Miss Brody come inside," Caroline said as she came in from the dining room. Her simple black dress was more fashionable than most widows' garb. "It's too cold to be standing there with the door open."

With her back to her employee, Mrs. Munson gave Charlotte a withering look that said one thing: Make it fast.

Charlotte smiled at the housekeeper, then at Caroline. "Thank you. I just wanted to ask where the Derenovs live."

Mrs. Munson shut the door, but stood near so she could usher Charlotte out as soon as possible.

Caroline considered it for a moment. Perhaps she didn't know. Employers weren't necessarily concerned with the home lives of their employees. "They have a small house not far from where you're staying. Down Third Street, the fourth alley past that big spruce. Blue and white. Flower boxes in the windows"

Charlotte couldn't keep the surprise off her face. It was a more precise description than she'd expected.

"I brought some things over when Mrs. Derenov was ill, God rest her soul," Caroline said. "They live humbly, but Mrs. Derenov and Rebecca kept the place quite clean and tidy."

"Thank you. And sorry to bother you at dinner." Charlotte turned toward the door, which Mrs. Munson was already starting to open.

"Just a moment, Charlotte," Caroline said. "Mrs. Munson, can you tell Mr. and Mrs. Adler I'll be with them momentarily, and please close the sliding door."

The housekeeper gave Charlotte another annoyed glare. Mrs. Munson nodded to her employer, then did as she was bade, closing the door and leaving Charlotte and Caroline alone in the entry.

"I'm sorry," Charlotte said. "I didn't realize you had company."

"It's fine." Caroline waved off her intrusion, obviously concerned about something else. "Adam told me his brother has been arrested for illegal transport of alcohol."

"He has. I have a small article ready for the paper tomorrow." Was Caroline going to ask her to pull the piece? Charlotte lifted her chin, ready for a fight. She'd had it with being told what the *Times* should be reporting.

But Caroline nodded thoughtfully. "Good."

Good? That wasn't quite the reaction Charlotte expected. There didn't seem to be much love lost between Caroline and Otto, considering how he distained his brother's relationship with Mrs. Fiske, but "good"?

"Shouldn't you at least feel bad for Adam's sake?"

"I do," Caroline said. "Adam was quite distraught when the marshal and the deputy came into their home and arrested Otto. They accused him of colluding with his brother, but Otto rightfully and truthfully said Adam had nothing to do with anything." She smiled wryly. "Though he claimed his own innocence."

"It's difficult to claim innocence when evidence is staring the marshal in the face." Granted, the method of obtaining that evidence wasn't quite as pure as the marshal believed, but that wasn't the point at the moment. "Do you know if Otto was competing with Lyle over this as well as the hardware business market?"

Caroline didn't say anything at first. Staring at Charlotte, her jaw tightened, then she said, "I have no idea what you mean."

Denial, of course, was expected.

"No, Lyle wasn't one to let you help with the business, was he? So how could you possibly know he was running contraband? And I'll assume you knew nothing of his pawn operation either."

Her face darkened. "I'll thank you not to come into my home and accuse my dead husband of such things, Miss Brody."

"Is that why you wanted the box?" Charlotte asked. "Because it had his contacts down in Seattle, perhaps the codes he used to order certain items? That would certainly help you to maintain your current standard of living. Perhaps you and Otto had considered going into business together after Lyle was gone. Did you ask Adam if Otto had the black box? Or do you think Adam really did know about Otto's dealings? How could he not, being his accountant?"

Caroline paled, but from shock or guilt it was difficult to say. "Get out, Miss Brody. And if you print a word of any of this . . . this nonsense without proof, I will sue you and Andrew Toliver for everything you have."

That certainly wouldn't amount to a hill of beans.

"I won't print anything that isn't true, Mrs. Fiske. I actually hope you *aren't* guilty, that whoever killed your husband did so without your knowledge." Charlotte believed Adam Kenner was innocent of killing Lyle, that Caroline was truly upset, for her own reasons, that her husband was dead before it would be in her best interest. But something didn't add up. "I can't exactly condone your affair with Adam, but I can see why you have a relationship with him. And why you chose to stay married. I sincerely wish you the best."

It wasn't much in the way of apologies for accusing the widow and her lover, though it was the truth.

Caroline opened the door. "Good-bye, Miss Brody."

Charlotte retrieved her flashlight from her pocket and left, barely clearing the frame as the door slammed behind her. She hadn't wanted to make an enemy of the woman, but there was still too much circumstantial evidence that Otto Kenner had killed Lyle. How could Adam not have known what his brother was up to? How could Caroline not have known Lyle was selling illegal goods?

But knowledge of running a black market was not the same as conspiring to commit murder.

Navigating the frozen path back down to more level ground, Charlotte turned up the side street, then turned again onto Third, as if she was heading home. She passed the big spruce tree she and James had hidden behind when they saw Ben

Derenov down the first alley. What had he been doing there? No evidence showed him to be interested in more than peeking inside Kermit's window, perhaps just looking for his friend.

Charlotte turned down the fourth alley. There were three homes squeezed together along the narrow lane. Her light fell upon a white house with a blue door and blue window boxes, peeling paint revealing the weathered gray wood underneath. The window to the left of the door had been replaced with a dozen or so green bottles roughly the same size, mortared together with mud. Window glass was expensive; it made sense that one would use anything at hand to replace it. Soft light filtered through the green glass from within. Someone was home.

Charlotte knocked. She waited a few moments, then knocked again, louder.

Ben Derenov yanked the door open. Dressed in dungarees and a flannel shirt, in stocking feet, he scowled down at her. "What do you want?"

She refused to flinch or back down. "Mr. Derenov, I'd like to talk to you, if I may."

"Nothing we need to talk about."

He started to close the door. Charlotte stuck her foot in the way, wincing when the heavy wood struck her instep. "Please, Mr. Derenov, I just want a few minutes of your time."

Ben's frown deepened, his dark eyes piercing beneath thick brows. "Wipe your feet."

He turned and went inside. Charlotte quickly wiped her boots on the woven fiber mat, followed him in, and closed the door behind her. Boots were neatly lined up under the coats hanging from pegs near the door. The front room of the house was half the size of her own, open to a small kitchen with a table and two wooden chairs. Some sheets of wrinkled brown paper and a ball of twine were on the table alongside a pocket knife. To the left of the kitchen, a staircase, hardly more than a ladder, really, led to the upper floor. There was a closed door behind the ladder.

The coal stove in the corner kept the tidy front room toasty warm. The divan and rocking chair, both with lace doilies on the backs, were nowhere near new, but appeared clean. It was a humble home, as Caroline had said.

Floral patterns and soft pillows suggested the more feminine touch of Rebecca and Mrs. Derenov. Ben lived here, but there wasn't much of him present.

"What do you want?" he asked, standing in the middle of the room.

Charlotte had no choice but to stay by the door. That was fine. She'd stand on her head if it meant getting him to listen to her. "I wanted to know how Rebecca was doing."

And Ben himself, but she didn't think he'd appreciate the suggestion he wasn't doing well.

Confusion joined the irritation on his face. "She's fine. Why do you care?"

"I saw her at the café this afternoon."

"So? Who are you, the new truant officer?"

She knew this wouldn't be an easy conversation, and couldn't blame him for his hostility. Not that it would stop Charlotte. "No, but I think she'd rather be in school."

"You know what I think?" Ben's hands closed into large fists. "I think she'd like to eat every day."

Her heart broke for Ben and his sister. "Mr. Derenov, I know it's difficult to find a good job in this town." She reached into her satchel for Rebecca's story. "Have you read any of her writing? She's very good."

"You don't know anything, lady. You have a job. Rebecca and I have each other, that's it. No one in this town gives a good damn whether we live or die."

"That's not true," Charlotte said vehemently. "I give a damn. I care whether you and your sister are eating and have a home. I care that she has to work rather than go to school."

"You think I don't?" His voice rose in volume and pitch. "I'm her brother. I'm supposed to take care of her, but I can't.

Not on the pittance they give me for wages. I'd leave if I could, but I can't until I have money. And I can't get money until I have a damn job."

His frustration was palpable, and difficult to argue against.

Ben had a chip on his shoulder the size of Mt. Eyak, but who could blame him? He was the man of the house, responsible for his little sister. But how could he get out from under the reputation of troublesome kid? That's what people remembered about him. The fact he was trying to turn his life around didn't seem to count for much with some, like Mr. Hanson at the jewelry store. Good jobs were scarce, and there were plenty of reliable young men clamoring for work.

"I wish I had an answer for your troubles. I know you don't want charity, but I'll buy the earrings if you still have them."

He narrowed his eyes, clearly not understanding what she'd meant. "Earrings?"

Charlotte frowned. How could he not recall trying to sell the earrings after such a to-do at Hanson's? Or was Ben so used to being treated poorly that all the incidents ran together?

"I was in the jewelry store when you were trying to sell them to Mr. Hanson, remember? Rebecca hadn't recalled your mother having any jewelry but her wedding ring and the ruby ring. The earrings were your mother's, weren't they?"

His face turned red. Anger at the accusation, or something else?

"It can be difficult to part with loved ones' possessions." Charlotte didn't have to fake the sympathy in her voice. "I'm glad you were able to find the ruby ring. Rebecca should be able to keep that."

He stiffened, eyes widening. "Damn right she should, after all that happened."

"After all of what that happened, Ben? Where did you get the gold-and-pearl earrings?"

He opened his mouth, but then shut it quickly on whatever he was going to say. Charlotte's stomach fluttered nervously.

The more she said, the angrier he became, but she couldn't stop now. What she said next would either lead to confirmation of her suspicions that the earrings weren't Mrs. Derenov's or bring her right back to square one in figuring out what had happened.

"Did you try to sell them to Mr. Fiske? Did he refuse to give you what you were asking? He wasn't one to give much, and he charged way more than he should have to get things back, didn't he?"

She knew that was a complete fabrication, and by the confused and anxious look on Ben's face, he was trying to keep up with his own lies.

Charlotte had a gut feeling about the jewelry. Ben hadn't had the earrings to sell to Fiske. Between Della's description of what one of the other girls had given of her transaction with Fiske, Rebecca denying her mother had other jewelry, and Ben's hesitation at Hanson's store, she was almost positive they were an item in the black book. Which meant only one terrible, terrible thing. But what had led up to it?

"That son of a bitch," Ben spat out. He was breathing hard, his face contorted with rage. "He gave her barely the value of the ring then wanted more than twice that back? Who has that sort of money?"

The knot in Charlotte's stomach tightened. She pushed a little harder against Ben's story. "Ring? You mean earrings. The gold-and-pearl earrings."

"No. I mean—" He ran both hands through his hair, the expression on his face one of realization that he'd slipped.

No, the earrings had come from Fiske's box *after* he was murdered. Ben meant another piece. The ring Rebecca wore around her neck. The ring Ben had given Rebecca after she'd been told by Mrs. Derenov it was lost. Their mother hadn't lost it at all. Ben had "found" it after Lyle Fiske had died.

"Your mother pawned her ring to Fiske."

"She sent me the money. When I came home, I promised I'd

get it back, for Rebecca. But Fiske wouldn't sell it for what I had." Ben spoke through clenched teeth, his face dangerously red. "Ma's wages he gave us went to bills and the funeral and some food. Fiske had me work off the price of the ring at his place. No wages. Didn't give a damn my mother was dead, that my sister was hungry. So I—"

"You what, Ben? What happened that night? Did you hurt Lyle Fiske?"

He shook his head. "Not on purpose."

"I believe you." She did, but with his temper, it was also easy to believe Ben Derenov had become so angry at Lyle Fiske that he attacked the man. "You have to tell the marshal."

Fear drained the color from his face, made him seem at the same time both years younger and years older. "No. They'll put me in jail again. What would happen to Rebecca? No."

"Ben—"

"You can't tell them!"

He lunged for Charlotte.

Chapter 15

Charlotte screamed and dashed to the side. She stumbled over the rocker's runner, her satchel tangling around her.

"You can't," Ben roared.

He was scared. Angry. Reacting. Dangerous.

She had to get away.

Ben grabbed for her. His fingers dragged down the sleeve of her coat, caught the material at her elbow. She twisted to the side, fell to her hands and knees. Seeking a path to escape, she kicked out blindly behind her. Her boot thunked into something. Ben grunted.

He was behind her, between her and the door. There was no escape through the front. Was there a back door? She launched herself forward, toward the kitchen.

Charlotte scrambled to her feet. Ben clamped his hand around her ankle and yanked. She landed hard on her chest, a half-grunt, half-whimper escaping her. She turned onto her back and kicked at his face. He blocked her foot with his forearm, then wrapped his arm around her lower leg. Charlotte kicked with her other foot. It glanced off his cheek, but didn't stop him. Strong as he was, he easily grabbed that foot. His upper body pinned her legs.

No no no no no!

Charlotte braced her arms on the floor and tried to pull free. No use. He was so strong.

Ben took hold of the front of her coat with one large hand. Keeping much of his weight on her, he threw himself up the length of her body, landing hard. The breath whooshed from Charlotte's lungs. She fell back, smacking her head on the floor. The world tilted. Lights burst behind her eyelids. His viselike fist gripped her throat.

"You can't tell them," Ben said, his voice rough. His rage-etched face hovered over hers. "They won't believe me."

She tried to say they'd believe the truth, but only a strangled sound emerged from her throat. She couldn't breathe. Her head swam.

"Ben, what are you doing?" Rebecca's voice, filled with fear and confusion. "Get off her!"

He loosened his grip slightly as he turned toward his sister, giving Charlotte a chance to draw breath. "She knows."

Rebecca came into Charlotte's line of sight. She yanked on her brother's arm. "Let her go, Ben! Let her go!"

Ben reared back, attempting to get his sister to stop without harming her, further loosening his hold on Charlotte's throat. She sucked in a breath and freed one arm. Making a fist, she swung, catching him in the nose.

He yowled and blood gushed. Rebecca pulled harder.

"No, Ben, stop. You have to stop!"

Whether from realization of what he was doing or his sister's words, Ben Derenov slid off Charlotte. He crumpled at his sister's feet.

Charlotte rolled away, coughing, her throat raw and bruised. Her heart pounded and her body ached. She lay on her side, her back to Rebecca and Ben. Was he going to hurt Rebecca or try to hurt her again?

She started to roll back toward them and heard sobbing. Not Rebecca, Ben. He was on his knees beside his kneeling sister, bent over with his head on her shoulder. Rebecca stroked his back, tears streaming down her face.

"Are you all right? What happened, Miss Brody? Why was he—" A sob broke her voice. "Why was he like that? Why was he hurting you?"

Charlotte sat up, legs bent and to the side. She leaned forward with one hand braced on the floor. "Ben," she said, the word rasping out of her injured throat. "Ben, it'll be all right."

She wasn't sure of that, but she had to tell him something.

"What happened?" Rebecca asked again, more steel in her now. Ben lifted his head. "I didn't mean it."

She frowned. "Didn't mean what? Why were you hurting Miss Brody?"

He glanced at Charlotte, his eyes wet and blood trickling from his nose. "I'm sorry."

Charlotte nodded. "What happened with Mr. Fiske, Ben?"

"I just wanted Mama's ring back." He spoke to Rebecca. "I promised her I'd get it back. I tried to talk to Mr. Fiske, but he put me off and put me off. Like I wasn't worth his time."

He was starting to sound angry again, and Charlotte braced herself for another outburst. Ben bowed his head, took a deep breath, and blew it out slowly in an effort to keep himself calm. For his sister's sake.

"I went to the store that night," he said, staring down at the floor. "Fiske was there. Alone. I threatened to hurt him, made him open the safe and take out the box. Mama told me that's where it was, in the box. All I wanted was the ring, but there were some nice things in there." He brought his gaze back up to Rebecca. "While I was looking inside the box, he took a swing at me with a hammer. I ducked and shoved him. He came at me again. That's when I grabbed the knife out of the display behind the counter."

Rebecca gasped, her eyes wide as he told his story. "Ben . . ."

"I had to do something. If they found out it was me, they'd take me away and put you in some sort of orphanage or something. I tried to make it look like a robbery, but the till was near empty when I opened it. Then I thought a fire would burn the body, cover the whole thing." Ben shook his head. "So stupid."

"What about the black box?" Charlotte asked softly.

He didn't look her way. "I must have just taken it after I set the fire. Didn't realize I had it until I was halfway home."

Rebecca's face was a mask of emotions. Sorrow, disbelief, horror. Charlotte couldn't imagine what it was like to hear someone you love admit to such a terrible crime.

"You were returning things to people," Charlotte said, trying to ease the pain they were both feeling. "You gave Della's cross back to her. She was so happy to have it again. What else, Ben? What else did you give back?"

"Walt Peter's pocketknife, one of those fancy ones, is on the table there." he said. "Mac Cahill's watch. Jackie Karnoff's World's Fair coin. Kermit moved. I was gonna send him his knife when I got some money."

Charlotte didn't recognize anyone except Kermit.

"You got their names from the black book."

He nodded. "Some people aren't around anymore. Dead or moved away. I figured I could sell those things if they didn't have family about." Meeting Rebecca's eyes, he winced. "It wasn't a lot, and I couldn't sell most of it. I just wanted money so we could go someplace else. Start over." Now he turned his head and frowned at Charlotte. "But we can't, can we? Not now."

Charlotte swallowed hard, wincing at the pain in her throat. The only people who knew what Ben had done were in this room, and she wasn't sure he'd be willing to let her walk out the door.

"Ben." Rebecca laid her palms on his cheeks and turned his head back so he looked at her, not Charlotte. "She won't say anything. We'll let Miss Brody go, and she'll promise to keep quiet. Right, Miss Brody?"

Charlotte clamped her jaws tight. She knew what Rebecca was doing, but she couldn't agree to what Rebecca was suggesting. She had to tell James what she knew, even if it hurt Rebecca by losing her brother.

Ben got to his feet and pulled Rebecca to hers. He pinned Charlotte to where she sat with his dark, hard glare. He'd killed a man and had tried to shut her up. Would he try again?

Charlotte's mind whirled. How could she escape? Which door would be easier and faster to access? Could she outrun Ben Derenov? Rebecca?

Her gut churned and her heart twinged at the thought of Rebecca being involved in that sort of thing. Would she turn on Charlotte to protect her brother? The fear and sorrow in her young face made Charlotte think not. Hope not.

"The black box is under my bed, upstairs," Ben said. "I'll go get it, then we'll head to the marshal's office."

Rebecca put her hand on his broad chest. "Ben, no. We can—"

He covered her hand with his and gave her a crooked smile. "No, Becs, we can't. I messed up. Again. I can't drag you off and expect you to have anything close to a normal life." His voice dropped to a rough whisper. "I promised Mama I'd do better, for you, and I couldn't."

Rebecca's breath hitched. She understood what he was doing, what he was sacrificing for her. Tears stung Charlotte's eyes.

"You tried," Rebecca said. "I know you tried."

He looked at Charlotte, anguish lining his face. "She needs to be taken care of, Miss Brody. You'll see to that, right? You'll make sure she stays in school and works hard and does her chores."

Rebecca buried her face in her brother's flannel shirt. Her shoulders shook with silent sobs.

Charlotte nodded. "I promise."

* * *

James gently shut the door leading to the jail cells behind him. He stood there for a moment, hands on his hips, staring at the floor. Charlotte tried to watch him from the corner of her eye, but Michael kept touching her jaw to encourage her to turn her head back toward him. When James had seen the bruises on Charlotte's throat, he'd insisted they call Michael as soon as he had Ben squared away in the cell next to Otto Kenner's.

"Just give me a minute to check your throat and I'll leave you be," Michael said in his doctor tone. "Now, open your mouth."

Feeling somewhat silly, but wanting to get the exam over with, Charlotte did as he asked, opening her mouth and making the obligatory "aaahhhhh" sound.

Michael flicked on his flashlight and pointed it down her throat. "Some swelling. Gargle with warm saltwater, and you can suck on some hard candies if you'd like."

"I think she has mints on her," James said as he sat at his desk.

Charlotte closed her mouth and stared at him. He winked. Did he know where she'd gotten them and why? Probably. It was becoming quite clear that Deputy Eddington played his cards close to his chest and wasn't quite the straight-and-narrow sort she'd assumed he was.

She smiled. He smiled back and touched his fingers to his forehead in salute.

"That would be fine," Michael said, oblivious to their exchange as he packed his satchel. "Are Rebecca and Ben all right? I'll take a look at them, if you think I should."

James shook his head. "Ben's got a bruised cheek and a bloody nose. Said he was fine."

"Rebecca's not hurt," Charlotte said, her voice gravelly. "Physically, anyway. This situation with Ben is going to tear her up. She thinks it's her fault."

"Nonsense," Michael said. "She didn't ask him to do anything."

"No, but he did it *for* her. You know how siblings can be." Charlotte smiled sadly when he met her eyes.

"True. And stop talking so much. You'll make your throat worse."

"Good luck with that," James muttered.

Charlotte stuck her tongue out at him.

"I can have someone come for Rebecca," Michael said. "I think Mary is a second cousin of some kind. She'll know who can take her in."

That made sense, of course, to have the girl stay with family. Yet there was a pang of disappointment within Charlotte. She'd promised to look after Rebecca, see to her schooling, and would do her best, but from a distance if Rebecca went to live elsewhere.

"We should ask Rebecca what she wants to do," Charlotte said.

The two men looked at her. Michael nodded. James seemed surprised.

"Then I won't talk to Mary until you let me know." Michael put on his hat and coat. "I'll check in on you tomorrow, Charlotte. Good night, Eddington."

"Good night, Doc." After Michael was gone, James leaned back in his chair and scrubbed his palms over his bearded cheeks. "I'll let Rebecca visit with Ben for a bit, then we'll figure out what to do with her for the time being."

"She can stay with me if she wants."

His brow creased. "You sure that's a good idea?"

"Why not? Rebecca and I are friends, and I promised Ben I'd take care of her." Did he think she couldn't handle a girl like Rebecca?

"You're pretty much responsible for her brother being in jail. Don't you think that will make things awkward?"

So he wasn't questioning her ability to take care of another person, just Rebecca's ability to understand what was happening and separate cause and effect. "She knows exactly who did what and why, James. Give the girl some credit."

"I do," he said, "but these aren't normal circumstances. Doesn't she have family nearby?"

Charlotte shook her head. "As Michael said, cousins of some sort, but no one close since the fallout with her father's family." She patted his arm, assuring him as well as herself. "It'll be fine. I'll see about some sort of guardianship, if you think it's necessary."

James didn't seem convinced. "She's a young girl whose life has come crashing down around her, Charlotte. It might get dicey."

"I think the family would take her in without question, despite the problems the father had, but I don't know. Rebecca should have a say in where she wants to live, don't you think?"

With a heavy sigh, he stared at the door marked "Jail." "I'm really not sure what the answer is."

"We'll figure it out." She laid her hand on his arm to get his attention. "And we'll abide by what she wants."

"She's just a kid," James said, frowning.

"And sometimes kids have to deal with very grown-up decisions and emotions." Charlotte couldn't help but think of Henry as well, struggling with his feelings about what happened to his family. "I think she's capable."

Silence hung between them. Charlotte ran her fingers over Lyle Fiske's black box where it sat on his desk. Caroline had been right about what was inside; there were insurance papers and a notarized will. Whether these were more recent than anything else Lyle had drawn up remained to be seen, but that wasn't James's or Charlotte's concern.

"I wonder what Caroline knew?" James asked as if reading her mind.

Also inside the box was the moleskin-covered notebook listing the pawned goods, the customers, and what Fiske paid. There were very few notations of items having been bought back by his customers and a number of notes on what was received as payment for items sold.

Pawning wasn't illegal, but Lyle wasn't licensed, and usury

charges for the interest rates he forced on his customers would have seen him doing time in jail if he'd been caught.

James had plans to search Fiske's inventory statements and storerooms as well, at least what he could recover from the ruins of the building or from any records kept at home. Indications he was ordering beyond his store's needs, as Otto Kenner was doing, could help prove his role in the local black market. But it was likely any illegal goods were now well-hidden, and more likely any evidence of whom he'd dealt with in town through falsified inventory and order lists had gone up in flames. Brigit would be grateful for that.

"You know someone will take the loss of Lyle and Otto as an opportunity," she said.

"I know." He nodded thoughtfully. "But anyone else bringing in unusually large shipments is going to have to take extra care. The city just hired two more policemen. The marshal and I will have more time to poke about the docks now."

"Should I write something up to let the smugglers know, or do you want it to be a surprise?"

"I think a surprise would be more fun, don't you?"

Charlotte laughed. Her throat stung.

Rebecca slipped in from the jail room. She cast a furtive glance at James as she walked to Charlotte. "Ben's gonna be all right, won't he?"

Charlotte held her arms open. Rebecca came to her. The two hugged, Rebecca's head on Charlotte's shoulder, facing away from James. Charlotte held his gaze as she spoke to the girl. "Deputy Eddington will make sure he's comfortable until they go to Valdez tomorrow. Then the courts will make sure he gets a fair trial."

God, she hoped so.

James winced, but recovered quickly, lest Rebecca see his expression. Ben was being charged with robbery, murder, arson, and several lesser charges. His prospects for anything less than life in prison were grim.

She'd already agreed to be a witness at his trial, hoping her testimony might mitigate his sentence. There were no guarantees, of course, but she had to do what she could, for Rebecca's sake.

Rebecca straightened and eased out of Charlotte's arms. "He told me to remind you the money he got for the stuff he sold is all in the box." She looked over at James. "He really tried hard to get things back to their rightful owners."

James's furrowed brow smoothed. "I know. I made sure it was in the statement I took down." He tapped the file labeled "Fiske, Lyle." "His lawyer and the judge will know everything."

Rebecca's smile was fleeting and uncertain, as if she wanted to believe it would all be well. Charlotte knew Rebecca understood that Ben would never see freedom again, but she still held on to a glimmer of hope.

Charlotte rose, and gathered Rebecca's hand in hers. "If you're ready, we can stop by your house and pack a few things for the next several days. We can see about having you stay with family. . . ." Rebecca made a face that said she wasn't keen on that particular idea. "Or you can stay with me."

Rebecca's eyes widened in surprise. "With you?"

"If you want to," Charlotte said, trying to sound welcoming but not so eager as to overwhelm her.

Worry crossed the girl's face. "Are you sure about this, Miss Brody? I mean, I like you, and we're friends and all, but I don't want to be trouble."

She'd been trying not to be trouble all her life, Charlotte realized. Rebecca had worked hard in school, was the good girl her mother needed her to be, not a burden, like her brother. And she'd succeeded. But now, Rebecca needed to succeed for her own good, not to please anyone other than herself. Not even Charlotte.

Charlotte smiled at her and gently squeezed her hand. "We are friends, so it will never be troublesome to have you around.

And I want you to call me Charlotte." Rebecca stared at her as if Charlotte had suggested dancing down Main Street in her small clothes. Good lord, she hoped she hadn't traumatized the poor girl. "Unless you're more comfortable with Miss Brody. That's fine."

After a moment, Rebecca gave her a tentative smile. "I've never called a grown-up by their first name. It might take some getting used to."

The whole situation would take some getting used to for the both of them, but if it meant keeping Rebecca safe, healthy, and in school, then it was well worth it to Charlotte.

"I'm sure you'll catch on quick," Charlotte said, winking at her. She met James's eyes, glad to see he was smiling too. Good. Now they could all get used to the idea. "If there's anything else you need, deputy, just let us know."

"I'll do that." He came around the desk and escorted them to the door. "Good evening, Miss Brody." Then, turning to Rebecca, "Miss Derenov."

Rebecca's cheeks pinkened. "Deputy."

Out on the walkway, Charlotte fished the flashlight out of her pocket. A light snow was starting to fall. They walked in silence most of the way down Main Street, hearing only the sound of their boots on the frozen, icy walk.

"Ben wouldn't have killed Mr. Fiske if he didn't have to get the ring for me." Rebecca's words were so soft Charlotte had almost missed them.

She stopped abruptly and turned Rebecca to face her. "No, don't think like that. Ben wanted to fulfill your mother's wishes, but how he went about it has nothing to do with you, honey. He told us that right off."

Tears welled in the girl's eyes. "I know, but I can't help it."

Charlotte wiped away the tear that ran down her cheek. "Guilt can be an insidious thing, Rebecca. You blame yourself because Ben did what he did out of love for you, but you can't be responsible for someone else's actions."

Rebecca nodded, but Charlotte wasn't sure she was convinced. She might never completely believe it.

"Oh, Rebecca." Charlotte drew her into a hug. "We humans are such fallible creatures, doing the wrong thing for the right reasons."

Rebecca looked up at Charlotte. "That's kind of what I told Ben."

Once again, she marveled at the girl's ability to see the deeper issue. "You were trying to make him feel better, but now it's time for you to believe it as well. This isn't your fault."

Rebecca stared at her for another few moments, then nodded again. Maybe she would start believing it sooner than Charlotte feared, but Charlotte was well aware of how guilt could worm its way into your brain and stay there. So far, the best remedy for Charlotte had been time, and learning to trust others when you felt at your worst.

"You can talk to me whenever you need to, Rebecca." Charlotte touched the girl's cheek. "It helps me to talk to friends when I'm feeling bad about things."

Where would she be without Kit or Michael or Brigit? Talking to them hadn't alleviated all of her guilt, of course, but they'd certainly helped her come to terms with what she'd done.

"I will," Rebecca said. "I promise."

"Good." Charlotte hooked her arm through Rebecca's and they continued down Main Street. "Now let's get back to the house. We'll have some tea, and I want to talk to you about that wonderful story you wrote."

Please turn the page for an exciting sneak peek of
Cathy Pegau's next Charlotte Brody mystery

MURDER ON LOCATION

coming in March 2017
wherever print and e-books are sold!

Chapter 1

The S S. *Fairbanks* made its approach to the Cordova ocean harbor, belching black smoke that quickly dissipated on the icy breeze. Anticipation from the crowd waiting on the dock was as thick as the aroma of tar, tide, and the exhaust from the line of idling automobiles. Sunlight glinted off the gray-green water and the bright white of the hull of the ship still one hundred yards away.

Charlotte Brody smiled at the memory of coming in on a similar vessel just six months ago. Still a "cheechako" in the eyes of Alaskans, she was settling into her new home. Plans to return East come spring—only a week or so away—had been indefinitely postponed.

The steamer's air horn blew three times, and the largest gathering of Cordovans Charlotte had ever seen in one place cheered in response, waving hats and hands.

"Isn't this exciting?" a woman standing beside Charlotte asked no one in particular. Smiling and starry-eyed, the woman brandished a rolled-up movie magazine like a member of the Signal Corps conveying messages to troops.

Charlotte didn't quite share the woman's or the crowd's

enthusiasm. Half the population must have turned out for the *Fairbanks*'s arrival. Who knew Cordova, home to some of the most practical people she'd ever met, would become positively giddy over a film crew coming to town?

Then again, given the cold, dark quiet of the winter they had just been through, the arrival of such unusual persons gave the town a boost to its torpid mood. Despite the calendar claiming it was mid-March, the more vitalizing days of the coming season were still a month or so away.

A frozen, salty gust blew in off the water. Charlotte shivered within her heavy coat and the trousers she wore. It was also a few tens of degrees from what she knew as spring.

Maybe more like two months away.

If she hadn't been assigned to cover the event, Charlotte would have happily stayed in her warm little house and avoided the whole thing. Or at least most of the fanfare and over-the-top events, at any rate. Andrew Toliver, her boss—and owner of the *Cordova Daily Times*—would have done it himself, but a fall on a slippery step had broken his foot. Being the only other writer on the paper, it fell to Charlotte to cover the most exciting thing to happen to Cordova since the railroad.

Toliver insisted she chronicle the visit by the Californians, painting Cordova in as positive a light as she could. He was sure the articles would be picked up by other newspapers, particularly those in areas where filmmaking was growing, and put the booming town in the minds of the rest of the country, if not the world.

Charlotte flexed her fingers within her mittens in an attempt to get them warm enough to use her pad and pencil when it came time to take notes. She would do her job and do it well, for the sake of the paper and for the town she now called home. The cast and crew would be here in Cordova for two weeks. Maybe she'd get caught up in the excitement.

God, I hope so, Charlotte thought as she watched the *Fairbanks* maneuver into position alongside the dock.

While she could admit interest in watching films—they were a great way to entertain or educate—she just didn't understand the growing popularity of the actors to the point that ordinary people seemed to put them above others. Many had excellent talents, and some poignant films had been made, but she saw no reason to elevate actors to an idealistic or romanticized status. There were plenty of other people doing real work who deserved acknowledgment and recognition.

Bells rang aboard ship. Several uniformed members of the *Fairbanks* crew threw thick lines over the rails to the longshoremen on the dock. Once the steamer was fastened and the engines throttled down to a low rumble, the gangplank was lowered and secured. Conversations in the crowd became random cheers and whistles, yet no one on the dock moved closer to the vessel. Charlotte noted a number of men facing the crowd now, standing at regular intervals and giving warning glares to any who dared to pass.

Security for the Californians? What did they think was going to happen in Cordova?

After several moments, a mustached man in a tweed cap and khaki trench coat with a motion picture camera balanced on his shoulder carefully limped down the gangplank. He set the legs of the tripod on the dock. After making a few adjustments to the box, he aimed the lens toward the top of the gangplank and checked the viewfinder.

He cupped his hand around his mouth. "Ready to roll!"

The cameraman turned his cap around, bent to look through the viewfinder, and began cranking.

A man in his forties strode across the deck and stopped at the top of gangplank. He wore a bowler hat, a thick white scarf around his neck, and a long black coat. The people on the dock began clapping and cheering. Who was he?

Behind him, a group of men and women gathered in a semi-circle. All were bundled against the cold and not recognizable. A few waved to the people on the dock, much to the delight of several onlookers by the sound of their exclamations.

Smiling, the man in front raised a megaphone and spoke to the attentive audience. "Thank you. Thank you, my friends," his voice boomed from the cone. "It's so wonderful to be back here in Cordova." He swept his hand in a gesture to encompass everything before him. "The most beautiful city in the Alaska Territory."

Cheers and whistles exploded from the dock dwellers, temporarily deafening Charlotte.

"Hey, Wally, you owe me a sawbuck!" someone shouted from the crowd.

Everyone laughed, including the man on the ship.

"And I'll pay it back, I promise," he said, still smiling. "Because with the help of all you fine folks and *North to Fortune,* we're gonna put Cordova on every map and on every mind in the country."

This man could run for mayor.

"For those of you who don't know me, my name is Wallace Meade."

The name was familiar to Charlotte, and now she had a face to go with it. Wallace Meade owned several properties in Cordova and was generous to local organizations. Meade also had business interests in other towns throughout the territory, including a gold mine in Fairbanks and a tract of land near Juneau where he ran a lumber mill.

Meade had been away for months, Charlotte had learned, busy in California and New York drumming up interest for the up-and-coming film industry to look north. According to Andrew Toliver, Meade had finally managed to engage the crew he needed to produce what was supposedly going to be a "truer than life" depiction of Alaska.

Whatever that meant.

"I know the good people of Cordova," Meade continued, "and I've assured the cast and crew that you're the friendliest bunch north of Seattle." The crowd cheered again, and Meade's smile broadened. "So let me introduce a few of these folks to you." He gestured for a tall, thin man to step forward. The man wore similar outerwear as Meade, but his coat collar was fur and his scarf was pulled up over his nose and mouth. "This here is Stanley Welsh, director of such notable films as *A Place in Their Hearts* and *Granger's Last Stand*. Stanley?"

Charlotte had heard of the films, but hadn't seen either of them. One was a murder mystery and the other something about battles during the Civil War.

People cheered, and Welsh took the megaphone from Meade. He tugged his scarf down, revealing his smooth-shaved face and narrow features. "Hello, Cordova!" Welsh waited for the noise to die down. "We are so very happy to be here and appreciate your fine welcome on a cold day."

Charlotte thought she detected something of an accent in the man's speech, but couldn't place it. Eastern European, perhaps?

"When Mr. Meade told us about your lovely town and showed us pictures, I knew right away it would be perfect for our film, *North to Fortune*. Some wanted us to wait a few more months until it warmed up, but I wanted to have my cast experience the real Alaska, cold and all. Authenticity, you know!"

"Only if you fixed the story!" a man shouted from behind the crowd.

Several people turned to see who had interrupted the director. No one stepped forward, and Welsh ignored the comment.

What was that all about?

"We will be here in Cordova for approximately two weeks," Welsh continued, "filming exterior shots of the mountains, glaciers, and lake. Our cast and crew are the best and ready for anything. I think some of you are familiar with our lead players."

Welsh smiled as a younger man stepped forward to wave to the crowd. His head was bare, his dark hair slicked back.

A woman shouted, "I love you, Peter!"

"Yes," Welsh said, "Peter York will be playing Lawrence Trumbull, our hero. And Roslyn Sanford is our leading lady." A petite woman came up beside York, waving. She could have been anyone; she was so bundled in furs, it was difficult to see her face. "We're all terribly pleased to be here, but we should let everyone get off the boat now. Thank you."

Welsh and Meade shook hands, holding the position as a still photographer on the dock took a picture. The photographer gave the men a "thumbs-up" gesture, and the two released hands. Meade took the megaphone from Welsh. "Tonight, we'll present a few brief scenes from the film and have some other thrilling performances at the Empress Theater," Meade said into the megaphone. "Eight o'clock curtain. Be sure to get your tickets."

"I have mine," the rosy-cheeked woman beside Charlotte said, flapping the movie magazine. "Goodness, that Peter York is a handsome devil, isn't he?"

"I suppose," Charlotte said, mostly to herself, as she jotted notes.

"In his last movie, he played a sheik prince." The woman sighed dramatically, and Charlotte wondered if she'd have to catch her should she faint. "So handsome."

The crowd parted as the cast and crew descended the gangplank, creating a narrow lane for the visitors to reach their awaiting cars. Cordova didn't have enough taxis to take them all, of course. The vehicles belonged to private citizens, hired for the sole purpose of transporting these particular VIPs. The audience would have to find their own way back to town.

Meade led the way, followed by Welsh and a statuesque woman holding his arm. Behind them, Peter York escorted Roslyn Sanford. At least a dozen more well-dressed people, obviously not Cordovans by the way they stared up at the surrounding mountains in wide-eyed wonder. A tall, bespectacled young woman gazed intently at her new environs as if absorbing every detail.

A few of the men broke away from the California group and moved directly to the longshoremen. One man gestured toward the ship, a crane, then to two waiting flatbed trucks. The shore man nodded, his cigar bobbing up and down as he chewed on the stub.

Shuffling across the slick dock with shoulders hunched against the cold, the visitors piled into the cars. The Cordovans followed as close as the security men would allow, some shouting requests for autographs, others their declarations of love.

"Miss Brody?" Mr. Jenkins, the Alaska Steamship Company agent, came up beside her, grinning broadly.

Charlotte took his extended hand and shook it. "Good afternoon. Quite the excitement today."

"Yes, indeed," he said, gazing out at the crowd. "We haven't had this sort brouhaha for some time." Jenkins focused on her again. "Mr. Meade was wondering if you would accompany him and the others to the hotel for an interview."

Charlotte stared at the agent. "Me? How does Mr. Meade know about me?"

Jenkins shook his head, shrugging. "He asked if there were any newsmen about. I told him I thought I saw you in the crowd. He asked me to fetch you."

The back of Charlotte's neck tightened. "Fetch?"

Perhaps she was overreacting, but she was a grown woman, a professional journalist, not something to be retrieved. And Mr. Jenkins wasn't a dog. She would not be at the beck and call of Wallace Meade, no matter what sort of do-gooder he was in the community.

"Um, I'm sure I misheard him," Jenkins said, eyes large with distress as he watched her reaction. "Yes, my apologies, I'm sure I did. Would you follow me, Miss Brody? Please?"

She should say no. She should tell Mr. Jenkins to tell Mr.

Meade to take a flying leap. But she shouldn't judge without facing the man himself. Perhaps he was just tired after a long voyage. There would be plenty of opportunity to see what he was like.

Giving the man the benefit of the doubt, for now, Charlotte forced a smile. "Lead the way, Mr. Jenkins."

Relief eased the tension lines from his narrow face. "Thank you. Over here."

He gestured toward the line of automobiles and started to make a path through the crowd. The onlookers reluctantly moved aside as Jenkins tapped shoulders and requested passage. When they finally reached the edge of the group facing the vehicles, Charlotte noted the men keeping the Cordovans from mobbing the visitors had closed ranks. Jenkins told the nearest one that he was escorting Charlotte at Mr. Meade's request.

The man gave Charlotte a quick once-over, then pointed a thumb toward the vehicle at the front of the line, a new deep green Oakland touring car that Charlotte recognized as belonging to Clive Wilkes, his Studebaker having given up the ghost in December. The passenger side front door opened, and Wallace Meade stepped out. The bespectacled young woman Charlotte had seen earlier sat beside the driver. She gave Charlotte a shy smile.

"Mr. Meade," Jenkins said, "this is Miss Charlotte Brody of the *Cordova Daily Times*. Miss Brody, Mr. Meade."

Meade stuck out his right hand. "Nice to meet you, little lady. Andrew Toliver speaks highly of you."

Little lady? Gritting her teeth, Charlotte offered a firm grip to counter the barely there pressure many men provided when shaking hands with a woman. "He's often spoken of you too, Mr. Meade."

Meade's dark eyes narrowed, then glinted with amusement when he realized she hadn't necessarily paid him a compliment. "Indeed. Please, join us for the ride back to town." He opened the rear door. Director Stanley Welsh and the woman he'd escorted down the gangplank sat on the leather bench seat. "Stanley, Carmen, this is Miss Brody from the local paper. Miss Brody, Stanley and Carmen Welsh, and that's their daughter Cicely up front."

"Pleased to meet you," Charlotte said, shaking the hands of each of the elder Welshes and smiling at Cicely, who peered over the front seat.

Mr. Welsh slid closer to the opposite side of the car, pressing himself against the other door. Mrs. Welsh made room for her.

Charlotte climbed in beside the Welshes, notebook and pencil in hand. Once she was seated, Meade closed the door and returned to his place in front. It was close quarters in the car, considering all their bulky outerwear, but not uncomfortable. Still, Charlotte was glad it was a short ride into town.

"Let's go," Meade said to the driver. He then turned to address the backseat. Poor Cicely Welsh. She was squashed to the driver's shoulder, angling her head to keep Meade from talking into her face. Meade seemed oblivious. "Toliver cabled me to say he was laid up with a broken foot, but that you'd be spot-on ideal for the job of writing up articles for the next couple weeks."

Spot-on ideal? Charlotte was amused with Toliver's fib. He knew she wasn't exactly thrilled with the assignment. But knowing Meade's success was due in no small part to his ability to soft-soap folks to get what he wanted, maybe it wasn't Toliver's wording at all.

"I don't know about ideal, Mr. Meade," she said. "I certainly enjoy going to the theater, but I'm not well-versed in the film business."

Stanley Welsh smiled. "Probably all the better for us."

Wincing suddenly, Welsh turned his head toward the window and coughed into a fold of his scarf.

"Are you okay, Papa?" Cicely asked, her brow drawn with concern. Welsh waved her off, the coughing less intense. Cicely frowned, keeping an eye on her father.

"Film is a marvelous world," Meade said as Welsh recovered from his bout. "Full of so much potential and growing every day. Why, I expect moving pictures will smother live theater in a few short years—"

"That would be a sad day," Carmen Welsh interjected. "There should be both."

Silently agreeing, Charlotte jotted down their exchange in short-hand, willing to let the conversation play out rather than interfere with questions for the moment.

"I should say so, my dear." Stanley Welsh patted his wife's arm. Charlotte couldn't tell if it was in true support or as pacification in front of a stranger. And a reporter, to boot. "What I think Wallace means is that as wonderful as live shows are, the ability to distribute film around the world will enable scores more to enjoy a story. Get the media to the masses."

"Exactly," Meade said. "Especially up here. It's cheaper to send reels of film than casts and crews for live shows. And by the same token, why shouldn't the natural beauty of Alaska be shared around the world?" He twisted further in his seat to better focus on Charlotte. "That's why I traveled from studio to studio, director to director, looking for someone who'd appreciate the natural wonder of the territory."

"And that's when you found Mr. Welsh?" Charlotte asked.

"Indeed." Meade beamed at the director. "Stanley talked to Roslyn about coming in, since she'd such a crowd pleaser, and Cicely here wrote a bang-up scenario."

Charlotte had read the credits titles on some films, happily noting how many women were involved in productions. "*North to Fortune* is your story, Miss Welsh? How wonderful. Have you written many?"

Cicely's cheeks pinked. "A few. Roslyn is under contract with the studio, but she's popular enough now to choose her films. I've written three other scenarios at her insistence. We work well together."

"Roslyn has the heart of the audiences and the ear of the studio head," Stanley said, chuckling. "If she requests a certain director or writer, then it will be done if it means getting her to agree to do a picture. Not to mention Cicely is quite talented."

"I'm pleased to see women with so much say in the industry," Charlotte said. "Have any of you been to Alaska before—besides Mr. Meade, I mean?"

"No, none of us have." Cicely gazed out the windscreen. "It's as beautiful as Mr. Meade said. I read up as best I could while writing the story and figured we could change things as needed to remain accurate. Right, Papa?"

"Of course, of course." Stanley waved a hand in dismissal, perhaps, as if they'd had that discussion in the past. "But we also want an exciting story that grabs the audience." He clenched a fist and raised it in enthusiasm. "Action! Adventure! Heroic deeds! That's what sells."

Carmen covered her husband's fist and lowered it. "Don't get overexcited dear. Along with that, we want characters that people can rally behind and believable plots."

Stanley pecked his wife on the cheek. "That as well."

"You see, Miss Brody," Meade said, "there's a lot involved with making a film on location. The production company was initially reluctant to help fund the trip, but Stanley and I convinced them authenticity was key."

"Absolutely," Charlotte said.

"We want this film to be made with the full support of the town," Meade continued. "Can we count on you to help with that?"

Charlotte made a gesture in the direction of the dock behind them. "You saw the crowd, Mr. Meade. I'm quite sure you have it already."

Meade grinned. "Yes, and it was a glorious reception. But the entire town won't be out with us when we do location shots. At least I hope not." He chuckled at his own words. "Which means, anything reported back to them, and subsequently picked up by other papers in the States, can potentially influence the success of this film or future projects brought up here."

Ah, so that was it. Meade wanted to make sure the *Times* painted things in a positive light. Charlotte couldn't blame him, of course, but she wasn't his publicist, she was a journalist.

"Do you anticipate any problems?" she asked.

"There's always some sort of difficulty or another on a film," Meade said.

"I'm not quite sure I understand what you're getting at, Mr. Meade. Do you mean the man who shouted about fixing the story?"

Meade and Welsh exchanged looks that Charlotte could only interpret as a brief, silent argument. Carmen quirked a slender eyebrow at her husband, and Cicely seemed as confused as Charlotte. Finally, Welsh appeared to give up, shaking his head and glancing out the window.

Meade focused on Charlotte over the seat. "A month or so ago, just after we announced our intent to come up here and revealed the basic plot of *North to Fortune,* I received a letter."

Charlotte's curiosity stirred. "What sort of letter?"

"Someone had revealed the details of the film and it found the ear of some lawyer in Juneau. There seem to be concerns that the portrayal of Natives may be undignified," Meade said.

Cicely's mouth dropped open. "Mr. Meade, you never mentioned that to me. As the scenarist, I want to make sure—"

"We took care of it, Cicely," Stanley Welsh said, his voice hard. "I told Wallace not to bother you with it."

"Not to bother me?" Cicely turned around as best she could without impeding the driver. Her face was red with anger. "If my story isn't accurate or someone finds it insulting, I need to know."

"It was just some blowhard." Welsh gave a dismissive shake of his head. "Everyone gets these sorts of letters. If we abided by every fool who got their feelings hurt, we'd never get a film made. Don't put that in your article, if you please, Miss Brody."

Charlotte had stopped taking notes, but she certainly took note of Welsh's attitude. "Who wrote the letter?"

Everyone but the driver looked to Wallace Meade. Did they not realize the man behind the wheel had ears and a mouth? Or was he being paid enough to keep mum?

"It was signed by the president of the Alaska Eyak Council, Jonas Smith, and a lawyer out of Juneau, Caleb Burrows," Meade said. "I know the men by reputation only, and they're no fools, Welsh, I told you that. Wrote back to assure them the film would be truthful."

Charlotte recognized Smith's name and the AEC, a small but growing group of Natives who were pushing for fair treatment and rights on their own lands. Though the majority of white Cordovans seemed get along with their Native neighbors, there were still tensions, especially in regard to land-ownership policies that had been handed down from the territorial or federal governments. The Eyak had been in the area for generations, but the overwhelming arrival of Caucasians had caused more than a few problems over the years.

Charlotte had overheard the occasional, all-too-casual remarks. She'd learned about a few past incidents, through conversations with Andrew Toliver and her brother Michael's new assistant, Mary, that had been physical, if not fatal.

"Considering how Native Americans in the States are treated in film," Charlotte said, "you really can't blame the AEC for their concern."

Stanley Welsh frowned at her. "We know the Alaskan Indians are nothing like that. *North to Fortune* will depict them as the simple, peaceful people they are. And everyone will admire how they survive in such hostile conditions with such primitive tools and ways. Why, in the scene where the Native saves Peter's character, the noble savage becomes the hero. For a short time, at least. And Peter teaches him to be civilized in return."

Charlotte wasn't intimately familiar with the Native culture, but she cringed inwardly at the idea of a white man "rewarding" a Native Alaskan by teaching him to be civilized. "Mr. Welsh—"

"The Alaska people are far from primitive, Papa," Cicely cut in. The frown lines between her eyes deepened. "I read up on a noted anthropologist's works and put it in the scenario. What scene are you talking about? I never wrote anything like that."

Again, Welsh offered a dismissive wave. "I thought the story needed a little more action. We'll talk about it later. I believe we're at the hotel. More fans—oh."

Charlotte peered out the window as the car rolled to a stop in front of the Windsor, Cordova's most prestigious hotel. A group of a dozen or so people bundled against the cold stood on the wooden walk. Several held signs that read, "Unfair to Natives," and "We Are a People, Not a Plot."

Meade glared out the driver's window. "Damnation."